WAR ANGEL

COPYRIGHT DISCLAIMER

Culmination
OF THE TALES OF TARTARUS

A.L. MENGEL'S BOOKSHELF

from THE TALES OF TARTARUS

Ashes

The Quest for Immortality

The Blood Decanter

from THE VEGA CHRONICLES

The Wandering Star

other WORKS

#Writestorm

The Other Side of the Door

Curtains and Fan Blade

AUTHOR'S NOTE ON WAR ANGEL

Bᴇʟᴏᴠᴇᴅ FRIENDS of *'The Writing Studio'*,

When writing this novel, which is entirely a work of fiction, there had been much turmoil going on in the world. One could argue that the "rapture" had somehow passed us by, that we all still remain Earthbound, our celestial destiny just a "myth". That accidents and terrorism, shootings, intolerance, racism, bigotry, violence and war, were part of the period of tribulation.

Before I started the manuscript, I remember a phone call I had with my mother one afternoon. The call took place when I was still writing *The Blood Decanter*. When I wrote that novel, I had experienced periods of anxiety, depression and frustration. I frequently found myself in a negative state of mind. I experienced periods of discouragement. And she explained to me that, when one is doing something good, interference is not uncommon.

That same day, she said something that remained with me while writing *War Angel*. We had talked about the issues facing the world today, and one day she said a single, solitary, quite profound sentence, that remained with me: "I think we all need a war angel in our lives right about now."

And so I present to you, the reader, the Beloved Friend, the one who I appreciate for adopting my writing and reading my words. It's the culmination of The Tales of Tartarus series, *War Angel*. This novel was first conceived in 2013 – way back when I was in the process of releasing *Ashes*. I knew, back then, that I wanted to write a story about angels. So enjoy, and let your wings soar across the sky…

The Thousand Years

20 And I saw an angel coming down out of heaven, having the key to the Abyss and holding in his hand a great chain. 2 He seized the dragon, that ancient serpent, who is the devil, or Satan, and bound him for a thousand years. 3 He threw him into the Abyss, and locked and sealed it over him, to keep him from deceiving the nations anymore until the thousand years were ended. After that, he must be set free for a short time.

4 I saw thrones on which were seated those who had been given authority to judge. And I saw the souls of those who had been beheaded because of their testimony about Jesus and because of the word of God. They[a] had not worshiped the beast or its image and had not received its mark on their foreheads or their hands. They came to life and reigned with Christ a thousand years. 5 (The rest of the dead did not come to life until the thousand years were ended.) This is the first resurrection. 6 Blessed and holy are those who share in the first resurrection. The second death has no power over them, but they will be priests of God and of Christ and will reign with him for a thousand years

The Judgment of Satan

[7] When the thousand years are over, Satan will be released from his prison [8] and will go out to deceive the nations in the four corners of the earth—Gog and Magog—and to gather them for battle. In number they are like the sand on the seashore. [9] They marched across the breadth of the earth and surrounded the camp of God's people, the city he loves. But fire came down from heaven and devoured them. [10] And the devil, who deceived them, was thrown into the lake of burning sulfur, where the beast and the false prophet had been thrown. They will be tormented day and night for ever and ever.

The Judgment of the Dead

[11] Then I saw a great white throne and him who was seated on it. The earth and the heavens fled from his presence, and there was no place for them. [12] And I saw the dead, great and small, standing before the throne, and books were opened. Another book was opened, which is the book of life. The dead were judged according to what they had done as recorded in the books. [13] The sea gave up the dead that were in it, and death and Hades gave up the dead that were in them, and each person was judged according to what they had done. [14] Then death and Hades were thrown into the lake of fire. The lake of fire is the second death. [15] Anyone whose name was not found written in the book of life was thrown into the lake.

War Angel

A NOVEL BY A.L. MENGEL

WAR ANGEL

FOR ALL OF THE WAR ANGELS IN THE
WORLD

THE

WAR

ANGEL

I

WHO IS THE WAR ANGEL?

Center of Silence

The path before me is clear —

I hold that there is truth in here

As I fight my way inside —

Where I have no place to hide

From myself.

By Shane Chase.

Tartare DÉPLIÉE

Will you love me? Until the hour of death takes your senses?

There comes a certain time for the choice – Will you accept your fate? The last encounter?

A final chance. Can I give it to you?

Whether it be on soil or the heavens, there always comes the moment of clarity.

When the warmth of the blood becomes real.

When the adrenaline stops and the sting pierces.

The flesh returns.

And wings are clipped –

But they are never truly gone…

T HERE ONCE WAS A STORY of a '*War Angel*'.

When the story had first been told, there were the many questions that followed. There were those who did not understand who the *War Angel* could be. While many wondered, there was an equally significant amount of people who were entirely unaware. But the questions remained, particularly in those societies who had a spiritual and cosmic connection. They asked the questions, over and over. Who is the angel?

Who is this mysterious, mythical angel of battles?

Was the angel male?

Female?

Did the *War Angel* walk among us? Protect us?

Stories had started to circulate among the populace. There were some people that claimed to have seen angelic figures and spirits, particularly at night. Pale, white ghostly apparitions in trees, watching them.

As if waiting for something.

Or someone.

But no one could be for certain if the phenomenon were a product of the *War Angel*. No one could tell if he (or she) were simply observing.

Or protecting.

And then there was the story of the immortals.

And their similar musings of the *War Angel*, and those same supernatural phenomena. The immortals, who had been peacefully coexisting with the humans for centuries, had come to a precipice in their existence: for they were dying and close to extinction. And so the same rumors of the *War Angel* started to circulate through their communities.

The same dinner table talk that the humans discussed penetrated their existence.

Initially, they were just stories.

Stories of angels.

And of demons, and of ghosts.

Throughout time, the stories had fueled the dinner table chatter among the immortals and humans alike. The immortals were on the brink of extinction after dealing with years of torment at the hands of the 'hooded man'. Some of the immortals had wondered who the *War Angel* could be. Perhaps a warrior to protect them? To triumph in their pursuit of goodness?

But the immortals had not been the harbingers of good. And there was no rest for the wicked. For centuries, the immortals were connected with sin.

And evil.

Debauchery and poison.

The humans who befriended them often found untimely deaths. And when they did not, those humans typically had great misfortunes befall upon them.

People started to talk about the immortals.

That they were sinful.

And that those humans who befriended them were courting evil; that those people who became embroiled in the wickedness deserved their fate.

Over time and recent decades, as the immortal society neared total collapse, there had been the advent of a mythical figure called *The Hooded Man*, a malevolent destroyer of the immortal foundation.

While no human being had ever been reported to have seen the robed figure, the rumors, which had initially circulated through the immortal communities, filtered over towards the human population, and not long after, were discussed in government meetings, on news stations, and media.

Immortals Targeted for Annihilation the headlines screamed. Artists painted renditions of *The Hooded Man* from long discussions with their immortal friends.

In Miami, which had long been thought to be the central battleground of *The Hooded Man's* wrath, immortal Antoine Nagevesh, who headed that "sector" of their society, had led a local effort, in joint conjuncture with the human population, to hunt down the hooded figure and destroy him before the immortals were wiped off the face of the Earth.

His drive made it across the Atlantic to France and Rome, where a large concentration of immortals lived, but it became futile. For *The Hooded Man* cast a seductive spell, and Antoine saw that the immortals were destined to wind up where they did: near extinction.

And so came the mystery of the *War Angel* in the society of the immortals. At the council of *The Inspiriti* in Rome, an enlightened society thought to be governed by a council of immortals, there were many discussions. Several members of the high council met over the course of decades to confer the possibility of a warrior, of an angel, and whether the angel posed a threat to the immortals or if it could be an ally.

And others, immortals and humans alike, argued about the mystery.

The *War Angel*.

Who could it be?

The apparitions continued.

Many during times of great distress.

Why the apparitions now? At this time? At this moment when the immortals were on the cusp of extinction? Certainly this being could not be sent to combat the immortals.

Could it have?

And so the questions circulated.

Did he or she travel along the sidewalks, and take a similar journey as the immortals and the people…or did he or she ride a horse?

Or was the story of the *War Angel* possibly in a modern time?

And did he or she sit in automobiles, ride on trains and ships and airplanes, and travel next to us…watching us…without our awareness of their presence?

Many questions permeated minds throughout the world.

And then, after the period of speculation, would follow the mystery of the angel's existence.

There were rarely answers, but the questions would always remain, regardless of the time period or amount of technology in the search: Would the angels only be seen in fleeting moments in times of distress?

Or could they be engaged with human beings in mundane, everyday situations, without our knowledge? Could the next interaction one were to have with another person be a conversation with an angel?

Or even a war angel?

The phenomenon remained a mystery.

There were those who did not understand who the *War Angel* was – nor did they choose to believe in something that they could not see nor prove.

And then, due to the lack of conviction, the world continued to evolve; man discovered science, and evolution. Industry, and technology.

The idea of a spiritual journey – and spirits who were sent from the celestial dimensions to protect – seemed increasingly foreign.

So the questions remained.

Was the war angel really there? Or was it an idea of stories and prayers?

For he or she who the angel was called to protect – would they *see* the angel? Would they even *know* the angel was there fighting a battle in their name?

Initially, there was no acknowledgement.

And complacency reigned, within the immortal populace but the human beings as well. Stories of the War Angel faded as time wore on.

Over the years, some did not believe the war angel actually existed. Man adopted the scientific mindset, and the world evolved. The Industrial Revolution proved to man – at least to a degree – that man was the 'Supreme Being'.

That man ruled the Earth.

God was not the ruler.

God was not the spiritual entity He once was; for man became increasingly self-absorbed.

The seven sins were prevalent. And because of that, man suffered the consequences.

According to Biblical history, Adam and Eve, after committing the first sin, were cast out of Eden, and ever since that time, a time which man had been birthed in the created World, there had been the stain of sin on man, like a fingerprint on a clean surface.

But the stain could be wiped clean.

It could be absolved, there *was* a method of cleansing.

Of redemption.

Man was given "free will" by God. And man, as a general entity, chose to focus on themselves. But that did not mean that man denied God, but, perhaps, rather, did not acknowledge Him. But He was always there, and He still gave man the tools needed for their survival – both physical and spiritual.

And then came a war angel.

A battle assigned angel.

One given to each and every living soul; in many cases (most, if not all cases) the presence of the war angel was completely undetected.

Their presence was ignored, and all spiritual connection was extinguished – and those who were to be protected continued their lives without any awareness of the war angel. But, and it was argued over generations, the war angel was still there, fulfilling their duties.

The story of the *War Angel* was told through generations – it was told again, and again, and again; over the centuries, no matter how many times the story had become diluted, it always reached the same conclusion.

And left the same questions.

Did the war angel actually exist?

But still, there were those who believed. Those who were insistent that the angel existed, despite a complete lack of evidence.

There were those who argued that they had seen the angel — whether it be in a night time vision or a specific summons — but, over the course of years, the awareness of the presence increased among the believers, over a slow period.

And so, with much uncertainty, there was a degree of comfort...in the midst of the turmoil, had everyone had a warrior? One to defend, one to conquer, one to protect?

Did everyone have a war angel?

And then, there was the moment when the piercing scream of a child, of a little girl, was heard across the land...

"He's dead! *Dead! Dead!*"

She shrieked and covered her eyes with her hands.

A patchwork of blood soiled her little white dress. It was still fresh and wet, and as she moved, tiny red droplets dripped to the hardwood floor. She smashed her palms over her cheeks and her fingers over her eyes, sobbing. Her palms were flat against her face as she felt the warmth of tears against her cheeks.

She shook her head back and forth, screaming. "No!" She dared not lower her fingers, and took a few steps back towards the wall. As each of her sobs and sniffles emanated through expanding portions of time, she chose to part her fingers – just a tiny, miniscule distance – and peek through them.

To let the sliver of light in.

And then there was the bright lake of crimson across the room.

Daddy's work boots.

And she saw his body on the floor.

It was Father.

His black pants.

A once white shirt stained with mud and drying blood around the edges, and a pool in the center of his chest.

There was a fresh pool of blood underneath his head, oozing into a larger, ever expanding lake. His eyes were wide open, but saw nothing.

She turned and ran into her room, slamming the door. She ran and jumped onto the bed, burying her face into the pillow, screaming a muffled scream. She didn't remember much after running away from the small sitting room where her father lay in a lake of blood. She lay, her face buried in the pillow, feeling the warmth of her breath against her face, and she thought she may have fallen asleep.

The room outside was silent.

But daddy was lying there.

Dead in a lake of blood.

As she hovered in the realm of sleep while not fully awake, she thought she remembered the sweet smell of fresh lavender, and when she opened her eyes, she was no longer in her room. As if magical, as if some mythical radiant hands carried her from her tiny bedroom towards an unknown darkness, there she was.

Was it a dream?

She looked down at herself; completely changed, a different being: long, flowing silver hair; a billowing robe, which appeared to be flowing with an unseen wind; a warm, glowing light emanating from behind her. But still, she could tell she was herself.

Her same self.

Her same mind.

Still who she was.

But so physically different.

She stood, but felt no floor. No stones beneath her feet, but she could stand. Her body was soft; grey, almost made of stone. Perhaps a certain angelic statue she could have been; but her, in this new, foreign form, in a world she did not understand, so different from the little girl who had fallen asleep on the bed next to the room where her father's body lay. But not here, in this cosmic realm, where there was a different sense of who she was.

She reached out and touched her robe.

Soft, supple.

And then her hands.

She looked down. No longer the hands of a child. But not working hands either. Her skin smooth, like glass. Brilliantly white, with the feel of ceramic.

And when she spread her wings, she looked up and saw them reach towards the sky. There was a certain sense of enlightenment; it was not as if there were a gigantic crash of demons falling from the heavens; it were as if music were playing in every dimension; a chorus of angels bathed in gold and in dreams realized, and love which was always understood.

Of tolerance, and acceptance.

And love.

Mostly of love.

She felt that wrap around her as her wings reached their full span, soaring across the sky.

The wings opened a world where all were loved and accepted, where the arguments were ceased and happiness endured; there was no longer any violence and the demons and the monsters were held at bay. She looked down and saw them chained below in the darkness.

Her vision was clearing. The mist that swirled below was lifting.

She could see a sea, a watery ocean below, waves crashing against stones. Her mind flashed, with images of darkness and blood, and she was standing on the large, flat stones.

The darkness swirled below her, and the stones which she now stood on – her feet, cold, tired, muscular and dirty – plastered over the rocks; her feet holding their stance; the wet, frigid boulders separated her from a field of skulls which the dark mist revealed below; but beneath that bit of earth – those same stones – were thrashing limbs; pasty white; arms which reached from a frigid sea from which they may never emerge. Faint light penetrated swirling, angry clouds.

But did she, when she stood, wrap herself in thorns?

Did she take the sharp assault willingly? Did she, as an angel, accept those transgressions as part of her being? The roping thorns appeared and she had no means to avoid them. As if tearing from the sky.

The thorns wrapped around her torso, tightly and leading up towards her bosoms, drawing a thin line of blood from the curves and under the arms where the thorns dug deep into her skin. She cried out as the thorns tore at her skin.

But the thorns she accepted.

The thorns were what she chose – under her own free will – to take on, to wear like a badge of courage, of commitment, and strength.

But it was in those thorns were the sins of those she saved, and even then, one can only take on so much. Can't they? And so she reached a point – a certain, quite specific time – with which she desired to be cleansed.

And then a thought permeated her mind.

Just a tiny, fleeting picture – a single skull in the sand on the beach. Far beyond where she stood above, she saw it far below on the sandy beach, amidst crawling bodies, their pasty limbs clawing through the sand.

But it was the skull that she saw.

Far below, but suddenly right in front of her face. She now stood at the edge of the water, and as the cool surf splashed over her bare feet, she turned around and looked at the skull, half buried in the sand. Beyond, in the center of the sea, were the stones she had stood on. Now, with just a fleeting thought, she was on the beach. But as she looked out towards the sea, she saw it darken. The water that lapped at the shores appeared clear. But she could see farther. Towards the dark center of the sea. Where the limbs were thrashing. She closed her eyes. She heard the dull roar of the surf. But as she concentrated, in the distance, she could hear more. A faint moaning. Screaming. She opened her eyes and looked out towards the center of the sea.

The screams were deafening.

Moans.

Crying.

Sobbing.

And where the mist swirled and covered the dirty secret. The lost souls. The forgotten ones. Those who she felt she must stand with. "I will stand with you," she said, looking out towards the sea. Another rope of thorns tore through her abdomen. She fell to her knees, crying out. She raised her hands up towards the sky and looked up for a moment. A beacon of light filtered down through a break in the clouds.

She looked back down at the tiny skull.

Could it have been that of a child?

Certainly not a full grown adult. Just lying in the sand, covered in dirt. It was slightly crooked; tipped on its side, with part of the head and eye sockets peering out from the sand.

She crouched down and crawled over towards it, never taking her eyes off of it. As she approached the skull, she bent down and tried to pull it out of the sand, but the ground was still wet from the high tide, and it took a great deal of effort to pull it out of the mud.

The skull was heavy, wet and muddy. But as she held it up, she could see the light shine behind it.

Who were you little skull? Who did you belong to?

She examined it closely. It had appeared to be intact. She held it in her hands, rotating it around. She ran her hand along the cranium, brushing the mud off. "Who were you in life?" she asked. "What was your mission?"

And then she was jolted back to the present.

In her dark bedroom.

The door to her bedroom swung open as she opened her eyes. How long had she been sleeping? She swung her legs to the floor and she stood. Looking up at a tall, shadowy figure in the door, she took several cautious steps backwards, towards her little window. A tall man dressed in a dark suit looked down at her. His face was plastered with an enormous frown. "Come with me, little girl!"

His eyes were wide and flaring as he lunged forward, reached down and grabbed her shoulder. She cried out as he dragged her across the room, out into the hallway, and into the living room.

"No!" She felt tears well up in her eyes. Father was still lying on the floor in a pool of fresh, bright red blood. It was not a dream, it was real. She could still smell the gun powder in the air. She turned and buried her face in the man's side. "No! Daddy! I thought it wasn't real!"

The man tightened his grip and pulled her away. "No, come with *me!*" He dragged her across the room to the front door as she turned her head around and looked at her Father's body. And then she was dragged away. She felt a powerful, muscular set of arms wrap around her, and hoist her off the floor. Her tiny hands fell with her arms to her sides, and she saw the horror: daddy was on the floor. His eyes were wide open and his face was motionless.

She screamed and buried her head in the strange man's shoulder. "Daddy! *Daddy!* Where have you gone?!"

Oh Father, why have you abandoned me?

The father of the little girl, Dion Arnette, was buried the following Saturday in a small, plain wooden coffin.

The townsfolk had taken a collection at the Church throughout the week. A small table was set outside the doors which led into the atrium; several of the ladies talked with parishioners as they exited after the services. Some gave.

Most did not.

The ladies spent days sitting in the chairs. But with Dion's reputation – of which word had traveled through the groups throughout Paris – had led to many saying "no, thank you" and walking past the charity table.

The little girl stood and watched the service conclude and saw the two ladies, sitting side by side, as the congregation filed out the doors and to the outside. She turned away as she heard the approach of a car.

A hand, in white gloves; an open palm reached out and she slowly placed her hand in the other.

She looked up.

The woman's hair blew with the passing wind as she fumbled through her purse. She pulled out a pack of cigarettes, and inserted one into a long, slender filter.

She placed the cigarette filter in her mouth and held it as she dropped her purse to the ground. She reached up to hold her hat down as a strong gust of wind blew through.

The sun, which shone from behind, cast a shadow on the woman's face, but it was a familiar face. "Come with me, little Delia. Poor sweet little girl. We must go bury your father. It's time to go. Pick up my purse for me, please."

The woman led Delia across the parking lot. As they approached the car, she tugged on the woman's sleeve. "Auntie Thelma?"

The woman turned around.

She looked down at Delia and smiled. Her face still appeared to be in a shadow in the bright sunlight. "Yes Delia?"

"Do you think daddy went to hell?"

Her mouth dropped open and her hands fell to her sides. "Why do you speak of such things, Delia? How could you think of such a horrid thing? Now shush and get in the car!"

The car ride was spent in silence as Auntie Thelma puffed on her cigarette. Delia could see her eyes in the rearview mirror as she looked up, and several times, made eye contact with Auntie Thelma, where they each would instantly look away. Delia was brought to the graveside services in a small, black car which pulled up as the mourners were gathering at the graveside. She stepped out of the back door and watched the people gathering amidst rows of small, white folding chairs.

The sun shined that morning – the warming rays filtered through the trees as her breath clouded out from her mouth as she exhaled.

The chill of the winter air had not left, although it was the era when the sunlight was warm and the shade had a chill. Rows of tiny plastic chairs lined the grass, as a small crowd of people huddled in coats and jackets.

But when she opened her eyes, she saw the many faces.

There were the faces of her lineage; the men and woman who had always seemed so familiar to her were present.

She had only seen them a handful of times in the short period of her life thus far; mostly at gathering such as this one. The group of the older generation mingled and chatted amongst each other, blocking her view. Some of the ladies reached up and held their hats down as the intermittent gusts of wind passed through.

During that time, she did not move.

She stood several feet away from the gathering, and watched them, as they nodded their heads in conversation.

And dabbed their eyes with wadded up handkerchiefs.

The ground still felt frozen.

There was no snow; yet the spring thaw hadn't quite begun. It was the time of year when the mornings were wintry and the afternoons gave a glimpse of the coming warmth.

She looked down at her feet.

She was wearing the dark blue saddle shoes that Mother had always liked on her. And the blue stockings. She looked up at the others again. The men wore black suits, some dark blue; the ladies in conservative, dark colored dresses. As they had mingled amongst each other, it seemed as if she were invisible.

She placed her hands over her eyes and stood in front of the gathering.

The space between her index finger and middle finger let a sliver of light through; she could see the blues and pale hues of the daylight.

She widened the gap and she looked at the adults. The coffin was being carried by six tall men. A small, plain brown wooden casket, nothing fancy. For he had very little money in the end anyway.

And then she bent down, and unbuckled the clasp on her shoe. She straightened herself out, reached her foot forward and wiggled the shoe off her foot. It fell in the grass. She looked up at the others, and they continued. Eyes were closed, as tissues dabbed at cheeks.

Hugs were exchanged.

She could hear sobs on shoulders.

But the feeling – so distant, so vulnerable; so seemingly insignificant – overwhelmed her as she looked up towards the sky. The sun was shining directly down on her, for she had to shield her eyes; the clouds meandered by. She looked back down, through the throngs of people, and saw the casket. She moved forward, unnoticed, as the others cried and spilled into each other's arms around her.

She stopped just at the edge of the rows of chairs and looked down at the small, wooden coffin. "Who are they crying for?" she asked, never taking her eyes off of the coffin. "They certainly aren't crying for you. Maybe they're crying out of relief that you're finally gone?" Fresh cut flowers surrounded the grave. The chatter amongst the adults was distant and inaudible behind her.

She paused and looked up towards the sky.

"I have failed you," she said. "Haven't I?"

She looked up to the heavens at the rolling clouds, and back towards the sun. She stared directly into the light. The clouds parted across the sunlit sky, and she covered her eyes with her hands. A warm, wet tear streamed down her cheek.

She closed her eyes and hung her head.

She could remember the light from before.

It had been the light which had once surrounded her.

In the realm where time had never existed, nor would it ever. Where she felt a determined happiness, a love, and fervent embrace. She covered her face with her hands as her tears flowed through her fingers.

"You gave me one task," she said, shaking her head. "You sent me to protect a monster. And with that *one single task*, I have failed."

She shrieked and screamed up towards the sky, shaking her fists. "Why did you give me this assignment?!"

Several of the others rushed to her side.

"Oh dear…" Auntie Thelma shook her head and put her arms around the little girl, and she leaned against her aunt. "Oh dear, sweet, Delia. Our little girl has lost her father. Come cry into Auntie Thelma's shoulder my sweet little one…"

Auntie Thelma picked her up and carried her away from the casket, as she continued her stare up towards the sky. She glared.

But the sky did not answer.

Still, without an audible response, there was a feeling that washed over her as Auntie Thelma carried her away. It was something that she had felt deep within her soul.

Like her sense of intuition, which, as a child, would be underdeveloped.

But she felt the feelings that a normal child would not have the ability to decipher: that she still did the right thing. That she completed her mission, no matter how abhorrent the subject may have been. She saw the clouds, but the light still filtered through. She followed the plume, down, and further towards her, and saw it touch her arm.

She could feel the warmth. "Is that how you speak with me? In feelings?"

Auntie Thelma stopped walking. "What did you say, Delia?"

But Delia did not answer Auntie Thelma, for she was still looking at the cascading light; the warm, inviting light that touched her, that made her feel the way that she did.

And the next assignment was still to come.

Later that same evening, Delia lay on her bed, her face buried in her pillow, her arms crossed before her. The pillow was damp. She heard Auntie Thelma's footsteps approach, in the old, familiar way her shoes would clap along the hardwood floor.

Thunder crashed overhead and rain fell, and pelted against the windowpane.

"Delia, you must eat some dinner," she said. "You need some strength. You're a growing little girl."

Delia turned around and looked up. "The darkness is returning, Auntie. I can feel it. I've failed God. I failed in what he called me here to do. But now, I know that I will be given another mission. Soon. I can tell. It's coming close."

Auntie Thelma stopped and stared at Delia. Her mouth had dropped open. "What did you say?"

The glow of the light caused Auntie Thelma to remain in a shadow. She bent down forward and scooped up little Delia. "Now how do you speak of such things? You speak like an adult when you are just a child! Are you in mourning? Do your tears still flow? Can I rock you in the chair over there?"

She carried Delia to the chair. She sat and held Delia on her lap as thunder rumbled overhead. She rocked in a rocking chair with Delia on her lap. "There, there, little Delia. Dry your tears my little one." She smoothed Delia's hair.

"We are moving into dark times," Delia said, raising her eyes up to look at her Aunt.

Auntie Thelma shook her head. "Oh dear, you must miss your father so very, very much. But how do you speak with such mature words?"

Delia straightened herself and looked up at Auntie Thelma. "The dead shall rise again. They will fight their way out of their graves, clawing through the ground with their hands. They will be judged. When the blood rain cometh…"

Auntie Thelma gasped and her mouth fell open. "Delia! Where do you hear such things! Such heresy!" She got up from the rocking chair and lay Delia back down on the bed, and Delia smiled, drawing the sheet up to cover herself. She burrowed into the pillow for a moment, and then sat up. She sat up with her legs crossed in the center of the bed. "Auntie, I speak because I know. I speak because I listen…"

Auntie Thelma stood and looked down at Delia with wide eyes. Her mouth gaped open. "You evil little child! How could you say such things?! Of bodies crawling out of the ground and blood rain? What is this, Delia? What has become of you?!"

Delia rested her chin on her hands and raised her eyes to look at Auntie Thelma. Delia glared up at her. "Do you not remember? What he did to mother?"

Auntie Thelma took a step back and shook her head. "No…no…you don't know what you speak of, little girl. He was a good man."

Delia wrinkled her forehead into a scowl. "You were not there. Not in the house, Auntie Thelma." She flopped back onto the bed, shifted around and buried her face in the pillow.

"You need some time alone. To grieve. I'm going to leave you to it and you can come out again in the morning when you have come back to your senses. No more of this talk of bodies rising from the dead. What speaking for a little girl!"

Auntie Thelma shook her head and headed out of the door. It shut silently, and the lock clicked just moments later.

After Auntie Thelma left the room, Delia turned back around and lay on her back on the bed, and stared at the ceiling. She noticed the warm glow that the lights brought to the plaster and studied a tiny crack near the hanging fan. She closed her eyes for a moment, and then she heard a creak in the silence.

Just a single creak.

But it was a familiar creak. One she had heard many, many times before.

It was the rocking chair creak.

She opened her eyes and sat up, and looked towards the corner, but it was covered in shadows. "Hello? Who is there?"

There was a crash of thunder and the rain fell harder as the lights flickered.

She laid back down, pulling the blanket up, covering her head. She shut her eyes tightly. The winds picked up outside and she could feel the house shake as the storm approached. The wind whistled around the corners outside her window.

And then there was another creak, and Delia flung the covers off her.

She propped herself up on her arms.

There was a deep, sinister laughter as the creaking started again.

It sounded masculine.

Grating.

"Who is that?" she called out into the silence, to no answer. Just the sound of fresh falling rain outside her window.

And then the creak came again – slow, methodic, determined. She looked over in the corner towards the rocker. Still bathed in darkness.

Utterly obscured.

But the creaking sounded heavier. Deeper than the first few times. As if someone were sitting in the rocking chair. Someone heavy.

She looked at the small, wooden chair. The darkness surrounded it, but a small plume of light highlighted the runners. The rocking chair sat across from the end of her bed, in the dark corner. In the same spot it had been for as long as she could remember.

Auntie Thelma sat in that very chair on many nights, singing her to sleep. And before that, there were muffled memories of mother sitting in that very chair as well. Nights when she lay her head on the comfort and warmth of mother's chest, treasuring the softness of her breasts, listening to her breathe in and out, and feeling the methodic rhythm of her mother's heartbeat against her back.

She could see herself reach around and twirl mother's long, brown hair as she lay her head on her shoulder.

But mother was gone.

And the small, wooden chair was empty.

Wasn't it?

She lay back on the bed, pulled the sheets up towards her chin and looked over at the door. A sliver of light shined from underneath the door, highlighting the wood planks. There were perhaps ten or fifteen feet of floor between her bed and the door.

Her vision was broken as thunder crashed directly overhead and Delia gasped. She jumped and gasped, pulling the blanket up closer to her neck.

The lights went out and Delia closed her eyes tight.

The creak filled the room, slow and methodical against the silence. Someone heavy was in the rocking chair. She knew it now. "Why can't I see you?" she whispered from beneath the sheets.

And then, without opening her eyes, she knew who it was.

"I have been watching you…" The voice was grating and deep. Masculine. Raspy.

Her heart pounded as the creaking continued, back and forth. She felt a rumble in the floor, which reached up towards the bed.

Back and forth…

Back…and forth…

And then the creaking stopped.

And then again there was silence.

All she heard again was the light falling rain pelting against the window pane. Was he teasing her? She shifted to her back, making sure not to uncover the sheet. She lay, her eyes now open, seeing the floral pattern that Auntie Thelma had chosen for her, and listened.

She covered her eyes with her hands, as she took her feet and pulled the sheet down.

She slowly parted her fingers to see. The long slivers of light, nestled between the dark columns of her fingers, didn't paint the picture that she had hoped. To the direction at the end of the bed, in the dark corner, where the rocker was.

She could sense someone was there. But still could only see darkness. Who was rocking in that chair?

And then a sense of fear washed over her.

She shivered.

But she didn't have to ask the question, and she already knew. She drew her knees up close to her chest.

The creaking stopped as the voice came again, deep, grating, and masculine. "So you finally recognize me."

She held her breath as she heard the methodic creak.

Back and forth…back and forth…

"Cat got your tongue?"

She heard him laugh.

It was deep.

Demonic sounding. She shuddered and peeked again. There was some movement in the darkness this time.

"I'm revealing myself to you," he said. "Only a blessed few receive this opportunity…"

Delia opened her mouth, face still covered with her hands. She could see the glimpse of a muscular leg towards the bottom of the chair. But it didn't look like a human leg. The skin was scaly. Red-tinted. Perhaps brown.

"I…don't believe in you," she finally managed to say.

He laughed again. "Oh, little Delia. You sweet little girl. You know I don't reveal myself to those who don't, right? You know that I work best when people deny me? But you…you believe in me. That I know for certain!"

She slowly drew her hands down and looked in the corner. He was still shrouded in darkness. She closed her eyes and turned her head away.

"Do you think you can come down here…to this Earthly, physical realm…where I reign freely…and think that you would not be called to serve *me*?"

She opened her eyes and looked over towards the dark corner. A sliver of light emanated across the room from the window. But little Delia did not need the light, but despite, it shined against what she had been struggling to see: the wooden rocker, the light hand rails moved back and forth like coupling rods on a locomotive.

She could now see his arm.

It was red, quite muscular.

Resting on the handrail.

She heard him breathe in deeply, chesty, full of mucous. Seemingly patient. Waiting for her?

Perhaps.

She sat up in the bed and her eyes adjusted to the darkness. "I see you over there," she said. Her voice took a harsh, commanding tone. "In the light. But you avoid the light."

"Do you not think that I knew that? That I would choose to reveal myself to you or not? Stupid, silly little girl."

She looked up at the light that was filtering into the tiny, dark room. It reached across towards the bed, and she saw it illuminate her arm.

She shuffled out of the covers and swung her legs from the bed. She stood on the cold, barren wood floor. "You have been following me! Why do you follow me? Why are you here?" Her head snapped around as she looked over towards the foot of the bed. She felt a stir in her gut as she saw the glint of light on the muscular arm. Red, roping flesh, leading up to a horn that caught the light for an instant.

"You will not capture me!" she shrieked.

Footsteps ran down the outside hallway, heeled shoes clicking on wood. The doorknob rattled. "Delia! Delia are you alright?! I'm going to get the key!"

But Delia did not listen.

She faced the rocking chair and looked at the muscular demon rocking back and forth.

"You come to me as if I have some sort of an allegiance to you," Delia said. "I do not. And will not."

"Tu credis in Deus?"
"Do I believe in God?! How dare you question my *faith*!"
He laughed. "I don't *have* to question your faith. It is you that is questioning. I saw you in the cemetery. I saw you look to the sky. I hear your thoughts. Of dismay. Of disbelief!"
Delia stamped her foot on the floor. Over and over. "You do *not* have authority to eavesdrop on conversations with *my* God!"

He leaned back in the chair and chuckled. "Oh, but I do. And I *will*. Just like He…I am always there, Delia. Always around. You can deny me all you want. It will just give me more power!" He laughed again.

Delia ran to the door and shook the knob. "Auntie Thelma! Where did you go? Come and get me!" She banged her hand against the wood frame. But there was no answer.

He rose from the rocking chair and the floor creaked under his weight. He shuffled over towards the windows, his hands clasped behind his back. Delia saw a set of horns at the top of his head; a large, muscular frame. He continued as he faced the window, looking outwards. "He was once my God too. And I know you are angry with Him. I share your emotion, little one. You are so…successful…in what you do. But you feel like a failure, don't you? Don't you, Delia?"

Delia loosened her grasp on the knob and looked towards the floor. "I have failed my God."

"You see, Delia…I don't think that. I think you are the perfect warrior. You are the one who is battle assigned. The perfect fighter. You were sent to protect…what? A violent man who had a knack for beating his wife. How many times were there bruises? And then he finally killed her. Now he's rotting in the ground in a coffin and you're free of that little assignment."

Delia shook her head and took several steps back. She glared at him. "Get out of my house. I am doing what I was sent here for! How dare you cast a seed of doubt!"

He chose not to listen. "But what if you were given a different cause to fight for?"

He threw his head back in laughter. "Oh, I will go little one. But don't be denied. I know you. I know where you come from. And I will visit you again."

Delia closed her eyes. *"Go, Lucifer, go!"*

She listened as the thunder crashed overhead. Lightning flashed, illuminating the room as he disappeared into the darkness. The rocking chair still rocked, now empty, as the winds increased outside. The house shook.

She shut her eyes tightly and saw a field of skulls under a red sky painted with black clouds. "Tartarus!" she screamed. "You will not take me! You will not keep me from my true mission!"

She opened her eyes and saw the field of skulls. She remembered the place. From her dreams, when she was a little girl. But she knew. She knew she had been there before.

There was a certain familiarity about the place.

She saw the skulls bulge in a small circular area. Some of them were displaced, as the skulls crashed against one another with deep thuds as the darkness penetrated the sky above. "Go! Leave me!"

Delia saw the tips of wings as an angel rose from underneath the skulls.

And there she was. She saw the angel rising from the field of skulls, reaching down towards the lake of writhing bodies, gently picking up each one, wiping the body down; taking the dirty, trying to make it clean.

As the angel rose further, Delia saw the wings were broken; the feathers made of stone and crumbling. A sullen angel. Broken, bruised, bloodied.

"Who are you!" Delia cried, as the darkness reached across the sky.

But the figure rose further, up towards the angry sky, and Delia saw her closed eyes, looking downwards, crying tears of blood. A rope of thorns shot out of the bed of skulls, tearing towards the sky.

Delia gasped but said nothing.

The roping thorns reached across the sky and tore across the perimeter, as they levitated in front of the rising woman.

There she was.

An angel.

Broken, bloodied wings. Sad, sullen eyes.

And then Delia saw the dark figure in the distance. Hovering like a dark cloud. It was far away, difficult to discern what or who it was, but she knew who the darkness was. It seemed to be moving towards her. She looked back at the angel, who rose high above the skulls, and then she gasped.

Then came the same dark, deep demonic voice: "Watch!"

She recognized that voice. The same deep, grating voice from the room that came from the rocking chair.

"This will happen to you!" he said.

The thorns roped around the angel as she cried out. Her eyes opened wide as the thorns pierced her skin, and she hung her head low as the blood flowed down her body. But Delia had not been prepared. Her mouth dropped open when the angel turned to stone, a monument rising from the field of skulls.

"*This* will happen to *you!*"

Delia took several steps back, and looked over at the dark figure, which had hovered next to the angel. "You will not take me! I will not follow you!"

The deep grating laughter came again. The dark figure gestured to the angel. "That is what *she* said," he said. "And do you see her? Do you see her now?! Bearing all of their sins! Thorns tear into her! She bleeds their transgressions into the sea of souls!"

Delia opened her eyes and looked up towards the sky. The black clouds swirled above her head, and the red sky seemed to darken. "Why can't I wake up?! Why am I not in my room?!"

"Because *you are the war angel*"

Laughter followed.

Delia paused and looked at the dark, misty figure. She shook her head. "No. I have not had any sort of directive from the divine!"

Laughter again.

"The war angel? You call *me* that? Who is this war angel?"

"I call you that because you are!" The darkness moved towards the stone angel, whose face was frozen with tears of blood, and wrapped in roping thorns. "And look over there! That is your fate! That is what you *will* become!"

"I will not become an angel wrapped in thorns!"

And then he appeared, instantly in front of her face. She shuddered. The horns above his head were real. They reached up toward the swirling black clouds, and seemed to have no end. He stunk of rotting flesh; like decaying bodies and excrement. She tried to hold her breath, wincing.

"Do you not see? You *are* the next war angel, Delia! You are the chosen one! Why do you think I come to you if not for a higher purpose?"

She opened her eyes wide. Her mouth dropped open and she stepped backwards. "No! You will not give me any fate! We will defeat you!"

"That's what you think!"

Delia took a deep breath and exhaled.

"Those roping thorns are the transgressions of those she saved. You cannot save everyone, Delia. Save yourself! Save yourself from this fate!"

She glared at the dark figure. "And how do I save myself? Why should I save myself above others when my mission is to protect?"

The dark figure bellowed out. "You will only save yourself by ignoring the others. You focus on yourself. You acquire nice things. Fanciful material possessions. And when you are given the opportunity to get money, you jump at it! Now go!"

She catapulted backwards and the sky turned black.

"Now go!"

Who am I? Go, Lucifer, go!

SHE OPENED her eyes.

She wasn't in the same little room with the wooden floor and the rocking chair. It still seemed dark, and it was hard to see. But it was different. Very different. She took a breath in through her nose. Smelled different.

It didn't even feel like France anymore. As the fuzziness in her vision cleared, she saw a small room with a dirt floor. Plain stone walls. It smelled of animals and cooking, although she could not place which food.

Her head was pounding and she winced.

Was she not having a conversation with the devil just moments ago?

Do you hear me? Do you listen to me? I am still speaking in your ear. I still live in your head…

She shuddered as the voice returned as she lay back down and groaned. And then she stopped.

Opened her eyes again.

She looked down at herself and saw herself laying on an earthen floor, on a thin mat. No bed. No sheets, no pillow. Across the tiny room, sunlight filtered in through a torn, red tapestry, blinding her for a moment. But there was some assurance to the light. Even though she felt so foreign in her surroundings, as she looked at her arm, the light highlighted the roping musculature. But she could feel the warmth.

And she felt that was right where she needed to be.

She could feel the warm air blow in from the window opening. She raised her hands above her eyes as she heard the creak of a door and the shuffle of footsteps on dirt and gravel.

And then a female voice that clearly wasn't Auntie Thelma. "How long have you slept? All night? Are you rested?"

She supported herself on her elbows and struggled to raise herself up. "Where…where am I?" She paused for a moment. Her voice sounded deeper. Adult sounding. Mature. No longer the shrill chirp of a little girl. She looked at the light that filtered in from the window.

Where have you called me to?

The woman had not yet revealed herself, but continued calling from the other room. "Are you awake yet?!" There was an opening in the wall that led to the next room, and she could see shadows against the stone of the opposite wall as the woman moved. Delia noted the dirt floors and called out. "Yes, yes!" The primitive construction and the plain stone walls. "Where am I?" she asked. "And *when* am I?"

The female voice spoke again, sounding more patient. "Oh, sweet one...give me a few moments. I will come to you."

And then she gasped. She shot up and looked down at herself. There was no small white dress. Or bloodstains. Or little buckled shoes. Her legs were long. Tall.

Muscular.

Adult.

The woman appeared in the opening in a long, black robe. She smiled, tilting her head to the side.

Delia thought she might have been someone's grandmother, for she was far more advanced in age than Auntie Thelma. As the woman approached her bed, Delia saw her golden brown skin. So different from Auntie Thelma's ivory white. The woman in the opening had small, brown spots on her cheeks.

"It's time to rise," the woman said.

The woman chuckled as Delia's eyes started to focus. "Where am I?" she asked. The woman walked towards the bed and leaned over, adjusted the sheet that Delia was wrapped in.

"What — "

The woman stooped down by where she was laying. Her eyes were wide. "Do you not know who you *are*? Do you know your origin? Or do you not?" The woman started folding the sheets and placing them neatly in a pile in the opposite corner. "They had told me that you would remember previous things…and bodies that you had existed in previously. And that sometimes you would have momentary lapses. Like this morning."

She lowered her eyes and shook her head.

"Well then," the woman said. "We shall get you cleaned. We shall wash you. And dress you. And I will tell you."

The woman was a silhouette against the light that spilled into the tiny room, but she could tell she was leaning forward and it looked like she was smiling. Still, her legs — adult and muscular. She could not wrap her head around it.

"I…was a child…"

The woman stood, away from the light. She looked up at her. Dark, matted hair framed her face. "You were. Yes. Or rather you're going to be."

"Going…to be? I don't understand…"

The woman peered around and looked Delia directly in the eyes. She smiled warmly. "There are many things which we do not understand, dear Delia. But you existed *here* before you existed in Paris. That is for certain. You are a chosen one. And for that, you exist on multiple levels. In different times. At the same time."

She shook her head, propped herself up against the wall in a sitting position, and winced again. A sharp pain shot through her back. "I cannot wrap my head around that! Why don't I remember you?"

"Anakin pierced you yesterday on your leg. You do not remember then?"

She looked down and lifted the sheet. There was a white cloth wrapped around her thigh, stained red. She closed her eyes and shook her head.

"Do you remember anything? Anything at all?"

The old woman shook her head again and leaned against the wall. "That's an unfortunate side effect."

She drew her legs up and clasped her arms around her knees. She looked up at the woman, who stooped down and looked her directly in the eyes.

"A side effect of what?"

"I was told you would wake up confused and disoriented." She moved about the room gathering clothes. She handed some to Delia and gestured for her to dress. "But," she continued. "In time, you will learn of your power. You will learn about how you woke up here, when, in your mind, you were just a child. How you traveled from Paris to here."

"Where is 'here'?"

Delia drew her knees up and wrapped her arms around her legs. "Clearly this is not Paris," she said. And then she looked around the room again. The stone floors, the small stone hut, the simple clothing, lack of furniture. "Where are we?"

The old woman clasped her hands in front of her waist. "Jerusalem."

Delia's eyes widened. "Jerusalem?! How did I get here? And how…for the love of *God*…did I age…what? *Thirty years*?"

Delia got up and fought her way into a flowing robe that the old woman held up for her. "Yes…the last thing I remember is lying in my bedroom. My tiny, dark bedroom."

The woman pulled out a small wooden chair, and gestured for Delia to sit. "But do you remember the conversation you had? That night?"

Delia sat in the chair, looked down at her legs. Her adult, muscular legs. She sighed and closed her eyes. And then she saw the room. The tiny, dark room with the wooden floors and pedestal bed. And the dark corner, where Auntie Thelma would rock her to sleep on nights when she had fallen ill.

Tu Credis en Dues?

She shuddered as the demonic voice penetrated her mind.

She took a deep breath and placed her hands on her cheeks. "Yes…" she said. "Yes, I remember."

And then she closed her eyes again. She saw the roping, muscular legs. The red skin. The horns against the moonlight.

"I remember…" Delia said, without opening her eyes. "I remember the room. Yes, the rocking chair. And the falling rain…"

The woman took a seat opposite Delia and leaned across the table, touching her arm. "But the conversation you had. Do you remember that? The specifics of it? And what happened next?"

"Yes…I was standing in a field of skulls…I saw an angel…and thorns were tearing into her…roping thorns…so much blood. *There was so…much…blood!*"

The old woman sighed. "Delia, come back. Come back to the present and I will explain everything to you."

Delia's eyes remained closed.

The woman started cleaning Delia's hair, smoothing it against the sides of her head. She explained that Delia had experienced a 'holding place' when she had left her room in Paris. That her assignment had completed.

"And we are in Jerusalem. Many hundreds of years before those days you remember in Paris. You will learn, and soon, I might add – "

"Why was I brought here? And how?"

The woman led her into an adjoining room that appeared like it could be an ancient kitchen. There was a small, wooden table and chairs at one end, several colorful tapestries laid out on the floor, others rolled in the corner, and a large pot in the center of a fire pit.

The woman gestured for her to sit.

"Sit, let me tell you about your mission."

Delia nodded and they sat opposite each other at the table. "Close your eyes, Delia," the woman said. "Let me tell you how you got here, at this very moment…this precise moment in time."

The old woman sat and told her about how she got to be in Jerusalem instead of Paris; how she became an adult after just being a little girl.

Delia closed her eyes as the woman spoke. Her voice sounded warm, reassuring, motherly.

Protective.

And then, she closed her eyes and her vision became so clear. The darkness was pierced by a tiny light. A small pinprick; a little sphere in the distance; so seemingly small and far that it seemed that it could be insignificant.

And then brilliant colors whooshed by her, as the darkness quickly returned. She could hear herself talking, though her voice sounded small and distant. "What was that? Those colors?"

She waited for an answer as she remained in darkness, her eyes focused on the tiny point of light ahead. Then the voice came; the old woman, that warm, reassuring voice. "I am showing you how you got here. You just had closed your eyes in Paris. When you were a little girl, lying in bed in your room. As soon as you closed your eyes you came here. Those colors were the lights of that period."

She kept her eyes closed

"Period?" Delia asked. "I don't understand…"

The warm voice returned as more lights flashed by. "Time. It's all about time, and how we measure our experiences. You will understand, dear one. You will understand your gifts, in due time. But your gift is unique, as is your mission. You have the power. You have the ability. You have the mission, dear Delia. You were in Paris as a little girl. You're now in Jerusalem and a full grown woman. You have the mission for which you have been assigned, which you will discover as you allow it to reveal itself to you. When you open your eyes. And your mind."

Delia opened her eyes and she was back in the small, stone room. The old woman sat at the small, wooden table opposite her, smiling. As Delia looked at the old woman, the brown skinned desert woman, whose dirty cheeks and mussed hair revealed that Delia truly was in a different time period, she noticed something about her. But she couldn't shake the thoughts out of her head. She had most certainly been in Paris. That much, she could remember. But now…it was a time that she hadn't experienced before. And with people she did not know.

Places she couldn't recognize or remember.

This woman, whom Delia had never encountered before, smiled. Her teeth, some rotted away with decay, seemed far whiter than her dirty skin.

She sat back and smiled. "Can I make you something to eat?"

Delia sighed and looked at the woman. "There's something about you," she said. "But I just can't place it."

The woman rose from her chair, neve r taking her eyes off Delia. She smiled again and she nodded, as she wandered over to the kettle. She started banging some stones together. "Do you know what it could be?"

Delia shook her head. "Here, let me help you."

"Open your mind, Delia." After several minutes of trying, the embers lit. Quickly, the room filled with smoke. The woman moved to a nearby table and started chopping vegetables and returned to rummage the wood in the fire under the kettle. "Open your mind and ask yourself…who was the one person who had the most impact on you, in all of time?"

Delia gasped and looked up at the old woman. "My mother. She did." She felt tears well up in her eyes as a wave of emotion chilled through her body. "Definitely my mother! She always guided me. Protected me."

The old woman sat back down at the table and smiled at her, as Delia brought her hands up to her face. Her eyes widened and rimmed with tears. She covered her mouth with her hands. "Mama?"

The woman looked down, then back up at Delia, and smiled.

Delia leaned forward and placed her hands on Mama's arms. "How did you...I don't understand!"

She looked up at Delia as a tear streamed down her cheek. "I was called to guide you...to assist you through your mission."

Tears streamed down Delia's cheeks and she leaned forward and hugged the old woman. She was in a time period that she had never experienced; in a culture that she did not understand, but here, in the midst of myriad questions and unfamiliarity, there was this little old woman. This lady of the desert.

"Are you an angel?" Delia asked, wiping her eyes and leaning back in the chair. "Called to protect...*me*?" Delia remembered the last time she saw mama. She was a little girl, back in Paris, in the days before her father was lying in a lake of blood. The last time she saw mama was at her funeral. Lying in the casket, just before the mortician closed the lid. She had run across the atrium of the church, as fast as her little legs could carry her. "No, one more minute! Wait! *Please*!" She remembered the tears falling down her face as she stood and watched the coffin lid being nailed into place.

And later, again the tears flowed, as the sadness overwhelmed her like a vice clutching her heart, as she watched the coffin being lowered into the ground. She had fallen to her knees in despair, deep in the cool dirt and she hung her head.

The woman leaned forward, reached out, and wiped Delia's tears from her cheeks. It was a simple movement, as her hands smeared the tears away, as her hands wiped under Delia's eyes. Delia opened her eyes and looked at the woman. "Are you my mother? *Are you really her*? How can this be possible?"

She smiled again as she leaned back. "Oh, Delia. We all have a war angel. Whether we know, or realize it, or not. And sometimes, they reveal themselves to us."

Delia's mouth dropped open. "You mean…what they have been talking about is true? That there is more than one of us? I am not the only one?"

She shook her head, reaching out to embrace her. "No, my little one. We are all war angels. We all have a war angel, protecting us. Guiding us, sometimes even without our knowledge. And we all have some power too. In influence, guidance, protection and knowledge. We are all a war angel to someone…"

Delia sighed. "So can I just leave? Close my eyes and go to another time period?"

The woman shook her head. "No, it doesn't work that way, Delia. When you close your eyes, you are sometimes called to another time period…but for a purpose. And you are here, now, to deal with your mission. Your purpose here. You are a war angel, Delia. This is your mission!"

She nodded. "I know that and we know the Atticus is pure. But they are doing everything in their power to muddy his name. To make him seem unfit for what he claims." Delia's mouth dropped open. She hadn't thought those words, only said them. "How did I say that?! I spoke as if I know this!"

Mama smiled and nodded. "It's coming back to you, Delia. Now go! You must go help him! They have taken him to the square and now they are coming for you!" She pointed to a small opening in the back of the hut. Mama fished a shawl that was hanging on a chair on the opposite side of the room and brought it over to her. "Here. There's a chill in the air. You must come with me though! They will be looking for you, dear one. I will protect you."

She swung her legs onto the hard, cold stone floor. Not like the floors in Paris. These floors were dusty, dirty. She looked down at her feet and saw her toes. No more painted nails. Crusted dirt. These were the feet of a worker.

"I am suddenly no longer a child…and I am starting to see a vision of a woman with red hair…"

They squeezed through the small opening and Mama paused for a moment and looked over at her. "She brought you here. You will remember in time."

Delia shook her head. "The last thing I remember…" Her mind saw darkness. And a red sky painted with black clouds. "I remember a red sky…"

"She rescued you," Mama said. "She went there to get you."

"The last thing I remember is being in my room. In Paris. And I was only a child!" She banged her palms against the exterior wall of the hut. "Why are the memories so choppy?"

Mama huddled close to Delia and smiled a warm smile. "Things will return to you. But you need to go to the square. Find Claret. She goes by the surname Atarah. She has figured in to your mission. She has called you here. But you are wanted. People are looking for you. Go now!"

There were several knocks on the door.

Persistent, deep thuds.

She raised her head and looked towards the other room. The small, wooden door across the room shook with the knocking. She returned her attention to Mama, who rose from her chair.

Three more knocks. Mama snapped her attention to the door and stared at it with wide eyes. Delia rose from her chair slowly and looked at Mama.

The old woman shook her head and started rushing around the room, placing items in a small satchel. The old woman dashed to the window and tore the tapestry down. The sun shined brightly through, as she grasped the stone edge and peered outside. "Where are they? How have they come?!"

She walked over to the window and joined the old woman. "Who?! Who are you talking about?!"

Mama snapped her head in the direction of the door as her eyes widened. She looked over at her. "Come with me, Delia! Let's go, it's time to go now!" She abandoned the cooking and rushed to the table and grabbed Delia's arm, dragging her across the room. "Come with me now! They want you!"

Delia grunted and cried out. "Who?! Who wants me?!"

The woman dragged her to an inner room and shut the door.

She looked at Delia with wide eyes. "The high priests! They say you have had relations with the chosen one!"

She looked back at the woman in horror. "What! The chosen one?"

"Atticus has been called to a meeting of the High Priests! Word is they are planning to stone him!"

Her mouth dropped open. "Who? Who is Atticus? Never would I whore myself out! Why would they accuse me of such heresy!"

"The High Priests said this. You are scheduled to go to trial today. They are calling you a whore!"

"How am I thrust into this? I did not! How can I leave?"

The old woman looked up at her with the same wide, frightened eyes. Sweat dripped down the sides of her face. "The watchers! They are coming! They are coming for *you*!"

AFTER THE DAYS Delia spent in Jerusalem with Claret

Atarah, when Delia learned much about who she truly was, she discovered the immortals.

And her gift for time-travel.

When Claret tutored her in the ways of the immortals, the light that still always found its way down to her, always continued to do so…at the graveside at her father's funeral, in her tiny bedroom in Paris, through the window in Jerusalem.

The light, however, started to dim over time; most often as she was becoming more deeply involved with Claret and the immortals.

The light would come less frequently.

And the phenomenon coincided with meeting Claret, who instructed her on how to properly use her time-traveling abilities. And because she felt drawn to do so, there came the day when Delia met a certain Antoine Nagevesh.

It was a day in the bright hot sunshine of Badulla, Sri Lanka, centuries after the days in Jerusalem. Delia had easily traveled to the time period, after the ancient years when Claret had transformed her with the dark gift of immortality; during those precious days in Badulla, when Antoine had just been a young man, a mortal human being, harvesting coffee in the fields, Delia watched him, as he tilled the soil, his dark, sweaty back muscles glistening against the sun and the searing tropical heat.

Antoine was not yet immortal.

He hadn't met his maker, a certain Darius Sauvage, an immortal who had been transformed in the Renaissance period in France. Antoine's ensuing affiliation with Darius had eventually brought Antoine to Lyon in the Southern side of that country, as they lived jointly in Darius' chateau.

But Delia was called from Jerusalem, found herself in Sri Lanka, and after she broke free from Claret, she felt compelled, despite falling towards the darkness, to complete her calling.

She still had a mission.

And she found herself drawn to Antoine.

She spent her first days in Badulla residing in a halfway house in the center of town, in the middle of the dilapidated, weatherworn construction, amidst muddy streets, cooling tropical rains and swaying palm trees.

But it was farther outside of the city where she would find Antoine.

On that same fateful night that Antoine had been transformed to be an immortal, when Darius, at that point already possessing the dark gift of immortality and darkness, Delia had also been there, watching...and waiting.

The Café, which Antoine frequented as a hustler for tourists, was situated in the middle of a patch of clear fields, and was only open at night. On the particular night that Antoine and Darius had met, the moon had been full, bathing the surrounding fields in pale blue light. Delia stood outside, huddled and shivering, for that evening there had been an unusual chill in the air, out of character for the region. She had waited and watched. Patrons darted in and out of the tiny door, some laughing, others walking briskly in the gravel. And as the warm light filtered through the windows to the cool ground outside below, she heard footsteps approaching the café from across the clearing.

It had to have been Darius, for Antoine was already inside.

Mama had instructed her well. Delia knew what time that she must arrive; for she knew that Darius would be transforming Antoine to the darkness on that very precise evening. And so Mama had told her how to identify the initial event when one would fall into darkness. As Darius approached, she squinted her eyes. He was dressed in a fine blue coat, which hung down to his knees. His brown hair was tied back behind his head. She saw him smooth his hair back as he approached the café door. She ducked behind several bushes, and kept her eyes focused on the door. As the crunching on the gravel became louder, she parted some of the branches. She heard the squeak of the door opening.

There was Darius.

In his heyday.

She got just a glimpse as he entered the door into the warm, yellow light, but that was all she needed.

Tall, slender, ruggedly handsome.

His long, brown hair waved down towards his buttocks, billowing out from the tieback. Her heart skipped a beat as he turned to face her, for a brief instant. She slowly exhaled as he turned back towards the inside.

He was so handsome in his early days. Precise bone structure. She could see dark stubble run across his cheeks and chin. But she dared not speak to him. Calling out to him would destroy her mission. For neither Antoine nor Darius knew that she was there; it was simply to witness their meeting.

And they wouldn't know.

Darius, at that point in time, would have a keen sense of his surroundings. But he would not have been able to have sensed her – which, she thought, couldn't explain why her heart skipped a beat when he turned, even if only for an instant, to look her way. Could there have been an inkling of a sense of her presence?

But she did outrank them in power. Both Antoine *and* Darius. She was able to navigate to the precise moment in time when they met, for it was Antoine and Darius, who became central in the history of the immortals. And her need to witness their first night together had become so essential in her fulfillment of her new mission.

For she was older than they.

And she was more powerful.

And Claret, her maker, passed several gifts to her, the time travel being one of them. And so she felt the need to guide them, both of them. But Delia continued her mission throughout the years, remaining close to Antoine and his closest friends, with the other immortals, Darius, Antoine and others…completely unaware of who she really was.

Still, there were times that Delia found herself in the years when Antoine had been alive, back in his youth in Sri Lanka, and later, as an immortal, with the dark gift, in modern-day Miami and also in France. She took special care, and with great determination, not to interact with Antoine, until they had a long established relationship while living in Miami, after centuries of living as an immortal.

Throughout the years, Antoine had risen among the immortals to a leadership role; he had been tasked with opening a club, called *Sacrafice*. Delia was there during all of those times, but she did not interact with Antoine until after Darius had lost his immortality, and had become mortal once again. During those years, Antoine was serving time in his coffin as Darius aged rapidly.

After Antoine was resurrected, it was Antoine that knew, probably long before the others, that Darius was about to die. It was during the days after they had returned to France from Miami that Antoine had seen the deterioration in his partner's demeanor: there were days that Darius could not even get out of bed, despite Antoine's efforts to open the windows, and let the summer breeze in. Antoine would wash and dress Darius, offered to prop him up in the chair by the window, but Darius always declined.

They didn't bother with doctors, because Darius had a quite unique condition which reached far beyond medical science: how could one explain a birthdate hundreds of years earlier to a general practitioner? Rapid aging? Had there even been a condition? And if so, could there have even been a cure besides death?

And so Antoine and Darius stayed at the chateau in France together, alone, except for their loyal houseman Giovanni, their blind, loyal servant, who ran into town and fetched supplies, and food, and anything else they might need, despite his disability.

The mornings became a ritual.

Antoine typically slept in the rocking chair at the foot of the bed and kept watch over Darius, who struggled to breathe and would frequently wake up in coughing fits throughout the night. In the morning, Antoine would assist Darius from the bed to the bathroom, and on some mornings, Darius would not be able to rise from the bed at all.

"Get me the bedpan, Gio," Antoine said. "And a pan of soapy water. And some fresh sheets. He has wet the bed again." Antoine sighed as he looked down at Darius. His eyes were closed and he still appeared to be sleeping. Antoine took a wet washcloth and smoothed it gently over Darius' cheek. His eyes fluttered as Antoine lowered his arm and leaned back.

"You awake?"

Antoine placed the washcloth in the bassinette and walked over to the rocking chair. As he sat, the runner emitted a creak, and he watched, waiting for Darius to reply. He was hovering under the covers, but his legs raised under the sheets as he shifted.

"Yes, I'm awake," Darius whispered. "Thank you for washing me. And changing my sheets. I know Giovanni is fetching them. I heard you."

Antoine didn't answer.

He looked over at the window and watched the curtains blow in the morning breeze as he felt tears well up in his eyes.

But there was a time when Antoine accepted Darius' fate.

For Darius had accepted his own fate long before Antoine. And Antoine discovered that he had no choice in the matter. This was not the type of coffin sentence that he had been condemned to; now, Darius was mortal. He no longer possessed the gift.

His time was coming to a close.

Giovanni returned with fresh sheets a few minutes later. "We can move him to one side of the bed as we change the sheets on the other."

Antoine nodded but said nothing.

Giovanni placed the sheets on the dresser and slowly turned around. He faced Antoine, and Antoine looked at Giovanni for a moment, studying his face. The white towel wrapped around his head, covering the ghastly holes underneath, where his eyes had once been, stood out brilliantly against the dull, grey interior of the chateau. "We are falling apart," Antoine said, grabbing one of the sheets and walking over to the bed. "Darius is dying, you have no eyes. Where did we go wrong?"

Giovanni shook his head and helped Antoine shift Darius to one side of the bed. Antoine continued as they unfolded a giant, white sheet.

"We immortals have endured so much," Antoine said. "Haven't we?"

He looked over at Giovanni, who was stripping the pillows and tossing the pillowcases on the floor. Antoine focused back on

Darius, whose eyes were closed once again. "Now we are dealing with this? With members of our community dying unexplained deaths?"

In the days after Darius had died, Antoine and Giovanni sat on a bench in the middle of *Les Enfantes*, the cemetery closest to their Chateau in Lyon, waiting for the sun to set.

Giovanni held a small, bejeweled handheld mirror, which he held in his lap for a few minutes. And then every few moments, he picked it up and examined his face. He placed a pudgy finger just below his eye as Antoine look at him. Antoine raised his eyebrows. "You've been examining yourself the entire time we've been sitting here."

Giovanni turned to face Antoine. "My eyes were once ghastly holes," he said. He shrugged his shoulders as he gingerly placed the mirror on the bench. "Can I not help but stare?"

Antoine smiled wanly, but his face was otherwise without expression. He faced forward again. "Do you remember when she took your eyes?"

Giovanni had received a new pair of eyes later that same year in Paris. Antoine had remembered when he saw Giovanni laying in the hospital bed with a wrapping of gauze covering his eyes. "Oh, to see again! I cannot wait. I cannot contain myself!" Giovanni paused and moved his head around a few moments. Some beeps from the monitoring equipment broke the silence. "Antoine?"

"I am here," Antoine said, rising from the chair he had been sitting in next to the bed. The light from the day waned, and Antoine took place at the side of the bed. Giovanni grinned. "They tell me I get this off on Tuesday!" He had exclaimed, just hours after the operation. "She took my eyes. These are from a killer. At least that's what I was told. But I don't care. At least I will be able to see again."

Antoine smiled. "At least you aren't walking around with that hideous handkerchief tied around your head anymore."

"Yes." He smiled and shifted his head up towards Antoine's voice. "Now I have gauze."

"But the gauze will be removed. And you will be able to see. Just think of what you remember. Of the world that you left behind so many years ago. Of all the beauty of it that you will be able to see again." Antoine returned to the chair and looked over at the bed. Giovanni lay motionless, his head facing the ceiling.

He was drumming his fingers on his stomach.

Antoine finally broke the silence. "How long have you been serving us?"

Giovanni took a breath and exhaled. "I – I'm not sure dear Antoine. I know it's been many, many years, though, dear sir."

He paused for a long while. "A *great* many years, I would imagine. Saw a lot of history with the two of you." Antoine looked up and could tell that Giovanni was shaking his head back and forth.

"What is it, Giovanni?"

He stopped moving his head back and forth. "I cannot remember. No matter how hard I try."

"Cannot remember? You can, Gio. I know you can. When you were transformed. You have to try. Wait a few hours, maybe? For the anesthesia to wear off? But certainly you haven't forgotten about when you lost your sight."

Giovanni shifted in the hospital bed as Antoine directed his gaze out the window to the fading Paris winter light.

Antoine and Giovanni had returned from Paris to Lyon and stayed at the Chateau. It wasn't until *The Inspiriti* had met in Rome to decipher the cause of Darius' death, that Antoine had pressed Giovanni to have the operation to receive a new pair of eyes.

And the inquiries in Rome continued.

Darius was among many immortals who lost their immortality, became mortal once again, and died a final death. *The Inspiriti* High Council spearheaded the investigation of a mythical figure, once known in the immortal community as *The Hooded Man.*

Antoine ignored the happenings in Rome and insisted Giovanni go and get the procedure for his eye transplant, for the trial would still go on, no matter what they did, and

Monsignor Harrison, the leader of the immortals, would be calling on Antoine at some point for questioning. But in the meantime, why would Giovanni not want to see?

Darius had already been dead and buried at that point, and Antoine felt that a short trip to Paris was in order. There were too many memories floating around the Chateau in Lyon.

After the procedure, months later, when Antoine and Giovanni sat on the bench in the cemetery, Giovanni nodded, moments after Antoine had asked him, again, about having a killer's eyes. "We're all just killers anyway, aren't we? I mean, faced with the situation. Of survival. It's kill or be killed, right?"

Antoine paused for a moment. "Do you remember when she gouged your eyes out? Do you remember when I asked you in your hospital room? When you couldn't remember the specifics?"

Giovanni nodded.

"So the memory returned?"

Giovanni sighed and looked out at the tombstones.

The clouds moved in and filtered the moonlight, giving a greyish hue to the markers. "I've never forgotten," he said. "It was the anesthesia, wasn't it?" He snapped his head and looked at Antoine, who fidgeted for a moment and looked back at Giovanni.

"So you blocked it? From your mind?"

Giovanni looked forward and closed his eyes. He then hung his head down, shaking his head. "I can still remember the gleam from the blade. The light had caught it. Reflected it back to me. That was the last thing I saw. And then she scooped them out. I saw the blade come closer to my eye, and then it was darkness. It wasn't the searing pain from the blade as it cut through my iris – but I did scream in pain. I did. But what tormented me so much was the darkness that followed. I heard her laughing afterwards as I lay on the floor. That sinister laugh that Claret always had. Like she was straight from hades. And I could feel the warmth of the blood gushing down my cheeks. I could feel it pooling on the floor. I felt its warmth through my toes. But I didn't hear her footsteps. I couldn't tell if she was still there. And you know how she can appear and disappear."

Antoine nodded. "Well, at least you can see again."

Giovanni looked up and around at the cemetery. It was the middle of the night.

The gravestones reflected on the pale blue moonlight. And the night was still and silent. "Yes," he said. "The tombstones are so beautiful. Each one representing a life lived. All at different times, different places. Just because one them had been buried here, it doesn't always mean they were born here. Nor even lived here."

"Or they lived here at the end of their life."

"Correct," Giovanni said.

They stopped talking as they heard the approach of footsteps in the gravel.

Neither could see in the darkness to whom the footsteps belonged, but they were expecting him. Without even having sight, they knew who it was. And when the footsteps stopped, they focused on the Italian leather boots, the blue tinted moonlight highlighting the leather in light pastel.

And then they looked up.

A pair of faded jeans.

And a black button down shirt.

But it was the long, flowing blonde hair, which had reached halfway down the back, and chiseled face, where it had been confirmed. "Tramos!" Giovanni exclaimed. "You actually came?"

He smiled, nodded and sat next to them on the edge of the bench. "Of course I did. You all are in torment. How many of you are left now?"

Antoine raised his head and Tramos looked directly back at him. "Not many, Tramos. Not many. We're severely injured. Almost gone. Darius was one of the first in my sector. And it just catapulted from there. It was like an infection. Like a virus."

Tramos nodded and looked around the cemetery. "Yes," he said. "*The Hooded Man*. What ever became of him?"

"We defeated him," Antoine said. "He is gone now. Forever. At least that is what we believe. But he left a trail of death."

Tramos took a seat next to them. He looked over at them, perplexed. "You defeated him? How?"

Antoine swallowed and placed his hands on his thighs. "You know of Claret? Claret Atarah?"

Tramos nodded.

"I know all. Continue."

Antoine nodded. "Well, when she was discovered to have orchestrated this assault on the immortals, she was tried and crucified for her crimes against her own kind."

Tramos leaned on his knee with his elbow. "And this 'hooded man'? Who was he?"

Antoine continued. "He was a puppet."

Tramos looked down and closed his eyes. He shook his head. "Oh, dear, oh dear. Whatever has become of my kind?"

Giovanni snapped his head over towards Tramos and grabbed his arm. "She took my eyes!" His eyes were wide as Tramos shifted his face and his mouth dropped open. "She gouged them out with a knife! She was evil!"

Tramos threw his head back and laughed. "And you two are not! Are you both so quick to judge? Do we know for certain that this was caused by Claret?"

Antoine stood and placed his hands on his hips. "She murdered our kind. She was hunting me for years."

Tramos shot a glance to Antoine. "She had reason to. I remember a night when you were in Cairo. Do you remember, Antoine?"

Antoine remembered.

He could still see the stars on that night, decades before the Tutankhamen expedition had been arranged and the tomb had been discovered in 1922. Antoine remembered being there.

He could still smell the pungent urine stench of the camels. And the feel of the hot wind blowing sand in his face. He could still feel the shoulder strap of the small leather bag that he had carried on his shoulder, with the weight of the cup inside.

Antoine sat and cleared his throat.

"You both don't know the specifics regarding Claret. All you know is speculation – "

"– And what she did," Antoine said. "What we saw!"

Tramos flung to his feet and spun around in Antoine's face. "You think you knew what was going on! But all you did was sit in those stupid little hocus-pocus sessions by that Harrison. That silly Monsignor. He has been a thorn in my side for centuries."

Giovanni straightened up and looked at Antoine. Antoine raised his eyebrows.

"Then what we need to do," Tramos said, "is for you to come with me. I will protect you both."

Antoine and Giovanni nodded.

Tramos snapped back around and looked at the two of them sitting on the small bench. "And Delia and the others know nothing of this, correct?"

Giovanni raised his head and looked at Tramos. "That's correct. *The Inspiriti* know nothing of this meeting."

Tramos looked at Antoine. "And what about you, Antoine? Why are you here?"

Antoine looked down and fidgeted for a few moments.

He finally looked up at Tramos, directly in his eyes. "Because you are my bloodline. Darius is gone now. He transformed me, you transformed him...but I think if we can raise Darius, couldn't he give us some answers?"

Tramos and Giovanni both looked at Antoine. Tramos placed his hands on Antoine's shoulders. "For what, Antoine? Do you seek redemption?"

Antoine sunk down in the bench. He sighed. "One day, this immortality, won't it all go away? I mean, a day has to come when all this...all this around us...ends. When we blow out like a candle."

And Tramos stood.

He looked down at Antoine and Giovanni, as they sat on the bench and looked back up at him. "You both are loyal," he said. "But it will take far more than your loyalty to our bloodline to redeem our kind." And then he looked directly at Giovanni. "You, sir, are from a different bloodline. Are you not? Who is your maker?"

Giovanni looked down. "Only recently. I was mortal for a long time. But I am part of the bloodline. Darius is my maker."

Tramos nodded. "How did I not see that? So you are part of our bloodline then. Interesting that I did not sense that."

Giovanni sighed. "Claret has placed a curse on me, dear Tramos. When she took my eyes. It was after Darius became mortal again. But before Antoine had resurrected. But she came. As I waited for them to return from Miami. I take care of their chateau, you see. But when I was waiting for them to return from Miami, she came to me! And she took my eyes! And she gouged them out with a knife!"

Giovanni cried and fell to his knees, hugging Tramos' legs. Tramos looked down at Giovanni, who buried his face in his thighs. Tramos could feel the warmth of the man's tears moistening his pants. Tramos closed his eyes, shook his head, and placed his hands on Giovanni's shoulders. "Get up," he said. "This is not something I would expect from you." Giovanni raised his head and looked up at him. "Master?"

Tramos smiled. "Do you know who I am?"

Giovanni shook his head and slowly rose to his feet as Antoine looked on.

"I am the eldest," he said. "The oldest immortal. I was transformed many thousands of years ago. Before Claret. Before Christ walked the Earth. And you will always call me Master, correct?"

Giovanni sat back on his haunches. He looked up at Tramos, who stood, looking down from the shadows. A faint light emanated from behind him.

Giovanni's eyes widened. "You cannot be..."

Tramos grabbed Giovanni's chin and yanked it towards his face. "And why do you think that?"

They paused for a moment and Giovanni said nothing, not until Tramos released his grip, and he sat back. He reached his hand up and massaged his chin. He shifted his eyes back up at Tramos. "Because Claret is the oldest."

Tramos lunged forward. He grabbed Giovanni by the neck with a powerful, muscular hand. "She is gone! Crucified! You crucified her without even really knowing that she even committed a crime! What makes you think that she was even guilty?"

Antoine placed his hand on Tramos' arm. "Because she recruited a man. A man named George Stanley. It was she. After the crucifixion, we spoke to George. He explained to us what Claret had done."

Tramos shifted his face towards Antoine. "What do you mean? You mean she did what she was tried for?"

Antoine shrugged his shoulders. "I hesitate to say this – but Monsignor Harrison – he was the one. He conducted a trial for her. He let the immortals make the decision. They voted, and chose to cast her away. They took her to Golgatha. She hung on a cross. And she served for her crimes."

Tramos took a deep breath and exhaled. He looked forward, out at the cemetery. "Well then," he said. "I will look into it. I have a mortal researcher who assists me. His name is Hector Tabares. Look him up, Antoine. He has been assisting me for years, and can be of great help to you. But use him to look into this Stanley character. I want to see what role he had to play in all of this. And also Monsignor Harrison. We have to clean up this whole mess with *The Hooded Man*. But if she was guilty…" Tramos shook his head. "Then that…that would be 'The Kiss of Judas', wouldn't it? The ultimate betrayal."

II

PREMONITION

IN THE DAYS before Darius had passed, Antoine kept his vigil in the Master Suite of their Chateau in Lyon. It had been a quiet evening; Giovanni was polishing silver in the kitchen as Antoine sat in the rocking chair next to the bed, his arm resting on the arm of the chair, his chin resting in his open palm.

He could never remember Darius being so close to death ever before. Not ever in the centuries they had known each other.

There was a knock on the front door as Antoine looked up.

He placed his chin back in his palm, hoping the caller would go away. He had instructed Giovanni to not answer for any visitors. Antoine sat in the rocking chair, watching Darius. The old and feeble Darius. Now lying on his back under a white sheet, looking like a snow covered mountain range.

The Darius who he had known for so many years, and who was a mere young man in chronological age – at least from when Darius had told Antoine of his transformation. Darius had been merely in his twenties when he encountered Antoine in Badulla, and then, the two of them had been frozen in time together for centuries. And then Darius had to drink from the decanter. That silly, crystal decanter. From that hooded man. Antoine shook his head and sighed.

But the knocking continued, as Antoine sighed and hung his head down, staring at his lap. He heard the clank of silver across the chateau and footsteps shuffle across the floor towards the foyer.

That certainly was Giovanni.

And he was clearly going to peek his head through to curtains from the windows that spanned the walls on the sides of the giant, wooden doors to get a view of the caller.

Antoine stood and headed to the bedroom door. He looked back once more at Darius, covered in white sheets, his head buried in the mountains of fluffy, white pillows. His eyes, sunken and dark. His skin looked pruned and wrinkled. Antoine closed his eyes. He could see Darius' jaw through his paper-thin skin.

"Darius?" There was no answer, just silence.

Antoine rushed to the bed. He knelt on the side and placed his hands on the side of Darius' feeble head. After a few moments, his eyes slowly opened and Antoine could hear his breath come quietly.

Antoine closed his eyes and let out a sigh as he heard footsteps in the hallway approach the door. He rested his head on his arms, lying for a moment next to Darius, when he heard Giovanni's footsteps approach in the hallway, and then the bedroom door click open. "I'm sorry sir. But it was Delia. And she insisted."

Antoine opened his eyes and slowly looked around his shoulder. "Oh, yes. Delia." He got up and nodded, turning around and saw Delia approach from the darkness of the hallway. Her hair had turned snow white. And her age appeared to be of an elderly lady. Had she drank from the decanter as well?

He looked at her directly in the eyes.

They were wide open and her face was shifted in concern.

Her face looked pained.

Her mascara was running down her cheeks, through the patchwork of wrinkled skin.

"I'm surprised to see you here, Delia."

She attempted a smile, but as she looked over and saw Darius dying in the bed, she bit her lip. "I came here to speak with you," she said.

"Does it concern Darius? Because that is all I am concerned about right now."

She nodded. "Will you join me in the front room?"

Antoine turned and looked down at Darius as he felt Delia's light touch on his arm. "Let me speak with you. Away from this room. I have something important to tell you."

Antoine never took his eyes off Darius as they exited the room, not until he crossed the threshold of the door. Darius lay in bed, as he been now for days. When Antoine had burst out of his grave, he first saw Darius. When Antoine clawed his way out of his coffin, Darius helped tear the wood away, and scoop the dirt out of the deep, dark grave. Antoine looked into the room for one last time. "You clawed me out of the earth with your own bare hands. I will do the same for you."

And then he heard a familiar voice in his head. It was dark, deep, and demonic.

I am coming for you, Antoine. I am coming to collect payment. Do you remember me? I will see you in your nightmares…

Antoine felt a chill rush through his body as he snapped off the lights and closed the door to the darkened room.

"What is it, Antoine?" Delia's face was shifted with concern.

Antoine closed his eyes and hung his head down. "I…I haven't heard that voice for many years…and it spoke to me just now as I was leaving Darius…" There was a quiver in his voice. "Just a moment."

Antoine dashed back into the room. He threw the drapes open as the bright afternoon daylight spilled into the room. He turned on each bedside lamp, as well as the overhead light. He stood for a moment. "No shadows?" He looked back at Delia. Her eyebrows were raised. Antoine took a few steps back towards the bedroom door as he scanned the room. "You don't see any shadows, do you?"

"What was that all about, Antoine?"

He shook his head.

"What voice were you talking about, Antoine?"

He shook his head and brushed it off. "Never mind. Let's go up front."

Giovanni was waiting in the front parlor holding a tray with two bulbous wine glasses. He stood straight and firm, and did not even reach up to adjust his blindfold. He raised his head towards the sound of their footsteps.

"I thought to open a Beaujolais? Perhaps might help?"

Antoine found his way to the sofa as Delia sat next to him. "Yes, Gio. That's fine." He looked over at Delia, directly in her eyes. "Now. What were you pressing to tell me?"

She took a deep breath and exhaled slowly. "Well," she said. "You know that Darius was aging rapidly after he lost his gift."

He nodded. "His immortality."

"Yes," she said, accepting a glass of dark red wine from Giovanni. He turned to Antoine, holding the tray with the remaining glass. Antoine picked it up as Giovanni sat on the chair across from them, placing the tray on the floor, as Delia took a sip and nodded. "Yes, Antoine," she said. "Well." She sounded exasperated as she set her wine glass on the coffee table with a slight clank. She leaned back and looked up at Antoine. "When you were in your coffin, after you had been burned on the altar…do you remember that?"

Antoine nodded. "Yes. I remember. It was after *Sacrafice* had opened. Asmodai had pursued me. I paid for resurrecting Darius by a coffin-sentence for years."

"Well, during that time, Darius went through a very difficult period. He lost his immortality that same day you burned on the altar. That was very significant for him."

Antoine nodded as he fingered the rim of his glass.

"Everything caught up with him," she said.

"How did you see this?"

"There were days that I would see him. And other days I didn't, of course. But it was those gaps that seemed to change most. I'd see him on a Monday. And then I might see him again on Friday or Saturday, and he would look ten years older."

Antoine shook his head, looking down at the floor.

"He was aging quite rapidly," Delia said. "But the real reason behind my visit today was to tell you about a conversation he had with me a while back. Before you were captured by Asmodai."

Antoine looked up and opened his eyes. "You mean when we were in business with the club? With *Sacrafice*?"

She nodded and took another sip of wine. "Yes, Antoine. He told me he had a vision."

"A vision?"

"A premonition."

"A premonition? Of what? His own death?"

She looked down at her wine.

Antoine scoffed. "Are you kidding me? He's still alive. In the back room. You know that, right?"

Giovanni interjected. "Antoine…"

Antoine guzzled his remaining wine and threw his glass across the room. It shattered on the mantle. He stood and started pacing. "Please, Delia! Stop sounding like a side show psychic! Just give me a straight answer!" Giovanni got up and rushed over to the fireplace and started picking up glass shards, placing them in a felt napkin.

Antoine sat on the sofa next to Delia and leaned his elbows on his knees as Giovanni brought Antoine a fresh glass of wine. Antoine looked forward and shook his head.

She looked down at his hand and placed her hand over his gently.

Antoine looked down at her hand, the wrinkled skin, the liver spots, and sighed. He brought his other hand to her chin. "Hey. It's me," he said. "Now I have a question. And we're talking about Darius. I know. But he's dying in the next room over there and I need to – at the very least – get some answers." He looked her directly in the eyes. "I'm not blaming you. Now about the conversation?"

She leaned back and sighed. There was a pause. "He came to me with a premonition of his death," she finally said. Antoine started coughing and spit some of his wine across the room.

Giovanni rushed over as Delia patted Antoine on the back. Giovanni leaned in. "Are you alright, master?" Antoine waved his arm. In his mind's eye, Antoine could see Darius lying in the room down the hallway. Huddled in a bright, white sheet. His chest rising and falling lightly as he took each breath. And then, Antoine hovered over Darius, locking his eyes near his face, when there was an interruption –

"Antoine what are you doing?"

Antoine took a deep breath through his nose but did not open his eyes.

"Giovanni, please. Let me concentrate."

Giovanni walked away from the sofa as Antoine exhaled through his mouth. "Very well then," Antoine said. He did not open his eyes. "Let me continue…"

Antoine recalled the days at *Sacrafice*.

When he and Darius would sit in the conference room, around the expansive wooden table (which was roughly the size of North Dakota) and wait. And watch each other, sitting at opposite ends of the table, and stare into each other's eyes. It was always Darius who would break the silence.

"And do you think that I am somehow – not – a part of this? Of this business venture of yours?"

The meeting of the investors had just concluded.

Antoine had leaned back in the chair and covered his face with his hands. "No, Darius. That's not what I'm saying at all. But there are rumors circulating that you have been visited by an angel of death."

Darius scoffed. He stood and slammed his palms on the table. "Who is saying that?"

Antoine walked over to the expansive window on the side wall that overlooked the nightclub dance floor. He looked out into the darkness of the club floor below, and then back over at Darius, who was waiting, arms still propping himself up on the table. "Where were you last night?" Antoine asked, eyebrows raised. "I know what you have been doing in Miami since I resurrected you. Did I make the wrong decision?"

Darius pushed the nearest conference chair down on the floor. "Are you serious?"

Antoine opened his eyes, as he was jolted back to the present.

Delia looked at him expectantly. She leaned forward. "Are you okay?"

Antoine slowly nodded.

"You were shaking."

Antoine took a deep breath and looked around. "I…I don't know, really. I remember Darius getting angry. On the night in the conference room. After the meeting of the investors. When I confronted him about the angel of death."

"*The Hooded Man.*"

Antoine looked up. "Yes. How did you know?"

Delia sighed and shook her head. "Because I think that's why he could be dying. I don't know yet. Don't circulate this with the immortal community. Just don't."

Antoine shook his head. "What is it?"

Delia set her glass of wine down as thunder rumbled outside. She clasped her hands over her knees and raised her eyes to look at Antoine. "This angel of death…this 'hooded man'…I think he is the cause of all this. Darius came to me, and felt that he was dying. He told me about *The Hooded Man*. And the night with the young Latino man in Flamingo Park. And the cops. He told me about it all, Antoine."

Antione looked down at his knees. "And he assumed then that he was going to die?"

Delia leaned back. "Well…" She looked down and appeared to study the magazines on the coffee table. "The encounter with *The Hooded Man* was the start. He just didn't have the heart to tell you himself."

Antoine stood and started pacing.

His face was shifted in anger. He breathed deeply through his nose. He guzzled his wine and held his glass out. "Giovanni," he said. Giovanni raised his head and adjusted his handkerchief. He dashed over in the direction of Antoine's voice and quickly refilled the glass.

"He certainly didn't," Antoine said. "And when I confronted him about it…when the rumors were circulating…he got defensive."

I am still alive.

Antoine shuddered. He reached out and grabbed the mantle, holding his stomach. "He is still alive!" Antoine said.

"Are you okay, Antoine?" Delia set her wine down on the table with the clank and rushed to Antoine. She placed her hand on his back.

He waved up towards her, still hunched over.

"He was always defensive," Antoine said, taking another gulp of his wine.

"Of course he was," Delia said.

Antoine stood straight again and looked over at Delia. "Because he was ashamed."

Antoine stared at the fire, crackling and popping in the fireplace. He didn't know that he had spoken those words. And in his mind's eye, he could see Darius. He could see Darius carrying an urn, filled with ashes, approaching *Les Enfantes*. He saw him standing on a shovel, breaking the ground under the tree, hoisting dirt over his shoulder until a grave was dug.

And he saw the ashes spread through the coffin. Antoine shook his head. "I can't believe I was so hard on him for it. He was carrying this dirty little secret for years. And it must have tormented him, knowing he was going to die."

Delia nodded but said nothing. She raised her glass as Giovanni refilled her wine.

"Dirty little secrets," Delia said. "They can eat you from the inside out."

Antoine returned his attention to the fire, watching Giovanni add a new log. "Darius struggled when he buried me," Antoine said, never taking his eyes off the flames. "I can see it now. He was no longer an immortal at that point."

"You mean when he had buried your ashes? After you were burned on the altar?"

Antoine broke his trance and looked over at Delia. She stood watching him, her skin taking on a deep glow from the reflection of the fire.

"Yes," he said, and slowly made his way back to the couch. He sat, staring straight ahead. "Darius was not an immortal when he buried me. I can see it in my mind now." He looked back up at Delia who joined him.

Antoine closed his eyes and sighed…

…And Antoine was hovering above Darius once again. As he experienced the visions in his mind, he spoke in small, simple words. "Darius told me about the decanter. He called it *The Blood Decanter.*"

Delia took notes furiously.

Antoine's eyes were still closed. And as Antoine looked down at Darius, seeing the vision in his mind, levitating above him, he stopped and looked at his partner of centuries. Darius lay back, his eyes were closed; there was no movement beneath the eyelids.

No REM.

He couldn't have been dreaming. He looked at Darius' forehead, not breaking his stare, as the room turned black around him. Darius' head seemed to levitate away from him, as Antoine was enveloped in total darkness, save Darius' face, which floated away from him, further; it got smaller and smaller, until it was a tiny pinprick of light in the sea of darkness.

"Darius!" he called out in the front room, eyes still closed. "Darius don't go. Don't fly away!" Delia set down her legal pad with a worried look on her face.

Antoine reached outwards towards the floating face, and he felt that he was in vast nothingness.

The bed, the sheets, the room, the chateau. Gone.

Seek me.

He stopped for a moment, just as Darius was out of visual sight.

The voice was masculine, but did not sound like Darius.

Follow me.

And then there was the moment that there was movement in the distance – what initially looked like it could be the return of Darius' face, it was quickly proven that it was not. There was movement.

A flash of red.

A crimson hue.

Come and follow me.

And then Antoine opened his eyes.

Delia's mouth hung open as Antoine jumped up from the couch and raced down the hallway. "Darius!"

Delia assisted Giovanni as they went through the parlor, through the stone foyer, around the fountain, and down the hallway. When they got in view, Antoine was fighting with the lock. He looked over at them for a moment and then right back down to the doorknob. "Damn door is jammed!"

Giovanni rushed forward and kicked the door. It shook in its frame.

"Come on!" Antoine said, yanking the doorknob back and forth. He kicked the door and it shook. "I knew I shouldn't have left the room. Now the door won't open!"

Giovanni took several oversized steps back and Antoine moved to the side. Giovanni lunged forward and threw his weight against the door.

Antoine could see the light emanating through as the door splintered from the frame. He reached up for a piece that was splintering off, and tore it away, throwing a section of the wood into the hallway. Delia jumped backwards, never taking her eyes off of the two immortals tearing the door apart.

"Darius!" Antoine screamed as they ran into the room. A shadowy, red figure hovered over the bed and disappeared into the corner behind the armoire just as they reached the bed. "Darius!"

Delia's heels clicked on the wooden floor as she approached the bed. Antoine covered his face with his hands. "I just know he's gone, I just know. He's gone! *Dead!*"

Antoine slammed the armoire and it crashed against the wall and corrected itself. He looked over at the bed. Darius lay flat on his back, covered in a white sheet, looking like a snow covered mountain range. He took a few steps closer to the bed, and looked at his former lover. He shook his head and felt his eyes well up with tears. "He looks dead. Should we check?"

Delia rushed over to Antoine and placed her hands around Antoine's shoulder as Giovanni stood at the opposite side of the room, hanging his head low, and crying softly. He sniffled several times as Delia loosened her embrace. Antoine wiped his eyes. "I can't even begin – to think – about where his soul may be now."

Delia dropped her arms to her sides. "He was not entirely evil," she said. "While you were in your coffin, Darius came to me, several times, when he was a mortal again."

Antoine looked up, eyes red rimmed with tears. "He came to you?"

Delia nodded. "He was trying to find a way to survive. Searching for an elixir. He called it *The Quest for Immortality.*"

Antoine slowly walked over to the bed.

He looked down at Darius, he appeared to be not only dead – but decrepit. His skin sucked to his cheekbones like parchment paper. Antoine shook his head. After a few moments, he looked up at Delia. She was standing just behind him. He hadn't even noticed that she had placed her hand, an open palm, in the center of his back.

"What was that?" Antoine asked.

Delia leaned in closer. "I mean I know of a manuscript. For a book he was writing. On his life. His story. And he called it *The Quest for Immortality.*"

Antoine looked up. "So you're saying I can read this? Where is it? About the years he was mortal and I was buried? And find out what happened?"

She nodded. "The location…not sure, Antoine. It was rumored to have been at your Estate in Miami when the fire struck."

"Was it destroyed in the fire? Is it finished?"

"The manuscript is substantial. Finished – I am not sure."

"Where is it again?"

"It is at the compound in Miami. He never brought it with him to France."

"Then we need to go to Miami. I need to get my hands on that manuscript!"

III

THE KISS OF
JUDAS

Delia Arnette.

She was the woman, the immortal woman, the one who was always present, but not always noticed. She would never die; unless she betrayed her own kind.

In the *Code of the Immortals*, death was a certain sentence for those who betrayed their own kind – whether it be for murderous intentions, the pursuit of power, or other reasons.

But when she left the Chateau, there had been a certain feeling that washed over her, like the Christ blood – that redemption, however far that it may seem out of reach, especially for members of the immortal community, could very well be possible, at least for some.

Even for the darkest of individuals.

Even for those who lived a life full of evil, like Darius, who had lived a life of sin and passion. But when Delia got into her car outside Antoine's estate, she made a mental note to find the manuscript for *The Quest for Immortality* for Antoine.

And later, as she sat back in her car as her driver navigated the small car-lined streets of Lyon, as she headed towards the airport, thoughts permeated her mind, and she wondered about the immortals as a whole society: could they be redeemed as well?

Was there hope for them beyond the physical world?

And after Darius died, after Delia had left for the airport in Lyon that one summer day, *The Hooded Man* struck the immortals with a vengeance.

Not far after that, the immortals were nearing death.

Extinction.

Even after defeating the villain, the wounds ran deep.

The blood was still fresh, and the many immortals who were seduced – the ones who drank from the decanter, were dying as mortals; final deaths.

No resurrection.

At least not in the physical world that they had come to know. Delia settled into her flight back to Rome from Lyon.

In the months and years after Darius passed, Delia remained close with the immortals.

She maintained her leadership role, and when *The Hooded Man* brought his assault against the immortals to a devastating crescendo, she was drawn to Antoine. Assisting him with navigating the leadership of a sector that was clearly the nucleus of the attack. And also comforting him when Antoine would shudder at the thought of Claret Atarah – or perhaps even Asmodai, the demon of hades, the demon of Lust, who had been pursuing Antoine for many years, ever since Antoine had resurrected Darius for the first time.

But when *The Hooded Man* was defeated, Antoine and Delia drew closer towards one another. Delia Arnette was now one of the most senior of the immortals, and she appeared aged.

Her hair had turned snow white.

Her hands and arms, appeared frail; but despite her outward appearance, she remained with the strength of her gift.

For she was still an immortal, she still would not die.

When Delia had first been transformed, when she was first given the dark gift of immortality, she had been young, gorgeous...a red lipped young starlet on the Vaudeville stage in Paris. And on that fateful night, when she took her bow at the end of the performance, she saw a man in the audience; a single pair of eyes in a sea of faces, staring right at her. Not merely watching the performance, or the bows, but staring directly at *her.*

Their eyes locked and the man nodded as the crowd stood on their feet and cheered as the rest of the cast took their bows. Delia slowly walked off stage, never taking her eyes off of the strange man. He seemed a bit out of place in the tiny Paris theatre; and she was strangely drawn to him.

Once backstage she rushed over to the makeup tables and started removing her glittering headdress. As she removed the bobby pins, she dropped her handheld mirror on the floor. As she leaned over to pick it up, she saw a pair of black boots. She paused, her hand on the mirror handle, and saw the man's dark face in the reflection.

She turned around and looked up.

The man smiled, removed his hat, revealing long, flowing golden hair. He smiled. "Pardon the intrusion," he said. "May I speak with you?"

She picked the mirror up and slowly placed it back on the make-up table. She leaned back in the small folding chair as the man moved around and leaned against the countertop. The other performers hurriedly removed their costumes and make-up, each picking up their belongings and leaving the theatre, one by one. Heels clicked against the hardwood floor, fading off into the distance. Several lights clicked off.

The man shifted his weight against the make-up counter and crossed his arms as they looked at each other in silence. Delia raised her eyes to look at him, as she still held the wadded up cloth in her hand. Bright red lipstick stained it.

"I know about you."

Delia's mouth opened. Her heart started beating fast. "Know…about me?"

"About you," he said. "I know of your origins. Where you come from. Where you have been. We have been studying you." He reached under some racks of costumes and fished out a small, wooden folding chair. He placed it on the floor next to her and sat facing her. "But first, please permit me to introduce myself," he said. He extended his hand, taking hers gently, and he drew it up to his lips and kissed it. "They call me Tramos."

Delia took a breath. "That's…an interesting name," she said, her eyes watching his hands.

He placed her hand gently back in her lap and leaned back in the chair. It creaked under his weight. Delia noticed how muscular he must be from the look of his large, powerful hands. "I know that you are special," he said. "You have a unique assignment. But you…what…have embraced the physical world, yes? And the ways of the immortals as well?"

Delia looked back in the mirror.

Her lipstick was smudged across her cheek. She dipped the cloth in a small glass of water and started to clean her face. "How do you know this? So much about me. Who are you affiliated with?"

Tramos removed his coat.

"I am one of the eldest immortals." He extended his hand as he told her about his origins. She got up and took his hand as they walked to the end of the stage. He spun her around, so that the room became blurred.

All was out of focus except his face.

Delia felt her eyes getting heavy. "Just focus on me," he said. "Don't lose sight of me…"

And then the stage turned black.

They spun as they lifted into the darkness. The lights cut out and they were bathed in black. The curtains soared down from the ceiling as they levitated.

Delia closed her eyes.

She was feeling nauseated.

But just as she closed her eyes, she felt Tramos put his powerful hands on her cheeks. "Stay awake, dear one. You will want to see this show!"

She struggled to open her eyes, but when she did, Tramos spread a pair of fine white wings from his back…so wide they reached far outwards from his muscular body. As the wings soared outwards, the spinning ceased, and Delia looked at an immense black mountain range, rising from an unseen land.

The green sky lent a foreign hue.

She looked down at an empty beach and surf from the sea. He flapped his wings as they hovered above the beach. He held her tight, and she felt his powerful muscles engulf her. She looked up at his piercing blue eyes.

Are you my war angel?

He looked down at her and smiled. "Shall I take us down to the beach?" She closed her eyes and rested her head on his chest.

Delia saw a small bonfire appear in the middle of the sand, burning and emitting a plume of dark, black smoke. She looked back up at Tramos. His long, blonde hair was blowing freely in the wind, and his eyes were closed. As his powerful arms were still wrapped around her, they gently glided down to the beach.

Tramos set Delia down gently on the sand. The surf splashed in the distance, crashing against stones and emitting a dull roar. Her mouth dropped open as Tramos extended his wings to full span. They reached from one end of the beach towards the other.

"You!" she gasped. "Are an *angel*"

Tramos leaped upwards and flapped his wings and they carried him into the sky. Delia looked up, her mouth open, her hand covering her forehead, shielding the sun from her eyes. He glided across the sky, as his wings soared out from his body. "Now you try!"

Delia looked up at Tramos.

He was hovering above the beach, his wings bent at an angle as he gently lowered himself down towards the sand. He watched Delia watching him in awe.

"Your wings…they're so beautiful!"

His wings were the color of ivory; but they caught and reflected the light in pastel rainbows. White at their crest; a bit darker in the inner parts of the wing.

But so bright and reflective.

Delia had to shield her eyes when she looked at them. And when he spread them, as they reached their maximum span, they appeared to reach across the entire sky, bathing the beach in celestial light and the colorful echo.

And then she heard what sounded like music.

"Is that music I hear?" Delia called up to Tramos.

He looked back down at her, and smiled.

Yes, there was music.

She could tell.

Just ever so faint. Like a hum. Or a chorus. The singing was faint but audible; and hit a crescendo when he spread his wings out to their maximum. A cascade of mezzo-sopranos from an unseen choir.

She watched as he drew his wings inwards to his back as the music stopped and the light faded.

They were as real as they could be. And when she had seen him gliding across the sky, she knew what she felt. She could feel their comfort. As if those wings were spread to protect her, and only her.

Tramos walked towards her as the singing stopped. The dull roar of the surf returned. "Time for you to try!"

Delia cocked her head to the side. "I…try? I've never been able to fly, Tramos. Why would you even think…"

Tramos put his arm around her shoulder. "Because of who you are, Delia. Because of *what* you are. You don't think that you were placed in Paris with your mother and father by chance, did you?"

She closed her eyes.

She saw father again. The blood was seeping across the floor. And then she saw mother. Her face in the casket. And before that vision, when mother had still been alive. He saw her father, whipping her with a belt as she bent over the kitchen table, clawing her way away from his assault, screaming and crying.

"No! Stop! *Stop!*"

Tramos embraced Delia as she shook. She looked up to him. "I have been blocking those memories…"

"There are no chances, Delia. No coincidences. Everything is planned."

Tramos lifted Delia's chin. She looked up at him and he smiled. "You were placed there for a specific purpose," he said, as he smiled warmly. "I know it was very upsetting to you. But we angels are never placed in easy situations. When others flee the evil in the world, we run towards it. We rescue those who cannot save themselves. We protect those who cannot do so for themselves. We shadow them from the storms, and shield them from the fire…"

And then she thought of Darius.

He saw his face, his long dark hair, his smile.

And then many times that he called on her, in her little apartment in Miami, those humid nights that he gently knocked on the door, when she sat with him on her sofa, sipping wine, reading the books that Darius had consulted with the hopes of saving himself.

But there had been no solution in the books they read together.

Tramos sensed her thoughts.

"You were a great influence on Darius," he said. "And have been equally so on Antoine as well. Do you see how you have been placed in their lives also, Delia?"

Delia thought of her time at the chateau. "Am I to protect Antoine as well?"

Tramos nodded. "In time, you will recognize your assignments more quickly. And your powers. You will learn how to use them. You have extraordinary power, Delia. And that's why I am visiting you. That's why I came to your dressing room at that precise moment in time. Because I have felt a significant need to guide you. You are having memories, in this vision with me, of events that you have yet to experience as a young starlet in Paris. But I felt the need to interject. To give you some guidance. And some knowledge."

"And take me under your wing."

"Do you want to try?"

Delia reached around towards her back. "I don't feel anything," she said. "What am I supposed to do?"

"Will it to happen, Delia. And it will happen."

She thought about father.

And mother.

Antoine and Darius.

And Atticus.

The images flooded her mind, flashing towards her and composing her cerebral vision. Again, and again, the images permeated her thoughts, until she felt her feet lift off the ground.

She opened her eyes and looked down. The beach was below and Tramos stood in the sand, looking up at her.

"I'm flying!" she squealed, laughing and crying at the same time. She looked up and saw the expanse of her wings, the same brightness, the same white, the colors and the music. They were moving, soaring and flapping and carrying her into the sky. "Oh they're so *beautiful*!"

Tramos spread his wings and joined her in the sky. They levitated above the beach as the chorale strengthened, and they held hands, floating across from each other, their sprawling wings reaching far across the sky, flapping up and down.

Delia beamed as she felt warmth. She closed her eyes as the sun brightened.

"The light!" Tramos said. "You are absorbing the light. Now look down below!"

Delia looked down and saw the beach, as it got tinier and seemed very dark, very black, like it was a film that was fading away to black.

"You are moving towards the light, Delia! Everything else will seem like darkness. You have found your wings! Oh, I'm so proud of you Delia!"

Delia threw her head back and felt the wind catch her hair, treasuring the warmth of the light on her face. Nothing else seemed to matter. Tramos let go of one of her hands so they were levitating together, next to one another, facing the sunlight. "It's time, Delia. Time to go and finish our mission. The immortals need us."

"I'm having a vision!" Delia exclaimed. "I see a cross!"

"That is part of your mission, Delia. It's time for us to focus on why we are here. It's time for you to focus on your mission, and for me to focus on mine."

They flew across the sky together, their wings spread wide and flowing, as Delia felt the wind against her face, she could not stop laughing.

"I am an angel! That is who I *am*!"

And then the clouds parted, as Delia envisioned Claret on the Cross.

The clouds retreated; leapt across the sky, as the sun fingered its way through, and down towards the rolling sandy hilltops. She remembered, so many times, a Ms. Claret Atarah. She had been an immortal who had the ability to time-travel. And the same immortal who had been responsible for Delia's descent into darkness and the ways of the earthly immortals.

But it was Claret who had taken Delia under *her* wing, back when she had first encountered her in the ancient, dusty streets of Jerusalem, and again in Paris.

How she remembered Paris.

She could still see the nights when Claret would watch her from the audience while Delia performed her stage routine. Over so many years, so many points in time…Claret would always be there.

Watching her, waiting for her.

Delia could remember the visions, and the days when Claret had walked the earth, searching for someone to be her successor. But it was the act of what happened in Gethsemane, on the night before the Messiah was to be tried by Pilate and hung on a cross, that she had first encountered Claret.

So many thoughts permeated her mind.

And from so many different points in time.

But when she looked down, she saw the result of *The Hooded Man*.

The aftermath of the destruction that he left.

The cross still stood at the crest of the hill, as those who had gathered stood below, were watching…and waiting. Was something else about the happen? Was some great prophecy still yet unfulfilled?

The body on the cross had slithered away.

Claret.

Delia knew now.

The body glided down the wood like a snake burned by a relentless sun; but then, after everything was said and done, and as the watchers stood and waited, it was a strange kind of silence.

And the rest of those who watched, who saw the death, who had watched her head raise to the sky, stood in solidarity as Claret had called out to her maker: *Why, oh why, have you forsaken me?*

But the watchers did not move when they saw her slither down the cross; they did not call for help. Nor did they look for the decanter.

Or for the blood.

But everyone searched for the truth to the conundrum: if she did not die on the cross, for if she were truly immortal, where did she then go? And who would then lead them?

Thunder crashed as the clouds retreated entirely. The sun shined with intensity. Delia looked down and saw herself, standing with the others at the base of the cross. And then she knew.

This was it.

This was her mission.

This is what she had been called to do.

Tramos was gone. She was now alone. Time to go to work…

…and Delia opened her eyes. She hung her head and looked downwards. On the ground lay, in a heap, a large, red cloak. It was lying in a puddle of muddy water.

And then, when Delia stood above the pile of clothing, next to the cross, as she looked down at the cloak, the dirty, torn fabric, she saw the glass shards. Tiny fragments of glass, millions of miniscule shiny pieces that caught the light; scattered all around the cloak and the ground, they seemed like tiny puzzle pieces of annihilation.

She bent down and inspected the pieces. She set her cane down on the ground next to her.

As she looked closer, she saw the top of the decanter, which was still intact; the crystal caught the sunlight coming from the sky and shined up towards her face, drawing a patchwork of light reflected against the lines on her skin; her tired eyes squinted, drawing more lines across her face, making her appear even older than her aged years.

She reached for it and held it up towards the sky. "It just looks like a plain wine decanter." She turned around and faced the others, who stood, watching her examine the decanter plug. "Do you see this? What I am showing you? It seems so powerless now."

Antoine joined her and brushed his long, dark locks aside. "I don't understand, Delia. But the power it had. Look around at us, Delia. We are barely existing. There are scarcely any of us left!"

Delia examined the decanter closely, holding it up to the light. The sun reflected through it. She brought it down and held it close to her heart.

And then she remembered.

She was forced to remember. As she closed her eyes, she saw the coming of the white mist on dirty, wet dark city streets. In the areas of town where one would never venture during the small hours of the night.

But she knew what the cloud of mist would signify.

For the man who would come – the villain – *The Hooded Man* …would follow shortly thereafter. The long, dark, red cloak would drag on the dirty pavement, splash through the puddles of muck. And when Delia stood on the pavement, barefoot and dirty herself, her feet still bled.

She looked down and saw her reflection in one of the puddles. Her lipstick had smeared across her face.

Her mascara ran down her cheeks. Too many tears. Too much sadness.

The music still wafted from the club's interior. Her burlesque show had ended hours ago, and she was alone in the alley. She could smell the stink of the trash in the cans next to her as she pulled the door shut. It locked with an audible click. Still wearing her heels, she clicked across the bricks towards the open street, where there would be more lighting and more people, even at this late hour, Paris seemed to always be awake.

And then she heard footsteps behind her.

Deep, heavy footsteps, coming from further back in the darkness of the alley.

She caught her breath in her throat.

The street still seemed so far away. For she could hear the deep throated and chesty breathing.

"I have waited for you for many years, Delia."

That voice.

So utterly familiar.

It could not possibly be, could it? Certainly, it was not *The Hooded Man*. So who was speaking to her from the darkness?

She faced the street ahead, her eyes still closed, as she held her bag over her shoulder. "You have been following me." She didn't even have to turn around to know who it was. She hadn't encountered him since she had been a little girl, in her tiny bedroom in Paris, back on the day they had buried her father's plain wooden coffin. In the days when Auntie Thelma had still been alive. Before the cirrhosis set in.

Delia took a deep breath and exhaled. She shook her head. "I don't even have to turn around, do I? To even know who you are? Correct?"

She heard shuffling and paper cups blowing in the wind. "Have you considered my offer? What I asked you the last time we talked?"

She sighed.

She could remember.

Back in her bedroom, when he had questioned her faith. And then she remembered the thorns. And the angel who stood in the field of skulls.

"I remember your proposal."

She turned around.

She could see a figure in the shadows, but it appeared to be far less than how he had appeared to her when she was a little girl. Not a monster, not a demon.

Just a man.

She cocked her head to the side, but the darkness obscured him far too much. "Yes..." she said again. "I remember our conversation. And I remember the visions you showed me after. I've had plenty of time to think about it too."

"But you haven't done anything about it."

She thought she saw the glimpse of a foot. A work boot, perhaps. "Why don't you show yourself? I know you're just a man back there. Don't see any horns this time…"

The man chuckled. "I'm keeping myself in the darkness. I'm not so sure you can handle this one, *little darlin'*."

"Try me." She shifted her bag to her other shoulder and stared intently at the darkness back in the alley beyond the group of small trash cans.

"Suit yourself, Delia."

And the man stepped forwards into the light, as Delia gasped. She recognized the sandy brown, mussed hair. The unshaved beard. The white sleeveless shirt and work boots.

Her mouth dropped open as she felt tears well up in her eyes. "Daddy!"

She turned her head around, closing her eyes and hanging her head down low. "Go away!"

He was closer now.

"Don't you see why you see me this way now? In the form of your father? Isn't he the one, single man who you loathed so much as to kill him? A little girl! Didn't think you had it in you, Delia…"

She shook her head, keeping her eyes closed.

"You're not really him," she said. "I know who you are." And then she lifted her head, and opened her eyes. Her fathers' likeness dripped away, pooling on the ground, like wax from a burning candle. And then she saw him again. The same red, beastly muscular skin.

But she only got a glimpse of the horns as he retreated back to the darkness. "Don't you worry! You can deny me all you want! For you will be traveling through time. I have those on the planet who will convince you to follow me. I already know it's going to happen!"

"Be gone!" she screamed. The wind blew trash around as the darkness fell silent.

Delia opened her eyes and saw she still held the top to the decanter in her hands. She threw the damaged piece back on the ground. She looked up at Antoine, who remained fixated on the shattered decanter. "It was pure evil," she said. "And this cloak. This horrible cloak. It must be burned. Destroyed. Buried. Whichever. The evil that surrounds this – must be extinguished."

A balding, older man joined Antoine and Delia. "Let me do it. Only I can do it."

Delia and Antoine looked at the man. "George!" Delia said. She shook her head and got up. She held her hand out and George assisted her to her feet. "How did you!? I have been to your grave! How did you?" She shook her head. "You must not touch that cloak," she said. "Or the decanter for that matter. Look at it down there. It still *resonates* with evil. The power that surrounds it is still there." She looked up and over at George. He stood, his hands clasped in front, fidgeting and shifting from foot to foot. He no longer seemed like the one who might have donned the robe. "And you, George, are still susceptible to that power."

George looked down at the robe as Delia placed her hand on his arm. "You can still be redeemed," she said. "You may no longer have a physical body. I know you are stuck in this world, away from reality. But you can still be saved."

George looked down at the robe he once wore to commit evil. And then, for a moment, as Delia remained focused on George, she could tell he was thinking about his life before the robe. Before the decanter. His shook his head and hung his head down, as he felt the warm wetness of a tear streaming down his cheek. "I had the cages in my basement," he said. "I still remember sitting in my driveway watching Nick."

And George had remembered Nick very well. It wasn't the tanned and fit torso, or the sweaty muscles that had glistened in the sun as the young man mowed his lawn and paused every so often to take a drink from his bottle of water. It was what had happened after that. For Nick was not the reason he was here.

He was here because of the decanter.

And because of Claret.

Delia looked at George as they made eye contact. She nodded as George smiled a tired smile.

They looked up as Monsignor Harrison, the leader of the immortals, walked up and joined the others. He was large, imposing. Overweight and balding. He wore horn-rimmed glasses. "Leave it there," he said. "Leave the cloak, leave the shattered glass. We have other things to worry about. We must get back to Rome at once. We are a dying race now. I must call a meeting of the High Council. This has gotten to a point where we cannot worry about trivial material items that may or may not hold a power."

He looked over at Delia and Antoine, who looked back up at him. Monsignor Harrison stood in confidence and authority, and his considerable heft and stature solidified his role as the supreme commander of the immortals. "We shall leave Golgatha and head to Rome. I have already sent Ramiel ahead to contact those who are still living – and still immortal – to organize their districts and prepare for a meeting in Rome. We all must attend. Every last immortal that hasn't been destroyed."

Delia stood and balanced herself on her cane as Antoine assisted her, taking her arm. "Are you calling a convention?" she asked. "Every last one of us?"

The Monsignor nodded. "There aren't many of us left now," he said. "We must band together. Join forces. We have to save our own kind."

"So we shall leave now?" Antoine asked. "Now that Claret is gone?"

The Monsignor reached his arms out. "Come with me," he said. "And remember, Claret may be gone physically from this world, but her soul still lives on. And because of that, she is never truly gone."

Delia paused and looked back at the cross as the group started to make their way down the hill. The sun shined from behind the cross, and it seemed, at least to her, that the sun had not shined that brightly in this world for a long time. At least not from what she could remember, during her time as a mortal or after she received the gift.

And then, as she looked up towards the light, she thought of Tramos and their time on the beach. She wondered where he had gone to. And what assignment he had been on. But one thing was for certain, she knew that they would soon cross paths again.

And then Delia looked down at the cloak, which lay just beneath the cross.

The heaping red mess of fabric that it had become. So dirty. So foul. The fabric which had once contained so much evil, now lying on the ground, amidst the shattered glass of the decanter. But as she navigated the rising stones and balanced herself on her cane, she looked back and could not take her eyes off of the cloak. Was it as powerless as they assumed?

Do you see my cloak? My blood decanter? My shattered glass? It will always torment you, I promise.

Delia stopped in her tracks. "There is still evil here. I can sense its presence. Antoine? Come here, Antoine. Stay close to me."

Before Darius had passed, Antoine often dreamed of him.

On most nights, he would sit, most often keeping vigil in the rocking chair across from the bed, and on the night after Delia left the chateau in Lyon, Antoine had dreams of Darius once again.

Antoine had closed his eyes, and there he was.

It was the same evening that Antoine had confronted Darius in the foyer, centuries earlier, when the chateau had been newly built and Antoine and Darius had but a short amount of time together.

It was the one night that stood out in Antoine's mind, which had haunted him throughout his existence: Antoine could still smell the smoke from the fire that had been burning in the fireplace in the parlor which adjoined the foyer. But it was a fire that had burned many years previously, during the age before electricity and ventilation, and the smoky smell hung through the rooms.

Darius was standing in the very same foyer, next to stone edge of the very same fountain that Delia would lay her purse upon, several centuries later.

Darius, known in those days as the vampire extraordinaire!

But was he a vampire?

Was he a creature of the night?

Darius had certainly been one who had embraced darkness. And in the early days, he would have been known in simpler terms, like that of a vampire.

Antoine had remembered the early days, rising from his coffin, on the night after he had been transformed, looking up as Darius had looked down upon him, bathed in the warm glow of candlelight.

Wake up, sleepyhead!

But Antoine remembered.

He recalled the days when Darius was thought of – at least among the Lyon populace – as the vampire extraordinaire.

That's what he was known by, at least, back in the early days when he and Antoine had lived in the chateau together, when gas lamps still lined the streets. Many years before they were to cross paths with Delia. It was in the early days, the days when Darius had been newly transformed, discovering the new ways of the darkness and immortality, that Antoine had remembered Darius with the most fondness.

Darius, the teacher.

Darius, the lover, the warrior.

Oh Darius, my war angel. My celestial docent. Spread your wings.

But in Antoine's dreams, Darius lived on. Tall, lanky, long, brown hair down his back. Always tied. There was a certain vision that remained with Antoine throughout the years. And as the centuries passed, it always penetrated his mind – the gleam of the light reflecting from the dagger. Antoine could still see that reflection of light, centuries after the night that Darius had stood next to the fountain, challenging Antoine to drive it through his heart.

Kill me! Murder me now! Do it, Antoine, do it!

The challenge.

Standing in the foyer in the flickering of candlelight. The shadows painted grey wisps across the walls as the grand chandelier, with its layers of candles like an orchestra of

157

flaming light, hung above the fountain, where Antoine stood, holding the dagger. He could see the burning candles the chandelier reflect in the dagger, shining back in his face.

Find your own way!

Darius had shouted to him in the dreamlike state, as Antoine had slowly raised his eyes from the dagger, looking at Antoine, noticing the reflection of his eyes, stark white, catching the light from the candles; appearing almost like a patchwork of shadows; a network of fingering branches.

It was before the days of electricity and transportation, in the days when Antoine and Darius had been together, living together, finding the ways of the immortals to be so similar to the ways of vampires, but discovering, together, that he and Darius were so much more, so increasingly complex.

Antoine remembered the night that Darius had cast him out of the chateau. When Antoine had been forced to find his own way in the world. Darius and his parting words had still rung in Antoine's mind, now so many years later:

Shed your skin. Find your own way. Do what is written, what must be done.

Antoine snapped awake and was brought back to the present. He struggled to catch his breath. He looked down, the veins protruding from his hands as they clutched the arms of the rocking chair. He looked over at the bed, and felt a wave of relief wash over him. He was still alive.

The chateau was silent save a ticking clock in a nearby room. He had fallen asleep in the rocking chair again. Moonlight filtered through the curtains as a light breeze moved through the room.

He focused on the bed. Antoine could hear Darius' shallow breathing against the silence of the room.

Darius was still alive.

That was what mattered now.

Barely clinging to life, most likely.

But alive.

He had the same look – like a snow covered mountain range. He lay, flat on his back. Immobile up to this point. But this time, there seemed to be some movement under the covers. Was Darius awake? Could he be improving?

Antoine stood as the rocking chair creaked backwards. He walked around the bed, and saw Darius lying back, eyes still closed.

"Darius? Darius are you awake?"

Antoine stood and watched Darius intently. His eyes remained closed, but there appeared to be a softness to his face that Antoine hadn't noticed before. A contentedness. His cheeks seemed slightly fuller. Had Giovanni's cooking helped?

And then Darius opened his eyes.

Antoine took a step back as Darius sat up in bed, and looked down at him directly.

Antoine dared not speak.

A smiled washed across Darius' face. "Do you remember your days in the coffin? After Asmodai burned you on the altar? Do you remember, Antoine?"

Antoine's mouth dropped open.

A flood of memories permeated his mind. He remembered the small, wooden coffin, the one that Darius had dug from the grave for him. The same grave in *Les Enfantes*, the one under the flowing, weeping tree; he remembered his ashes being spread through the casket. And his heart, which still beat.

I am still alive.

Darius smiled. Antoine noticed his teeth were rotting, his mouth riddled with decay.

"You were still alive, Antoine. Burned to ashes, but your heart still beat. Do you remember?"

Antoine slowly nodded and took a step towards the window. "Darius…."

Darius chuckled. "Antoine, when you were gone, I was fighting to live. Now that you're back, you need to listen to me." Antoine sighed and examined the curtains. Darius coughed. "When I am gone, I will no longer be alive. Dead. Damned. For all of eternity!"

"Is that why, Darius? Is that why you were fighting to live? For fear of damnation?"

Darius coughed, it was a deep, chesty hack. Antoine grimaced. "My time is near," Darius said.

Antoine turned around. Darius was attempting to raise himself on his elbows. Antoine rushed over to his side. "Giovanni! Come, help me!"

Giovanni appeared at the door and rushed to the bedside, reaching out and assisting Antoine. Giovanni held Darius in a sitting position as Antoine adjusted the pillows against the headboard. Darius again started a fit of coughing, more phlegm, deep, wet coughing. "I need to sit," he croaked. "Just one last time…"

Antoine shook his head. "What is it, Darius? What do you need to tell us?"

Giovanni opened the closet across the room and got some oversized white pillows. He propped the large, fluffy pillows around Darius and leaned him gently back against the headboard as Darius closed his eyes and let out a breath. Darius threw his head forward in another fit of coughing. Tiny blood droplets tinged the edge of the cover.

"What is it Darius? What is it you need to tell us?"

He looked down and sighed. "My body…is catching up to my soul…my heart…is nearing its final beat…"

Antoine sat on the bed and put his arms around Darius. "Do you think the end is truly near? Is there something I can do to thwart this? Can I call on Asmodai?"

"No," Darius said through labored breaths. "No demons. No rituals. It's time for me to go."

Darius raised his head slowly and looked up at Antoine. His eyes were clouded. "I am almost ready," he said. Antoine hugged him close, shuddering at how frail Darius seemed now. He had once been rugged and muscular; he was now a shell of his former self.

"I had been cursed with vanity," Darius said. "The sickening self-obsession. And where has that gotten me?"

The young years are few and fast.

"Antoine, do you remember when you first saw me?"

The café in Badulla flashed through Antoine's mind.

He remembered the bartender, the boisterous crowd. The small, wooden tables and chairs. The tiny wooden tables and chairs, the dim-lit corner booths with the paintings on the wall. And he remembered Darius, sitting in the corner, watching…and waiting. But Antoine also remembered his occupation at the time. And he remember Darius watching him, as he took tourists and regulars to the rooms up above the bar.

"I remember…" Antoine said.

You can only use your body as your means of existence for so long. And then you have to figure out what you're going to do in this world.

Darius' exhaled a deep, labored breath.

Each breath took on a raspy tone, as he signaled for Antoine to lay him back down. "Do you remember when I carried you? In the urn? Your ashes?"

Antoine nodded. "I felt your presence. But yes, I remember."

Antoine thought of the sea of souls. That horrid lake full of putrid bodies, writhing at the entrance to Hades. He remembered the face off with Asmodai, the lumbering demon of Lust, the monster who had been sent to the *Les Enfantes* cemetery in Lyon when Antoine was trying to resurrect Darius. And Antoine remembered watching him ride away on black clouds in a red tinted sky.

"I remember Asmodai," Antoine said. "When I was digging up your grave in *Les Enfantes*. How could I forget?"

Darius attempted a smile. "Yes, but those were different days, Antoine. I was lying in that coffin in *Les Enfantes* for centuries. After you drove the dagger in my heart. But I was immortal then, Antoine. I still existed. It will be different now, Antoine. So very different."

Antoine scoffed and shook his head. "You still exist now! And why wouldn't you exist then?!"

Antoine sank into the rocking chair and rested his chin on a balled up fist, shaking his head, as Giovanni quietly left the room and closed the door with a slight click. After a few minutes, Antoine looked directly at Darius, and they made eye contact.

Antoine felt a tear stream down his cheek. "I know you're dying, Darius. No one has to explain it to me. But I was able to resurrect you back in *Les Enfantes*, and I can do it again. I know I can."

Darius looked down. "Things are different now, Antoine. I no longer have the gift. This is final, Antoine."

They sat in silence for a few minutes, as Antoine leaned back, rocking and looking at the window, saying nothing.

"When you were gone, I fought for you," Darius said, breaking the silence. "They may have burned you on the altar…but I fought for you. I got you out of there. Out of that wretched underworld."

"Yes, Darius. I know you did."

"And I brought you here…back to France…in your urn as I started to age."

Antoine sat in the rocking chair across from the bed. "Why did *The Hooded Man* come for you, Darius? Why did he choose *you*? Why did he choose *us*?"

"My mouth…it's so dry. Like cotton…" Darius shifted. "I don't know, Antoine. I truly don't."

Antoine got up and reached for a glass of water and a straw that were sitting on the bedside table. He held it down in front of Darius, as he leaned forward and took a long sip.

After a few minutes, Darius laid his head back on the pillow. Antoine looked at Darius' eyes; the cataracts had clouded them, but he could still tell that Darius was looking at him.

After a period of silence, and as Antoine returned to the rocking chair with a slight creak, Darius finally spoke. "We were chosen…why were we chosen? We were all so evil. We still are."

"Tramos transformed you?"

"Yes, back when I was a young man. Here in France. He would visit me in the early morning. He feasted on me for months before he finally transformed me."

"You never told me that story, Darius."

"The sheets were always covered in blood when he left. He would always tear through the window and fly away."

Antoine raised his head. He had been leaning on the arm of the rocking chair, listening to Darius, resting his chin on his open palm, but then he looked back up at Darius. "He could fly?"

"He has many powers which we do not."

Antoine sighed and returned to resting his chin on his hands.

"So do you see now?" Darius said. "Why we had been chosen?"

Antoine shook his head.

"We are evil, Antoine. *The Hooded Man* selected us for annihilation."

Antoine scoffed and stood. He started pacing around the room. "Darius…that is preposterous." Antoine's nostrils flared as he took in a deep breath. He looked back at Darius with an intense stare. "We are who we *are*," he said. "This is who we *are*. How we were *created*. We didn't ask to be this way."

Darius raised his arm, pointing his index finger up towards the ceiling. He bobbed his arm up and down as he spoke. "When I first saw you, in the café in Badulla, what type of life were you living, Antoine?"

Antoine stopped pacing.

He looked back at Darius who returned his gaze.

And then, the old, decrepit Darius, lying on the bed in front of him, seemed to transform to the young, vibrant, muscular Darius whom he had seen so many years ago in the tiny café, at the table in the corner.

Antoine remembered that Darius had been laughing, wildly. Right across the tiny table as they nursed drinks together. Darius had been telling jokes, and Antoine was enamored with his sensuality. He looked down and saw that Darius was touching his hands, fingertips touching.

"Don't you *see!*" Darius had said on that one night. "You must join me! Come with me, Antoine! I will show you the world. You are here, existing on a life of debauchery in this tiny town. Harvesting coffee! I can take you to Paris. And the world! And beyond!"

Antoine thoughts were brought back to the present.

Darius shifted in the bed.

"Do you remember what happened after we met? After I proposed that you come with me?"

Antoine thought.

He remembered walking along the banks of the New River, watching the reflection of a full moon in the still, calm waters. He remembered the silence of the night. The crunch that their feet made in the gravel as they walked, slowly together.

And he remembered Darius' voice that night. So warm. Reassuring. "Do you see the lights of Badulla up ahead?"

Antoine had looked, through the darkened fields, past the blue moonlit reflections on the tops of the coffee plants, and saw the tiny, box-cutter buildings. There was a warm, yellow glow against the night sky in the distance.

"Such a tiny town. In Paris there is so much art," Darius said. "It's a big, cosmopolitan city. You could be a star there."

"A star?" Antoine laughed. He looked back at Darius who smiled back. "Doing what?" Antoine asked.

"There's many things you could do," Darius said. "I have watched you. Observed you for quite some time now. And I see how you are with people. How you interact. They are *drawn* to you, Antoine. They're captivated by you. You can certainly build on that. You're meant for so much more than this, Antoine. You were meant for bigger things than harvesting coffee and keeping tourists happy in the tiny rooms above the café."

"And what about America?"

Darius smiled as they stopped walking. He turned and faced Antoine, looking at him in the eyes. "I will transform you, if you let me. You will become immortal, Antoine. You will never die. And then we will spend some time in France. For you will be what's known as 'new Baal'. You will need your time to adjust. But after France, I will take you to America."

Antoine opened his eyes and went back to the rocking chair. He could hear Darius' labored breathing.

"You never took me to America. I went there myself. You had me drive a dagger through your heart right over there in the foyer."

Darius seemed out of breath. "No…no, I didn't. But things changed, Antoine. I had to…*had* to die then. I had no choice. You had to find your own way."

Antoine leaned back in the chair and started rocking back and forth. He sighed and looked out the window. The sun was about to set, as a light breeze blew the curtains inwards. The room fell silent, save the creak of the rocker.

After a few minutes, Antoine looked up at the bed. Darius was motionless. "Darius?"

No answer.

He got up and went to the side of the bed. Darius was lying flat on his back, his eyes closed, his body motionless. "Darius?"

Antoine covered his eyes with his hands. Thoughts of Darius flashed through his mind. The laughing in the Café, the walking on the river, the days in the conference room that overlooked the dance floor at Club Sacrafice in Miami…it was a flood of images of Darius, flashing through his mind's eye.

After a few moments, Antoine took his hands away, his cheeks moist with tears. He looked at Darius, lying on the bed as if he were asleep, a look of peace on his face.

The dark ones didn't come, my friend. They didn't come.

Antoine walked to the door, looking back at Darius. He reached for the doorknob, opening the door and moving out to the hallway. He kept the door open as he looked up towards the foyer.

It was by that same fountain that Darius had stood, challenging him with the dagger, so many years ago. "Kill me! Kill me now!" Darius had said. "Drive it into my heart! Don't wait! Shed your skin! It's time! *Shed your skin!* Find your own way in this world! You must!"

Antoine closed the door without a word.

I AM DEAD.

There was a time, when I lay in a room, in a chateau in France, when I had been clinging to life. I had taken each breath as I could, and the breaths that I did, were labored. I scarcely could take in the air.

I could remember the sweet summer air. The breeze flowing into the room through the curtains. How the air would smell so fresh, like linen hanging on a clothesline. And the air, how it tasted. So floral. So wonderful. Refreshing. And then, there was a certain silence to the room. I could even hear the buzzards outside the window.

And I could smell the storm coming on the horizon.

But there was nothing I could do about it.

I couldn't close the window. Or pull the drapes back together. Or even swing my legs around the side of the bed to rise.

I lay on the bed, simply, and that's all I had been able to do.

Flat on my back, spread out, covered by a sheet, and unable to move.

I was in Miami recently, I had remembered that.

My mind still worked at that point, I knew that. But there was a point when I disconnected. When there was no longer a reality; when the others in my life were still there – I could still sense their presence – but it was in a different way.

They were still in the room with me.

The armoire had still been located at the end of the bed, and it was still made of dark wood. It was blurred, but a dark object against a pale, white background.

Still there.

The rocking chair still sat next to it, and Antoine, as far as I knew, still sat in the chair regularly, when we were in our chateau, to sit and enjoy a glass of red wine.

Usually a Cabernet.

Sometimes a Beaujolais.

I could feel the sheet being pulled up and over my body. Soon after, the world became white, for my eyes were still open.

It was placed gently over my face, and moments later, I could hear Antoine start to cry.

I knew it was him.

I wanted to get up. To swing my legs over the side of the bed, to let the sheet fall gently to the floor. To walk over to him, to place my arms around him, as I had so many times in life, to hug him and let him know that everything was fine, everything was alright.

I am here! I would say. *I was never dead! You don't have to cry! There is no reason to be sad! For I am sitting right here next to you, alive, talking and well!*

Antoine eyes would most certainly widen.

His mouth would drop open, and would wipe the tears from his face.

As soon as he would figure out that I was actually sitting there on the bed, living, eyes open and seeing; ears hearing, he would rush to my side, taking me into his arms.

But that isn't what happened.

For I was dead.

And even though I could still hear, even though I could still feel, there was something that I had been unable to do. I could not move. Nor could I speak. So I would wait, and listen. After some time, as the room grew silent, and Antoine's sobbing had subsided, I could hear him breathing, slow and steady.

He might have been sleeping.

But after the silence, I could hear the methodic creak of the rocking chair. The same, old rickety wooden chair that had sat in that room for over a century. And in my mind, I could picture Antoine sitting in the chair, moving his legs up and down, his knees moving upwards, powered by his toes, rocking the chair back and forth, his face buried in his hands. He'd be slumped over the side of the chair, because I would know that Antoine slumped over the side of that very same rocking chair each and every time he would grow sad.

But after some time, the creak of the old, rickety wooden chair ceased, and the room grew silent again. I felt as though the days were passing through the window on the other side of the room.

The door creaked open, and I heard the slow shuffle of footsteps approach the side of the bed. And then a second set of footsteps followed.

"We must bury him tonight. He has been lying here for days. It's time to decide what you want to do."

It was Giovanni.

I could recognize his gravelly voice. It was quite distinct. There was a certain dialect that Giovanni spoke with. A certain accent he had.

And then, the other set of footsteps could only belong to Antoine, now the Master of the House. "Yes, yes," Antoine said. "We should take him to *Les Enfantes*. We have a crypt there. No sense now in burying him in the plot under the tree. I am taking him to his family mausoleum."

"Just a moment, Antoine. I have some papers that Darius had me guard when he became ill. He told me it was his wish, and to be opened only by you."

I knew where I was being taken.

It was over.

For I was still residing in the same bedroom, listening to them in the hours after my death.

I had yet to cross over.

But I knew.

It was time.

I had been lying in the room long enough. My body was decaying.

Starting to decompose. Certainly a stench was starting to permeate the room.

It was time to bury the body.

I couldn't feel the arms which wrapped around my torso, hoisting me off of the bed – but the amazing thing – the part that was truly wondrous…was that I didn't have to rely on senses.

For at that moment, when my body was touched by another pair of hands, I stood on the side and watched. I was able to hear, see, and witness all of it. It was as if I weren't even dead at all; as if I were watching the removal of my body take place in a strange, supernatural show, where I was the star but my eyes would be closed and my lips would be pursed in silence.

I would open my mouth, but the words could not come out. I tried to scream, to place my mouth by their ears, but every time, they went about their business and I was unheard.

But one thing was for certain.

Antoine had been right.

During my final days, I had always been looking over my shoulder. My mind, as it sank into a sea of uncertainty as the age of my body caught up with the passage of time, had an increasingly difficult time deciphering reality versus things that were taking place in my mind. Or in alternate dimensions of existence.

I remember running from hellhounds.

Yes, I remembered the hounds.

They had stood watch over Antoine's estate in Miami, like a marrying of the supernatural with reality. They patrolled the front yards, and the front doors to the mansion, which at that point, had been a burned out shell. But that part – the fact that the building had been covered in ashes and surrounded by bright yellow police crime tape – did not matter.

It was what was inside that the hellhounds were protecting.

I'd remembered that house.

So many times, living there with Antoine. That palatial Miami house. A mansion, really, in any better sense of description. It was the house where he had introduced me to Roberto, his young Latino lover, and Sheldon, the director of *The Astral,* a paranormal research society with offices in nearby Coral Gables, who had sat in the front room, on many occasions, sipping whiskey and talking to Antoine about a book he'd been writing. I'd stayed there on many occasions, but had never truly moved in. I'd always been most connected to our chateau in France, but still, I loved the Miami estate.

Loved it there.

Miss it.

Tried visiting it, several times, when I was mortal and dying, trying to say a goodbye. But as soon as I managed to duck under the crime scene tape, I heard the growl in the bushes.

The rustling.

And I remember, on multiple occasions, running from those viscous supernatural dogs. And I would jump into my car and head to Delia's apartment.

But I knew what they were protecting.

I knew, Delia knew, everyone knew...

Antoine and Giovanni stood at the foot of the bed.

Antoine had thought Darius, completely covered under the sheets, resembled a snow covered mountain range. "I can't get that thought out of my head," Antoine said. Giovanni raised his head towards Antoine. "Hm, sir?" After a few minutes of silence, Giovanni raised his head up and over in Antoine's direction. He placed his hand on Antoine's shoulder.

The curtains blew inwards.

"Close the windows," Antoine said. "We do not want him to rot here in the heat."

There was a breeze that found its way through the windows. It was late in the fall, and southern France had experienced an unusually warm period.

Giovanni shuffled over close to Antoine, and placed his hand gently on Antoine's arm. He raised his head up towards Antoine.

Antoine could only see the white handkerchief wrapped around Giovanni's head. His thin and wispy hair hung lazily along the sides of his head.

"She may have gouged my eyes out," Giovanni said. "But I can see when you are suffering."

"We must get you soon to get your vision restored, Gio."

Antoine lowered his head, nodded slowly, and found his way to the rocking chair, and sat as the chair emitted a slow creak. He leaned the chair back as far as it would go. He closed his eyes and hung his head for a moment. He could feel the warmth of a tear cascading down his cheek. He reached up, wiped it away, and looked over at Giovanni, who had sat at the foot of the bed. "Do you think Darius can hear us?" Antoine asked. He leaned forward slightly as the runners gave an audible creak against the otherwise silent room.

Thunder rumbled in the distance.

Giovanni looked down at Darius as Antoine waited patiently for an answer.

"You don't see anything, Giovanni."

He raised his head towards Antoine's voice. "Oh, but I do, Antoine. I do. And even though I may have lost my vision, my sense of remembrance is so much stronger."

"So you didn't answer my question, Gio."

He nodded. "Do I think Darius can hear us? What we are saying?"

Antoine nodded as Giovanni turned around.

He shuffled over towards the rocker, dragging his feet along the hardwood. He stopped just short of the chair, and leaned down, closer towards Antoine's face. Antoine could smell the wine on his breath. Gio leaned towards the side, and as he spoke, Antoine felt the heat of his breath.

"Darius can hear us. He can hear everything. He is lying under the sheet listening to our every word!"

Do you love me?

Do you hear me calling your name through the howl of the winds? Through the storms and the rain? Did you watch as I fought through the skulls towards the altar? Did you see me thrash through the sea of souls?

As Nesmaron waited for me?

As Asmodai assaulted me through the clouds?

My genesis; the epoxy of my mind…has only just begun…

…Darius opened his eyes…

All he saw was darkness.

Total blackness.

He took a deep breath and sighed. Where had he just been?

He could not remember. He closed his eyes (not that it mattered, given that he was in total darkness) and tried to remember.

There were fleeting images of Antoine.

And visions of the Master Suite at their chateau in Lyon. Yes, he knew it was their Master Suite. He recognized the soaring pedestals from their dark oak bed; the cranberry colored drapes and how they spilled to the floor.

But not much more.

Under normal circumstances, the solitude might have been inviting, but in this case, the coffin lid had been closed. He had heard the creak and the lowering of the wood, and the click of the lock.

How long must I stay buried this time, Antoine? How long until you will rescue me?

He could hear Antoine's muffled screaming as they carried coffin lower into the ground. Towards the crypt. And to be sealed for all of eternity.

There had not been such a travesty of emotion pouring out of his partner the previous time he had been buried –

Drive the dagger, Antoine! Into my heart! Do it! Do it now!

Kill me, kill me, kill me!

Antoine hadn't driven a dagger into his heart this time. There hadn't been a challenge of death in the foyer next to the fountain like there had been before.

There was no call for death.

No need for the darkness. But he tried to remember. An attempt to get his mind to work. To recall the last days of his life. For the last thing he remembered, he had watched Antoine burn to ashes on the bleeding altar.

What had happened after that?

It was a blur.

Like a blackout of memories perpetuated by an overindulgence of alcohol, there was the fight to remember.

And nothing.

Just blackness.

Darius waited for a resolution.

And then, in the darkness, far off in the distance, appeared a tiny pinpoint of light. His pain was gone. The headaches that had plagued him later in his life no longer existed. But this body…was it there?

He struggled to focus his eyes in the darkness, but the only thing he could see was the tiny pinpoint of light. Was it a sliver of his life? Was he floating through space? Through the heavens?

The dark ones didn't come, my friend.

He had heard Antoine's voice. Speaking to him just after he had passed. There was a certain point, when he lost consciousness, that the room became black. But he could still see. There were snippets – the armoire in the corner. And they flashed before his eyes, amidst the blackness, like old photos on a projector. He saw the rocking chair. Even the light seemed different. He saw the nightclub conference room for a fleeting moment.

They didn't come.

And then there was Antoine.

Standing at the foot of the bed.

He was looking down at the bed. And Darius knew…he knew what was under the white sheet…

Darius looked up and saw Giovanni.

Giovanni raised his head. "Master Antoine, I hear a car. I think it may be pulling up."

Antoine ran for the door as Giovanni followed. Darius remained standing at the foot of the bed, still looking down at his body covered in the white sheet. He listened to the front doors opening, and he struggled to hear what Antoine was saying.

Muffled voices followed.

He turned, glided across the room, noticing that the floor felt different now. He looked down. He saw his bare feet. He saw himself standing on the hardwood, but he couldn't feel it. It was like he were standing on air.

Antoine parted the sheer drapes that hung on the expansive windows that bordered either side of the heavy, double wooden doors. He pressed his nose against the glass and saw a long, black hearse pull up in front of the chateau. It was quite long, slender, and sleek. This was no ordinary hearse, as all of the windows were tinted dark back.

As he heard the driver cut the engine, he went to the front door. He clicked the lock and turned the oversized brass handle.

The big, heavy wooden door slowly opened inwards as the brilliant daylight spilled inside. He looked out, as the driver's door opened and an unusually tall man stood and turned around.

Antoine recognized the man from his photo: his dark hair was plastered to his head; combed over in the front and parted on the side. Kind of a greasy look. The man was quite thin and lanky, Antoine thought. The driver spun around and watched Antoine. The tall man nodded as he slowly walked around the car towards the front steps. He said nothing, but remained focused on Antoine, who stood on the front porch, his hand still on the oversized brass doorknob. The man stopped at the base of the stairs and reached into his coat pocket. He fished an overly long, white cigarette and produced a small, silver lighter. After he lit the cigarette, took a long drag, and exhaled a cloud of smoke, and he finally spoke.

"I'm here for the body," he said, as the passenger door opened. But Antoine's mouth dropped open as he looked beyond the man at the car. The lanky man turned around as Antoine gasped. Another man stepped out, dressed in a similar black suit, dark brown hair plastered to his head in a similar fashion.

"Ramiel?! Is that really you?" Antoine said, returning his attention to the man on the steps. "I thought you were coming alone?"

"Ramiel insisted that he come," he said. "And I am Ned McCracken. My apologies. So rude of me to not introduce myself." He extended his hand once reaching the top of the porch steps.

"Yes, yes. I remember from the document that Giovanni gave me."

Antoine looked into the man's eyes. There seemed to be something a little "off" about the man, but he couldn't quite place it. He had heard about the mortician, back in Miami. But never had met him in person until this one time. Ned looked back at Antoine with unusually large, brown eyes. Antoine took his hand and shook it as Ned ran his free hand through his dark, greasy-looking hair.

"I was instructed to come as soon as Darius passed," Ned explained.

Ramiel joined them on the steps. "And I came to investigate his death. With all the talk in Rome about *The Hooded Man* rumors, *The Inspiriti* is going to conduct their own investigation." Ramiel extended his hand.

"No," Antoine said. He grabbed Ramiel and hugged him tightly. "You don't think you are going to get off with just a handshake, are you?"

Ramiel chuckled. "No, my friend, no. How long has it been now?"

Antoine looked upwards, as if to search the sky for an answer. "I want to say…hmmm…back in Badulla? Did I see you then? Back when I was newly transformed?"

Ramiel shifted his face. "I'm not sure…Antoine. I think we met much later, no? Were you not already transformed?"

Ramiel moved close to Antoine as the three entered the foyer. He moved close to Antoine, and hugged him from behind. Antoine froze, accepted the hug, and placed his palms on Ramiel's muscular forearms. Ramiel moved closer, and pressed his body close to Antoine's. He could feel that Ramiel had been working out. His chest was far more musclebound than Antoine had remembered. He felt Ramiel's hard member press against his buttocks as Ramiel wrapped his muscular arms around Antoine.

Antoine spun around. "No!" he said. His eyes flared. "His body is still lying in the back room! How can you attempt play at a time like this!"

Ramiel took a few steps back.

Ned approached from the foyer, stood silent, motionless, with wide eyes. He looked at Antoine and Ramiel, and then back at Antoine. "Did I miss something?"

Ramiel had a grin plastered across his face like a Cheshire cat. "No, nothing at all, Ned. Just remembering old times, that's all."

Antoine looked at Ramiel and shook his head. "Let's go upstairs and keep focused on the task at hand."

Back in the days when Darius had just died, and despite Tramos' intervention and his tutelage, Delia did not notice her gift as much. She did not realize how important she had become to the immortals and their destiny. It was before the days of the hooded man and his assault on the immortals. When Darius had just died, Delia did the exact thing that she had been doing for years: be a close friend to those who were closest to her.

And after Darius was gone, she chose to focus on Antoine. But still, she always felt a very close connection with Darius, even after his death. And she still felt a connection with Antoine and Darius together.

As if they were two beings, interlocked through the pursuit of immortality; their destinies intertwined as a singular spirit.

Those two, she felt, she had the most connection to.

Her connection to Darius, however, spanned a greater length of time. She was instantly drawn to Darius when they had first met in Paris.

She and Darius had both been transformed with the gift already, and Delia was performing on the Vaudeville stage. When her number was over, she looked out into the audience. To the dark sea of faces as the applause rang through the auditorium. She was not focused on the sea of people. She couldn't even hear the applause. It was as if she were wearing a pair of muffs, for all the sounds seemed so distant. When she took her bow, she closed her eyes for a moment. And when she snapped back up, she saw the one face.

But there was one man that stood out.

But she knew differently this time.

For the man in the audience was not a familiar face. It was not Tramos, and although she knew that she was special, that she was chosen, and others were pursuing her to raise her awareness of her gifts, there still the mystery of this particular man.

A face who stared directly at her, that spoke to her.

That connected with her.

Her mouth dropped open, just slightly, as she stared directly into his eyes, watching him watching her. As she turned with the other performers to exit the stage, she kept watching him, and he kept watching her.

Just like before.

I know you are just like me.

She broke her trance as she skittered off the stage with the other starlets. Once in the dressing room backstage, she sat in a small folding chair wiping the heavy layer of make-up off of her face, when she heard approaching footsteps on the wood.

"Delia? Delia Arnette?"

It was a strange replay.

Who was the visitor that watched this performance?

The voice was masculine, yet sounded young. Not like Tramos at all. Still working on the confidence. She turned around, and saw him.

Tall, lanky. Long, brown hair tied back. Still yet to fill out. But clearly a man. "Yes?"

"I'm Darius Sauvage. I caught your performance."

Yes. That was it.

He was clearly the one.

The face in the crowd.

The eyes that had stared back at her when she took her bow, when she lifted her head and saw that one, single solitary face looking back at her in a sea of darkness.

"I saw you watching me. Somehow we made eye contact. I hope you liked the show. How may I help you, young man?"

He stammered, and fidgeted with a hat, which he held at the front of his waist. He looked down at the floor. "Are you…who I think you are?"

Delia scoffed and returned her attention to the mirror, and dabbing at her make-up. She continued to look in the mirror as she spoke with Darius. "And who do you think I am?"

He looked around the room and grabbed a small folding chair near the hanging heavy black drapes that concealed the back of the stage. He slid the chair next to Delia and sat. He faced her, although she could see him in the mirror, she did not turn around. She stopped wiping her face for a moment, watching him in the mirror, as she waited for an answer. When she saw him looking down towards his feet, she tossed the cloth on the table. "Who do you think I am?!"

He looked up.

She watched him and made eye contact with him. It didn't matter if he answered or not. Because she already knew. He was the same as her. Maybe on a different level, perhaps from a different bloodline, but still on the same level.

Delia sighed and turned back around to face him. "You already know who I am, don't you?"

Darius leaned forward, placing his elbows on his knees, raised his head to look at her, and his eyebrows.

She stood. "So if you know who I am…which you certainly must know, since you came to my performance. Where are you from?"

"I grew up in Lyon."

She shook her head as she circled the area where Darius sat. "Yes. Lyon. But now you're in Paris. And now you're a man." She leaned close down towards his face, and met eyes with him. "Now you're a man and now you're calling on me. So do you know who I am or not?"

He leaned back. "Yes. I do."

"And why did you come calling? Why did you come to my show?"

"Well, we're the same. I wanted to find others like me. I was transformed and abandoned."

"Abandoned?"

"Yes. My maker left once I was transformed. He visited me for weeks and weeks up until the night he transformed me, but once that happened, I never heard from him again."

She turned around.

The look on her face softened.

A young, scared, abandoned immortal sat before her, looking at her with wide, open eyes. "Are you scared?" she asked, her head now cocked to the side, a smile now warmed her face.

Darius looked at her and bit his lip. "I..." he stammered. "I don't know what to make of this. I feel this hunger inside of me that I cannot explain! I have desires that I never thought I would have! Things look different to me now...when I look around, all I see is *death*..."

Delia leaned forward and took his hands. She looked down as he intertwined his fingers with hers.

They sat, facing each other, holding hands, looking down in each other's laps, and sat there as the theatre closed for the evening around them, as the lamps were shut out and curtains were drawn closed.

Darius kicked his feet against the hardwood floor. He leaned back and forth, as if searching for an answer. "Well," he stammered. "I have heard rumors about you. That you are the protector. You guide and counsel the immortals. I thought you might do the same for me."

She stood, walking around the chair, and around over to Darius, and leaned down to look at him face to face. She placed her hands on his chin, as he raised his eyes to look at her. "You have heard that? Who have you heard it from? And if they told you that, then certainly they told you of the requirements?"

He leaned back and shook his head as she continued back towards the makeup counter. "I didn't know there were any requirements. I was told that you were protective of all."

She paused and sat back in the small folding chair. She hung her head down, looking down at the floor between her legs. "You know, despite what they all say, I am the same as you. I am just an immortal who got transformed. Just like you. I am scared and worried about my future. Just like you."

"And they told me to come to you."

She snapped around. "Who are *they*?"

Darius leaned back, looking up at Delia with wide eyes. "Uh…they…well…Tramos had mentioned your name. And when I saw it on the billboard, I bought a ticket to the show. But the word on the street is that you're a protector."

She looked down for a moment and then back up in his eyes. "And then you thought I could be your salvation? From what? Who is chasing you, Darius?"

Darius looked up. He leaned back.

"Chasing me? No one is chasing me. I was just compelled to contact you. Was I wrong?"

Delia fidgeted with the items on her makeup tray, looking down, and sighed. "No, Darius. No, not at all. I am sorry for the chilly reception. I can help you. I certainly can. And know that there are no coincidences, my new friend. Everything that happens is meant to happen. And Tramos was meant to mention my name to you. And you were meant to purchase a ticket to my performance. And I was meant to see your face looking at me from the dark crowd. There are no coincidences, Darius."

As Antoine meandered through the kitchen, Ramiel followed, watching Antoine's every move. Antoine kept looking back at Ramiel, who was always nearby, watching him closely. Antoine could feel Ramiel's intense stare, and as they sat at the wooden table, directly across from each other, Antoine thought he might have remembered when they had first met.

"I remember a night in Badulla," Antoine said, folding his hands, his eyes staring straight into Ramiel's. "You were one of my suitors, weren't you?"

Ramiel let out a small laugh and looked down at the table, then back up. "Your suitors?"

"Well you know I was a prostitute for tourists."

He nodded. "I think that might have been what it was. But that isn't the reason why I came to Badulla. Or why I was waiting for you in the café. You don't remember?" He leaned back, as his eyes darted around the room. He paused for a moment.

"Do you think Ned needs help? He might. But I think we should explore it a little bit."

Antoine nodded and poured some tea for Ramiel, who continued. "I had just gotten in from Rome. And the Monsignor had already retired. We'd finished our meeting with the Southeast Asian sector of the immortal commune, and I was feisty."

Antoine nodded. "You certainly were."

"But I knew you were important, Antoine. I knew about your destiny."

Antoine looked up from stirring the sugar cubes in his steaming tea. He raised his eyes towards Ramiel. "My destiny? How did you know that?"

Ramiel chuckled. "Antoine, I'm much older than you. I was transformed many years before you. And I work directly with Monsignor Harrison in Rome. Do you not think that I would have a vast knowledge of our immortal kind? Of all those in the lineages and ancestry that we have?"

Antoine nodded.

"And so you need to realize," Ramiel said. "We were meant to meet. That I can assure you. There are those of us who are rumored to be much more than immortals. Our dark gift, as we have called it throughout the centuries. There are those of us who are rumored to possess the dark gift but also have other celestial connections."

Antoine's eyes widened. "You mean…"

"There are those of us who could be angels."

AFTER THEY HAD LEFT THE HILL of Golgatha, Monsignor Harrison settled into the backseat of the large, black sedan and started thumbing through a book, as Delia looked out the window on the opposite side, through the muted view of the tinted glass, and saw the sandy, brown hill in the distance.

The cross still hung. She could see the shadow.

But the sun wasn't as intense as before. She could see dark clouds on the horizon.

Delia lay back in her seat, leaned her head against the headrest, and closed her eyes as the car pulled away for Ben Gurion International outside of Jerusalem. As she listened to the tires crunching through the gravel and dirt, and then the eventual hum of the engine as the dirt roads gave way to pavement, she remembered Paris from her days as a little girl, back in the days before Vaudeville had come to town.

She remembered the words of mother.

"We all need to have a little courage," she had said, as she braided little Delia's hair. Still a child in those days, she looked up towards her mother's smiling face. "Mama, do you have courage?"

Her mother's face fell and she stopped braiding.

The door crashed open and father spilled into the room. He was drunk again. "You forgot, didn't you?"

He lunged forwards and grabbed mama's arm and tore her away from little Delia. She held her hands up in defense as her eyes were wide with terror. "I – No – !"

"You stupid fucking *bitch!*"

But little Delia had been accustomed to her father's repeated assaults on her mother. She started to cower backwards – but stopped. Little Delia stood and started slapping on her father's hip, as his head snapped down and glared at her. "Lay your hands off me you little child!"

Delia looked up and scowled at her father as her mother eased back towards the wall and flopped back under the window, holding her hands over her face. A stream of blood ran from her mother's nostril.

"Leave her *alone*!" Delia shrieked.

Little Delia maintained her stance, her arms against her hips, her neck craned upwards, and she glared up at her father, as he looked down at her, his eyes rimmed red, his hair mussed and oily. Drool spilled out of his mouth as he bent down towards her. "Don't you think you can save her?! She is a whore and doesn't need any saving! So you think you're a fucking *angel*? Just look like a little child to me! Now get out of my way!"

And he stumbled across the room, slamming the door behind him, as Delia flew to her mother's side. Mother leaned her head back against the wall, crying, holding Delia in her arms. "He's drunk again…he's drinking every night…"

The car's suspension fumbled over a speed bump as Delia was roused from her dream. She rubbed the sleep from her eyes, and stretched her arms. She felt the warmth of a solitary tear stream down her cheek, as she smeared it away with her hands. She took a breath and cleared her throat as she leaned forward. "Are we close?" She looked up at the diver as he turned around once the car was at a stoplight. "Not far yet, ma'am. Not far yet."

She took a deep breath and exhaled, and looked out the window. They were still in broken territory. They weren't in modern Jerusalem yet, so she could have only been asleep for a few minutes, at the most. The palm trees rose from the dry sands on the sides of the streets, amidst dilapidated old houses. She sighed and looked down at her hands. Her hands shook as she fumbled with the zipper on her purse. She fished her plane ticket out and examined it. "How, after so many years, can you still make my hands tremble?"

The Monsignor looked up from his book and over at Delia and raised his eyes. "Are you okay?"

Delia made a fist, never taking her eyes off of her hands. "I...I will be okay. Yes." She raised her head for a moment. And then looked over at the Monsignor. "Yes, I will." There was more confidence in her voice. More determination. "Let's catch our flight, your Highness. I have so much more to tell you once we get to Rome."

"You can't tell me now?"

Delia shook her head. "No, your highness. I need some more time to face it. To process what I have running through my mind. Once I've had a chance to sort it all out, I will speak to you about it. I think once we get to Rome I will feel better about everything."

Monsignor Harrison nodded and returned to his book. "Understood. Fair enough."

As the car approached the terminal, it slowed in front of Departures. Delia looked out the window and noticed it was teeming with activity. Lines of people stood and waited with bags of all sizes at curbside check-in. Others dashed in and out of oversized, glass revolving doors, as cars sandwiched their way down several blacktop lanes. The car pulled up in front of the large revolving doors and the driver exited the car and slammed his door shut. He swung around to the rear of the car and popped the trunk, fishing out their bags.

They made their way through the boisterous activity and crowded terminal, and not long after, boarded their plane. Once settled in their seats, Delia settled into the flight as Monsignor Harrison sipped on a whiskey.

Delia closed her eyes as the rumble of the plane shook her seat as it barreled down the runway.

Her arms felt heavy.

She unfolded the small, blue blanket across her lap and settled deeper into her seat as the plane shot higher into the sky. As the pilot turned starboard, she leaned her head on the side headrest and opened her eyes for a moment, and looked over at Monsignor Harrison, who sat just across the aisle.

"Your Highness," she croaked.

He looked over at her and raised his eyebrows.

"Do you think my past had anything to do with this?"

"With what?" The Monsignor asked. "The whole deal with the 'Hooded Man'?"

Delia nodded.

The Monsignor looked at his lap for a moment and then back up at Delia. "I think not. You were what — just a girl weren't you? When Claret found you?"

"Still a girl but still a woman," Delia sighed and turned back towards the front of the plane. She pulled the blanket up towards her neck. "Oh, those days back in Jerusalem seem so distant now. I remember waking up. So lost. But my mother was there. She was there for me."

She closed her eyes again.

"And the rest that happened while you were there, including meeting Claret for the first time, you'll certainly remember them," Monsignor Harrison said. "Just close your eyes, get some rest on the flight, and we'll talk about it more in Rome."

As the plane turned starboard into the fading daylight, Delia dozed off. As the quiet conversations, nearly drowned out by the hum of the engines, faded away, she started to think of Darius. And their time in Paris. When they had first met, in the theatre, after her performance. And when she could no longer hear the hum of the engines, or the announcements on the p.a. system, she started to feel a chill.

And hear the clap of hooves from a horse drawn carriage.

She looked down as her breath emitted a cloud in the chilly Paris night.

After the theatre had closed for the evening, Delia stood with Darius outside on in the chilly, night Paris air. They huddled under the awning of the theatre, next to the expansive doors.

"Stay in touch with me," Delia said. "There's talks of immortals going to America. Would you be interested?"

Darius met eyes with Delia. He huddled and shivered, wrapping himself in his coat. "You mean? America? Immortals are crossing the Atlantic?"

Delia nodded, her eyes brighter. "Yes Darius. America is calling. I can feel it. I think the future of our kind could be there. There are others who've said they'd been there."

Darius looked down. "I…" he stammered. "I don't know what to say, Delia. This is not what I expected."

"Well certainly you need to travel. To find yourself a partner. Right?"

Darius nodded. "Yes, yes. I have my sights on someone, though. I see visions of him in my dreams when I am in my coffin."

Delia's eyebrows raised and she cocked her head to the side. "Really? Someone you fancy?"

They started walked from the theatre, huddled close together, as if they had known each other for years. "I don't know if I fancy him just yet," Darius said as they approached a cross street. "But I definitely feel a connection with him. I've been watching him. Been going to Sri Lanka. Spending time observing him. But all I really know is that he harvests coffee in Sri Lanka of all places."

"Then you should go to him," she said. "Go to Sri Lanka, find him. Tell him about the gift, the transformation. Who wouldn't want immortality?"

Darius nodded. "We shall see."

"And after," she said. "Introduce me to him, and we shall all go to America!"

Darius smiled and vowed to stay in touch with Delia. Delia stood as he started walking towards the central city. He huddled in a long, black coat, his hands shoved in his pockets, walking away from her. Steam rose from manholes as the moon filtered a blue light over the city like a warming blanket.

After they bid their farewells, Delia returned to her tiny apartment, several blocks away. She struggled with the key in the lock, shifting it back and forth before it went in completely and turned.

The apartment was silent and cold. One single room with a small kitchenette off to the side, and an adjoining bedroom. She stopped in the center of the room, tossed her bag on the couch, and headed towards the window.

She grunted as she rose the window, and shivered as the sting of cold air spilled in. The curtains blew inwards as she stepped aside from the window. She leaned her head against the wall and looked at a full moon shining a reassuring light down on the city.

Ah, the nights in Paris.

Such a blessing.

The crisp, yet sweet smell of the air.

The puzzle pieces of buildings set in rows like colorful dominoes bathed in blue, lined up down the avenues, reaching towards the Eiffel Tower.

Oh, how she loved living in Paris.

Such a city with so many bad memories, but the beauty of the moonlit nights next to the window, were what Delia looked forward to after her shows.

The bad memories would just wash away.

And even then, so many years later, when she was now a woman, long from when she had grown in the world, she found herself once again in Paris. The Paris of her childhood seemed increasingly foreign. No longer were the nights spent hiding in her room under pillows and sheets, listening to the screams and to the chairs toppling over. No more would she wait for her father to pound on the door yelling at her to get to sleep.

But Paris, once again.

She didn't know exactly how she wound up in Paris once again. Except for the possibility of a mission. It was just like the old woman in Jerusalem had explained to her, "You will be called to a time period that you are needed in."

And sitting under the full moon, listening to the silence of the city in the predawn dark, she realized what Mama might have meant. And then she thought of Darius. And thought that her mission in Paris might just be complete. Had she only been called to Paris again to meet Darius? Was his attending her performance part of the celestial plan?

Still, she appreciated the changes in the world – automobiles had replaced carriages, lights had overtaken and candles had become a novelty. And it was the light of the neon sign outside of her window, the sign hanging from the dark, brick façade that reflected against her face; her skin, pillow white. She was still wearing the bright red lipstick from her show earlier that evening.

When there was a knock on the door.

She broke her stare and looked back at the door, and waited. The silence that followed was impenetrable, and even the hum of the electric sign outside the window could be heard. But she continued to stare at the door...watching...and waiting.

Knock! Knock! Knock!

The door shook in its frame.

"Who is it?" Her voice reverberated against the stark white walls. There was no answer.

Just the same hum from the sign hanging outside her window.

Her heels tapped on the hardwood as she walked to the door. She leaned forward and peered through the peephole, which gave a broken view.

There was a small, dark figure outside.

Looked like something shifting back and forth, like a man shifting from foot to foot.

"Who is it?"

Delia stood in front of the door, looking at the small peephole. Should she dare lean forward and look through again? She stood a few feet away from the door as three deep thuds pounded against the wooden frame. She took a step back, never taking her eyes off of the door.

Delia...listen to me. I am just on the other side of the door. Do you hear me calling you?

She paused.

Her eyes were wide. She could feel a drop of sweat flow down the side of her cheek as she took a cautious step forward. Her heels clicked on the hardwood.

I'm here, Delia. Just on the other side of the door.

She stopped walking and shut her eyes tight as the image of her father's body flashed into her mind. His eyes were wide open as he lay in the lake of blood. And then her voice as a little girl rang through her mind:

"You're dead! Dead! *Dead!*" She slammed her palms against the door.

And she saw her father.

Lying in his wooden coffin, his face macerated and drained, maggots feasting on his flesh. "No!"

Three deep knocks on the door rattled the wooden frame once again. She reached for the brass knob, as the door handle turned.

She slowly opened the door with a creak…

DELIA AWOKE WITH A START as the plane touched down in Rome. Monsignor Harrison adjusted his seat. He leaned over to Delia. "You must have been tired."

"I have good reason to be."

They said nothing to each other once they had landed in Rome after their trip to Jerusalem, which had been spent investigating the crucifixion of an old and highly ranking member of the immortals, Claret Atarah. They had also spent time there defeating *The Hooded Man*, who, at that time, was believed to have been stopped.

They grabbed their bags and headed to the waiting cars outside baggage claim. The ride in the car was in silence, as they each traveled in separate cars, and during that time, Delia rummaged through her purse.

The cars pulled up on the small avenues that bordered the Piazza San Pietro, the plaza which borders Rome, part of the papal enclave. Delia looked outside the smoked glass and saw the rising columns frame the fountain. Statues soaring into the sky above the columns; a tall, reaching obelisk in the center hinted of a relationship with ancient Egypt. But Delia was in *Citta del Vaticano*, in the plaza, bordered with the giant colonnades, surrounding the elliptical cemented area. Tourists mulled about, posing for photos in the plaza around the fountain and walking about; clergymen walked, two and two, in flowing black cassocks, towards the Sistine.

Once they had arrived in the square, Delia stood in front of the chapel doors and looked upwards, towards the roof spire. Framed by columns, she entered through the heavy, grand doors, into an atrium under the arched ceiling. Her heels clicked on the marble as she walked past sets of rising columns, Monsignor Harrison took a phone call. His voice echoed against the masonry and fought against soft organ music. She found the small, wooden door in a discreet corner and waved the Monsignor over. They navigated the creaky, wooden stairs and emerged underneath the Chapel and into the brightly lit catacombs. She found the nearest restroom and gestured to Monsignor Harrison that she would be a few minutes. She closed the door and clicked the lock. She leaned against the wall and closed her eyes. "I cannot take this anymore! Why *must* you haunt me with these nightmares?!"

She raised her eyes to the ceiling.

There had been no expectation of a celestial light shining through the women's restroom. Or a Heavenly doorway appearing over near the stalls. But Delia had never, in her entire life, felt so distant from God. There was the time, when she had been a child, when she thought that she had been away from God. In the days when her father beat and killed her mother; in the days when she would hide in her room, at night, in the darkness, and listen to the arguing. She remembered huddling under the covers till it got too warm and sweaty, and then, the muffled voices grew louder and more insistent, and she would climb out of bed, ever so quietly. She would always remember to avoid that one spot on the floor that would creak.

And then she would peek through the door.

And on that one night – that one fateful night – when the screaming had just been too loud. When the furniture sounded like it was being moved across the room – was the night she remembered. The night when the blood pooled on the living room floor. And the police came. And when she had stood in the middle of the living room floor, watching her father bleed to death.

"You bastard," she said, under her breath. "I was sent for you? The slime of the Earth…"

Delia opened her eyes, and saw herself in the bathroom mirror.

She reached for a tissue and blotted her mascara.

Those days were so long ago. But the pain still felt so real. She turned around, and leaned forward and examined herself in the mirror. She fixed her hair and reapplied her makeup. It had been a long, tough life. A difficult assignment. But her perseverance won, and she exited back towards the hallway. Monsignor Harrison stood, patiently waiting, but his face was shifted with concern. "I heard you in there. Everything alright?"

Delia glared at the Monsignor. "Yes, everything is fine. Let's just get inside. I know they are waiting for us with the news from Jerusalem.

Delia and Monsignor Harrison waited patiently in a stark lobby area lined with plain black leather chairs. There was a small television perched up in the high corner across the room, with a local news station playing; the ticker that flowed across the bottom of the screen read in Italian.

Delia sighed and sat further into her chair as Monsignor Harrison examined his fingernails.

After a few moments, the Monsignor shifted his glance over towards Delia. "So you understand why I did it, right?"

Delia stopped and looked up. She looked at the Monsignor. "Why you crucified her? Yes, I understand. I know why it was done."

He nodded. "And do you think she deserved it? That she was a betrayer to her own kind? It was the ultimate betrayal, right?"

She shrugged her shoulders. "I don't know, your highness. I don't know why she would have so much contempt for her own kind...and on the other hand, I also can't understand why she didn't really present a defense."

"There wasn't much of a defense for her to present, Delia."

"Do you think they'll agree?"

Monsignor Harrison shook his head. "I don't know, Delia. I just don't know."

A door next to them opened as a nun, dressed in full black and white habit, gestured for them to come inside. Delia looked at Monsignor Harrison and squeezed his hand. As they were about to enter the door, the Monsignor touched Delia's arm and whispered in her ear. "Do you think I acted too harshly? I was protecting our own kind! *The Hooded Man* had to be stopped!" His eyes were wide as he stood and turned, heading into the conference chamber.

They were led on separate sides of a large, rectangular conference room. The High Council sat on a long table that spanned the opposite end of the room, as other members of the delegation sat in fields of chairs on either side of a wide aisle that led from the double doors which Monsignor Harrison and Delia had entered. They found their seats and a Cardinal in the center of the long table banged his gavel and brought the proceedings to order. The old man glared directly at Monsignor Harrison as Delia looked on from the opposite end of the room.

Monsignor Harrison stood in front of a small upholstered chair, which faced the High Council. Elderly men, dressed in flowing red robes with black sashes lined the table. In the center, a man removed his glasses and placed them on the table. "I am Cardinal Angelo Klemmson. I am here, along with the rest of the High Council, to determine your guilt in the sentencing and resultant crucifixion of Claret Atarah for suspected crimes against the immortal kind."

"I have been reading this file for weeks now," he said, looking directly at Monsignor Harrison as the room hushed. "Ever since Darius Sauvage passed. And I'm troubled."

Monsignor Harrison sat directly in front of the High Council and removed his glasses. He placed them on his notebook, sat back in his chair, and folded his hands. "I am the last of my kind."

The aged Cardinal leaned forward. "Come again?"

"My ancestors have all died and are gone from this world. Now, everyone looks up to me. I am the leader of the immortal race. There is no one older than me."

The man leaned back in his chair. "Would you care to elaborate? I am not sure – and I am certain that there are others in this chamber that agree – that I follow what you are claiming. Are you saying that you are the last living member of your bloodline?"

The Monsignor looked down at his hands. He clasped them about his waist, and fidgeted with his fingers. He could feel the sweat on his palms. He reached up and pulled his collar out. The room felt warm.

The Monsignor sighed. "Do you understand who I am or what I am about?"

"Just a moment," the eldest Cardinal said. The Cardinals huddled and chatted amongst each other as the Monsignor sat back and watched. After a few minutes, they stopped, returned to their seats, and sat back and looked directly at Monsignor Harrison. The one who appeared to be the eldest, and who had spoken with him up to that point, spoke to him again. "Monsignor Harrison, we have called you here because of the great…misfortune…that has befallen us. Do you understand the charges you face?"

"Um…the charges?"

The eldest raised his eyebrows. "If you are certain that you are the eldest of your kind, why do you question what the charges may be? Shouldn't you already know?"

The Monsignor took pause.

He placed the pen that he was fidgeting with gently on the table, next to a yellow legal pad. He looked up at the eldest Cardinal, and studied the man. He certainly had to be well into his nineties.

But could he be an immortal?

"Yes, I question the charges, your grace." His voice quivered as he stood. The High Council members all focused on him. "I question them. Because I led our kind through the threat of annihilation. When a hooded figure…some mysterious man…or creature…was attacking us. My assistant Ramiel and I flew to Miami. We offered our assistance to those affected." He looked at the panel, his eyes wide. "They were attacking us! We were targeted. The hooded man approached unsuspecting immortals and convinced them to drink from a decanter which proved to be an imposter of salvation!"

"Under your watch," Klemmson said.

Monsignor Harrison nodded and let out an exasperated sigh. "Yes, yes, under my watch your highness. Many immortals met their death during this time. But *The Hooded Man* was very seductive. And many of our kind are surrounded by darkness. He was offering a false route to the light."

"I have no desire to move towards the light."

Monsignor Harrison nodded. "Yes, maybe not, but many immortals *do* have a desire for the light, and redemption, and a different state of existence that isn't always washed with evil. *The Hooded Man* preyed on that."

The Cardinal looked down and examined some paperwork. "It says here that this 'hooded man' was a member of our society?" He looked at several of the other Cardinals as he waved the paperwork around. "And if so, how could that be possible? And why wouldn't have we have heard about the man? Especially working so close with him. It says here that he was a church going man in Miami, Florida. His house was raided by the FBI for keeping young men in cages in his basement."

Delia stood and raised her hand. She looked over at the Monsignor, then back at the Cardinals. "If I may, your highness."

Cardinal Klemmson looked over at Delia. "Approach."

Delia eased her way behind the others seated along the table, and towards the center of the room. She sat a small chair next to Monsignor Harrison and faced the council.

"My pleasure to the council." She looked over at Monsignor Harrison who looked back at her. "And your highness."

"I have quite a bit of information on this man," she said, looking back at the council. "And he was *not* an immortal. He was an ordinary man. He's dead. Buried in Ascension

Cemetery in Miami. We can't hold him accountable, in any way, for this eradication. He was a supernatural pawn. That's it. Literally a pawn. The one who is responsible is a Claret Atarah. She was tried for crimes against the immortals and crucified."

"Yes, yes, thank you Ms. Arnette." The Cardinal gestured for Delia to return to her seat. "We will be examining Ms. Atarah's case in detail." He looked up and directly at Monsignor Harrison. "You have to understand that we investigate all instances of immortal death and sentencing. Regardless of who carried out the proceedings or alleged trial. It's standard operating procedure for *The Inspiriti*, and it's been in place since the existence of the Immortal kind."

He nodded.

"And so your trial of Ms. Atarah may have seemed fair and just at the time, Monsignor, however we are the third party who is now charged with examining the case

Delia look at the Cardinal, and watched the way he carried himself mysteriously. His hair was stark white, receded to a large, shiny forehead. The lines on his cheeks indicated his advanced age. This Cardinal – this mysterious man. Could he be immortal? Certainly he was not affiliated with the Catholic Church. But how was this man tied to their organization?

The Monsignor, Monsignor Harrison, headed *The Inspiriti* – which was not affiliated with the Church at all. Could this elder have slipped through the cracks? Could he have been hiding in the Church all along and be the eldest immortal?

Sister Ignacious looked up from her computer and looked at Monsignor Harrison. "How old are you, Monsignor?"

"I lived many years before Christ," he said. "I'm alone. I have had that question in my mind as I would stand in the center of the hilltop and look upwards towards the sky. But now, as I sit before you, I ask myself the same question."

"So you do not know your age? How far back your ancestry reaches?" Ignacious stopped typing and leaned back in her chair. She folded her arms and adjusted her glasses. "You don't know when you were given the gift? Or how about who gave it to you?"

The Monsignor paused for a moment, and looked onward toward the group of questioners. Ignacious sat towards the left, and the group, the High Council, sat at the table opposite of him, to the right of Ignacious, and looked at him, some leaning forward, raising their eyebrows, and patiently waiting for him to answer the question.

"Very well," Sister Ignacious said. She rose from her chair and walked over to him. She stood directly in front of Monsignor Harrison as the Cardinals sat at the opposite table and looked on. "We are going to have to hypnotize you," she said. "Explore your mind for a bit. So we can see into your past."

Monsignor Harrison scoffed, leaned back in his chair and looked up at Sister Ignacious. "What is the purpose of this? Am I on some sort of trial?!"

"You have led the immortals for centuries now," Klemmson said. "That is why it is necessary for us to explore your history. During your tenure, the hooded man attacked us. Some salvation imposter he was."

But the Monsignor did not see those questioners who sat in front of him. For his mind was painting a different picture, and, even as he stared forward, the scene before him changed. Those who were in the conference room did not notice that Monsignor Harrison was leaving them; they saw the questioning proceeding as normal.

Except for one.

Delia.

And when she looking over at the Monsignor, who sat staunch, and still, with suddenly short, one word answers, she knew. His bilocation was something that only he possessed, and it proved handy in situations like the inquiry, for he could return to an event and remember minute details that others could only commit to memory.

Monsignor Harrison was not looking at Delia, however. As his eyelids grew heavy, the voices of the questioners seemed farther away each time they spoke. For a time, he could still make out their faces – he still recognized Ignacious and her silver-white hair; but it grew increasingly out of focus, as if he were looking through a camera and someone had been toggling with the focus.

And as his vision clouded, there was a rip in the fabric of time, a tear in the center of his field of sight, which stood out in clarity and opened to darkness: the black vision increased in size, as the rips were bright, white and glowing; and they increased in size, as the Monsignor felt like he was floating towards the mysterious rip.

When he looked down, he saw that he was still sitting in his chair, and when he looked back up at the rip, it had increased to such an immense size that it surpassed him, and he was sitting inside the darkness. As he looked behind him, he could see the stark walls of the conference room, and the vision decreased in size, as he felt like he was entering further into the oblivion; and then, within a moment, or even less, he saw nothing, for the rip closed, and he was alone in the silence.

WHILE WAITING FOR NED THE MORTICIAN to
retrieve and load Darius' body, Antoine sat on the overstuffed
side chair that Darius used to always sit in and read his National
Geographic magazines. "I think I can still feel his imprint on
the fabric," Antoine told Ramiel, who was helping Giovanni
cover the remaining furniture with white dust cloths. Ramiel
looked up at Antoine but said nothing. Antoine returned his
gaze out the window, and watched the body being loaded into
the hearse. Ned was quite strong.

He was lifting and hoisting the body by himself.

Antoine turned back to face Ramiel again. "He doesn't need help?"

The coffin had been prepared by Ned McCracken, along with the body.

Antoine had looked through Darius' file cabinet, and found Ned's contact info. Antoine learned that Darius had a close relationship with Ned. Antoine didn't understand the relationship in the least, but after reading the document that Giovanni had presented him the other day, Antoine opted to ask Ned to fly to Europe to personally handle the preparation and burial of Darius' body. Later as Darius was cleaned and wrapped, Antoine rocked in the same rocking chair that he held vigil in during Darius' final days.

"I've changed my mind," Antoine said, as Ramiel and Ned wrapped Darius in a white sheet. Ramiel looked up and over at Antoine.

Antoine made eye contact with Ramiel. Ned continued wrapping the sheet around Darius' body, attaching safety pins in several locations where the corner of the sheet met the seam. Ned looked up. "Come again?"

Antoine took a breath and sighed. "I'm saying I no longer want him embalmed. I want him buried naturally. Don't embalm him." Antoine looked over at Ned but Ramiel was the one who made eye contact.

Ramiel knew.

Antoine could see it in his eyes.

There was a pleading as Ramiel shook his head. Ramiel bit his lip but did not protest.

"Yes," Antoine said, as he stood. "No embalming. And let me know when you are finished with him. I need to get him buried at once."

While they were waiting for the body to be bagged and loaded, Ramiel took Antoine's hand and led him through the chateau. "You aren't planning to do what I think you are, are you, Antoine?"

Antoine let out a short breath. "That's none of your business, Ramiel."

He reached up and grasped Antoine's shoulders, looking him directly in the eyes. "But yes it is, Antoine. Do you remember the mess from last time you tried to resurrect him?"

Antoine took a breath and released it. He looked down and then back up at Ramiel. "Yes," he finally said. "I remember."

"And Asmodai still searches for you. We've been in charge of your protection for years. Don't you think it's a terrible waste of resources to try this again?"

Antoine shook his head and pushed Ramiel away. He hugged him tighter.

"And Darius died a mortal, Antoine. He died a mortal. Do you even think the resurrection could work?"

Antoine sighed. "I just don't know."

Ramiel stood back and looked around the foyer. The dustcloths had been placed on the furniture and the drapes had been closed. Ned appeared in the doorway informing them that the body was loaded and he was ready to go.

Ramiel lifted Antoine's chin so their eyes met. "Do you need to check anything? The windows and doors? It's best you leave for a while."

Antoine shook his head. "No. Everything is secure."

"Delia is meeting us in Frankfurt?"

Antoine nodded. "That's how we left it when she was here. As far as I know, things haven't changed."

Ramiel grabbed Antoine's arm as Darius was loaded into the hearse. "Do you know what you are trying to do?"

Antoine scoffed and pulled Ramiel's hand off his arm. "I know perfectly well. Either you will help me with it or you won't."

Ramiel stood back as Ned closed the hearse rear door. He looked at Antoine, directly in his eyes. "Are you sure you want to attempt this?"

"I've done it before."

Ramiel nodded. "True. But then, Darius was immortal. His heart still beat in the coffin. He was sentenced to a punishment."

Antoine's mouth dropped open. "A punishment? I never knew that."

Ramiel nodded and placed his arm around Antoine's shoulder as they descended the steps together. "Yes," Ramiel said, quietly, close to Antoine's ear. "Back when you drove the dagger into his chest, that, my friend, was all planned."

"Well, I figured that may have been, at least to a degree."

Ramiel nodded. "Yes. But the extent of it, you do not know. Until now. Now that I am telling you."

They stood outside the passenger door as Ned slid into the driver's seat.

Ramiel turned around to face Antoine. He looked into his eyes. "Antoine. Things were different back then."

Antoine nodded. "Yes. The early days. Back when Darius had just taken me here."

"Yes," Ramiel said. "And there are still things which you do not understand. But Darius was instructed to spend some time in the coffin. That's where you came in."

Shed your skin.

"I must admit I found myself when he was gone then," Antoine admitted. "But it didn't take long before I needed him again. That's why I resurrected him."

"And you paid a steep price for it. For his sentence had not ended. So you took it on. That's why you were pursued, burned at the altar, and had to finish the coffin sentence."

Antoine sighed.

"Yes, Ramiel. It's common knowledge, isn't it?"

Ramiel shrugged his shoulders and looked off to the side. "Well…yes…to a degree, Antoine. We have been monitoring you with your situation not only with Asmodai but also with Claret."

Antoine shook his head and groaned. "Of course you have. Who's been doing this? Harrison?"

Ramiel placed his hand on Antoine's arm. "Come now, Antoine. You know how everything works. All with *The Inspiriti*. When they hear of immortals being conquered, being removed from the planet, they listen. They investigate. They're here to protect, Antoine."

Antoine stood and faced Ramiel. "So what are you saying then? They don't like that Asmodai is after me? Or Claret is following me? Come on, Ramiel. They've been after me for generations!"

Giovanni waited in front of the chateau holding the rear door open to a large silver Mercedes sedan. He handed the keys over to Ramiel. "If you don't mind, sir. I don't get my operation for another couple of weeks."

Ramiel nodded and headed to the driver's side as Giovanni helped Antoine into the back seat. As the car engine roared to life, Antoine felt the cool air blowing from the vents. "Hot this time of year," he said, his eyes transfixed on the large wooded front doors of the chateau. He felt so small, looking up the cement walk-up steps, and looking at the large, expansive windows that soared up towards the second floor.

The car pulled away, and he craned his neck to keep his eyes on the chateau. *When will I see you again?*

The ride through the French countryside towards Germany took several hours. Ramiel remained focused on the road, as Giovanni could be heard lightly snoring in the back seat. Antoine sat, watching the patchwork of farmland and bright, lush green fields flash by, his chin resting on his open palm, and as he felt the warmth of the sun through the windows, he felt his eyelids grow heavy. He looked over at Ramiel, noticing his salt and pepper hair on the back of his head as he remained focused on the road. And not before long, as his mind drifted off, he was with Ramiel again…

…Antoine stood in the clearing near the large angel headstone and watched Ramiel approach. He was smoking a cigarette, and walked through the grave makers, back and forth, in a zig zag fashion, smoking and smiling. His hair hung just below his forehead, slightly covering his eyes on one side of his face. Antoine thought that he looked like he just stepped off of the magazine pages of Milan.

"So you finally made it," Antoine said as he heard Ramiel's footsteps through the gravel. "Are you ready for what I am about to show you?"

Ramiel nodded and took a drag on his cigarette. He blew out a cloud of smoke, as Antoine stood motionless before him. "Yes," Ramiel said.

Antoine nodded and turned around. "Well thank you for joining me."

Ramiel followed Antoine across the cemetery. Antoine turned around and looked back. "Where we are going is beyond the main burial area. On the other side of these trees."

"Okay," Ramiel said.

Antoine could scarcely remember the first days when he met Ramiel. But in his mind, when he saw the moonlight reflect on the river water across the road from his house, he remembered the nights – after he had met Darius – but before he had been transformed, walking along the river bank, in the cool, blue moonlight, heading towards his haven. He remembered looking up and seeing the warmth of the lights from the Café, like an oasis in a dark, blue desert.

The door opened without him having to touch the handle. He had recognized the bartender's salt and pepper hair, how it wisped out from around his ears like pulled cotton and how his head was shiny and bald on the top.

"We were waiting for you!" He boomed in his usual deep, baritone voice.

And there he was.

Standing on the other side of the sea of cocktail tables and small wooden chairs. It was the man he saw; the olive-skinned young man, watching. His eyes. Intense.

Beckoning.

Antoine took a few steps inside the Café and looked back at the bartender. He still stood holding the door open, watching Antoine. "He insisted upon you," he said. "And only you."

Antoine looked back over at the man. He held his hand up, extended his index finger, and beckoned him over. Antoine looked back at the bartender again who simply shrugged his shoulders, closed the door, and walked back over to the bar, slinging a small, white towel on his shoulder.

Antoine returned his gaze to the mysterious young olive-skinned man, and felt his feet start to move. He didn't feel that he had much control over the situation whatsoever, because part of him felt that something about the man was like heading into the unknown.

When Antoine finally was in front of the man, they met eyes and both nodded and smiled. Antoine saw he had been drinking a glass of red wine. The man gestured to the small, wooden table and leaned against the wall. The man picked up his glass and took a sip, again holding out his arm to gesture Antoine to sit.

"Please sit," he said. "I must discuss something with you."

Antoine pulled the chair out slowly, never taking his eyes off the man.

He smiled as Antoine looked at him. He raised his eyebrows.

"We've been watching you for quite some time," he said as he leaned back in the chair. He grasped the stem of his wine glass with his index finger and thumb, drew it to his mouth slowly, and never took his eyes off of Antoine.

Antoine stammered.

"What do you mean you have been watching me? For what purpose? Who are you?"

The man chuckled, set down his wine glass, and leaned forward. He extended his hand. "Permit me to introduce myself. I am Ramiel. I represent a group of immortals in an organization called *The Inspiriti.*"

Antoine smiled and nodded. "You…are so beautiful…" he ran the back of his hand along Ramiel's cheek. "Oh your skin…it's so soft! I've never experienced a man's skin so supple."

Ramiel smiled. "I'm quite flattered, Mr. Antoine. And I know what you have been up to here in Badulla. We have been watching you and would like to recruit you."

Antoine stopped and looked up at Ramiel. He smiled and leaned back, placing his hands over his crossed legs. Antoine leaned forward, placing his chin in his hands. Antoine turned around, glancing up the stairs, to the doors above. He then looked back at Ramiel.

"I will not accompany you to one of those rooms," he said. "I come here with a proposal. There will be a young suitor who will show interest in you. A certain Darius Sauvage from France. He will offer you a gift – a dark gift, rather. One of immortality. If you accept it, you will never die."

Antoine thought of his father. And the day he found him dead, lying in the barn next to the coffee fields. And then of his mother, sitting inside their small cottage, sitting on the chair in the kitchen, crying, waiting for Antoine. "Never die?" Antoine asked. He leaned in closer. "How is that possible?"

Ramiel took Antoine's hands. "It's possible. But you will live in darkness, my friend. You will live isolated in darkness, but you will have others. There are others like us. We're spread across the world. I have been watching you. And have seen how you interact with the patrons here. Everyone loves you. They look up to you. I see those natural leadership qualities. The immortal kind needs more like you."

"And what if I do accept this gift? What is entailed?"

"In the beginning," Ramiel said, "it will seem similar to vampirism. In the beginning, you will crave blood and flesh. But you will quickly evolve, and that's where the similarity ends. Your human form will die, as with vampirism. But again, that's where the similarity ends. You will be a much higher form, of an order we call the Baal, and a member of our enlightened organization *The Inspiriti*."

Antoine looked back at Ramiel but said nothing. They listened to the clanking of glassware as the bartender cleared the glasses from the night's business. After a few minutes, Antoine reached out and took a sip of Ramiel's wine. "I have to die but in the end I will live forever?"

"Essentially, yes."

Antoine nodded and stood. "I best be going."

Ramiel also stood, calling out to Antoine "Think about it, Antoine. Darius will be visiting you soon. Think of immortality. We can use a natural leader like you."

Antoine left the café as the door swung closed behind him.

In the catacombs underneath Vatican City, in the offices of *The Inspiriti*, Delia Arnette fished her phone from her purse as the sessions went on break. She looked up and saw Monsignor Harrison wandering over to the vending area with his hands in his pockets. She pulled up Antoine's information and typed him a message:

WE MUST GET TO MIAMI. IN ROME. MEET ME?

She spent the next few minutes reviewing e-mails as she noticed, in the corner of her eye, a pair of work boots. As if a man were standing next to her, facing her. Who had started this dark vision?

She looked up, gasped and covered her mouth with her free hand. "No! It isn't you!"

The room darkened and they were alone together.

His eyes were wide open and the mysterious man stood above her, saying nothing.

His face was pleading. A tear streamed down his cheek. "I...I don't know what to say..."

The man smiled. "You could start by letting me in."

Her face shifted. "Let you in? To where? Who are you?" She put her glasses on. The man had short cropped dark hair, parted on the side. He wore his black suit well. But the darkness that surrounded him still offered no answers to where she suddenly was.

"I am back for you, Delia. I have been following you all these years. You know that don't you?"

Her mouth dropped open. "Oh..." She removed her glasses as the man's image softened. "You're no man."

"I'm going to leave you a minute, don't you worry your pretty face," he said. "Although I see you've grown old."

"Thanks to *The Hooded Man.* I lost my immortality and aged."

"But you're immortal again."

"Yes," she nodded. "I am."

The man took a step back. "Do you remember the night in Paris? That night so many years ago when you had the mysterious visitor at your door?"

Delia nodded slowly.

"It was the night after you met Darius," he said.

She nodded again.

And then she remembered. The man faded into the darkness, as she saw it play in her mind's eye, like the celluloid of the past.

She saw herself in her apartment in Paris.

Delia took a breath and stood aside. She reached her arm out and gestured for the man to come in. He was dressed in traditionally cut coat and hat, typical dress for the men in Paris of the era. She showed him in to the small sitting area, and he sat on the couch. She went to the kitchenette and boiled some water for tea. The man sat still on the couch, almost motionless, as her clanking of china filled the otherwise silent room. When she approached the sitting area, she placed a steaming cup of tea on the table before him and sat in a small wooden chair next to the sofa.

She stirred her tea and placed the spoon down silently. She raised her eyes to the man. "I let you in because you claim you are my father. I buried him years ago."

"I am your father, Delia. That was not me you saw in the pool of blood on the floor."

"It wasn't you?"

He lifted his cup to his lips and took a sip. "No. It wasn't me. I wouldn't be sitting in front of you if I were dead, would I?"

Delia leaned back and studied the man who claimed to be her father. He had the same wispy hair. Broad shoulders. Facial features. But there was something in her mind. Deep within her soul, that told her to proceed with caution.

Delia's expression softened. She hung her arms at her side and took a step backwards. "How are you standing here? When you are dead and buried?"

But the vision did not stay.

She opened her eyes and saw the harsh overhead lighting of the conference waiting area. She still clutched her phone in her hand, her purse had not moved from her lap.

Monsignor Harrison approached with a small bag of potato chips, his face was shifted and he bit his lip. He sat in the seat next to Delia and placed his hand on her shoulder. "Are you okay, Delia? You look like you've seen a ghost!"

She turned and looked at Monsignor Harrison. "Was I out for a few minutes? Asleep or anything?"

The Monsignor tore his bag of chips open, leaned back and started crunching. He looked around the room as Delia patiently waited for an answer. He swallowed his chips and took a large gulp of soda as he looked back at Delia. "No. You've been sitting here. But we just got out of session. I mean, I just walked over and bought these chips. You sure you're alright Delia? You look pasty white. No ghosts?"

"So no time has passed? Not ten or twenty minutes? Nothing like that?"

Monsignor Harrison shook his head. "No, I went and got the chips and came right back. What is going on, Delia?"

She looked down at her phone. "I sent Antoine a message. Let me look at the time stamp."

Delia pulled up the message she sent to Antoine:

WE MUST GET TO MIAMI. IN ROME. MEET ME?

And then checked the time stamp. She looked up at the clock and gasped. "I...just sent that a moment ago."

Monsignor Harrison leaned closer to her. "What happened, Delia?"

"It appears I've had a visitor. Somehow he came to see me during the seconds between when I sent that message to Antoine and when you came here."

"You look pained."

Delia looked down and then back up at Monsignor Harrison. "This visitor is bringing up old memories. From so long ago. And my life has been so...erratic."

The Monsignor leaned in and whispered in Delia's ear, his voice almost completely concealed by the ambient noise in the waiting area.

"I know, Delia. About your history. I know you exist in different time periods. And how you travel between them. I know who you are."

She opened her eyes. "So…you know." She straightened up and tossed her phone in her purse. "Of course you do. You're Monsignor Harrison. You're the eldest, aren't you?"

He nodded.

"I know what you have done. For our kind. And I am forever grateful for it. You protect us, Delia. Now why don't you lie back and rest yourself? We still have some time before we go back inside."

Delia settled deeper into the small, leather chair and closed her eyes. She didn't notice the noise around her; the chatter of random conversations, the heavy thud and clank of a soda can tumbling out of the vending machine, or the chatter of a news report on the television perched in the corner. She was fading, away, and, then, when she opened her eyes, she looked down and saw her hands.

Dirt was caked underneath her finger nails.

"Come on! Come with us!"

Jerusalem.

The heat and the dust could only be.

But where was she?

In a state of a dream?

For when she looked, when she viewed the film in her mind, she saw herself. She wore the same robe that the old woman had put on her that very first morning that she had awakened on the mat. She moved through the crowds slowly like a lost fish in a vast, overpopulated sea, in an ocean of unknown faces and foreign, dusty roads.

And then came a bright flash.

Delia shut her eyes, raising her arms across her face.

The winds roared, and she felt she was moving, perhaps to another time, or to another place, but the tiny, fragile woman, who sat, silently, in the waiting room in Rome, her eyes still shut tightly, tears streaming down her face, as she found herself, again, now through the darkness.

Antoine woke as the car pulled to a stop.

Ramiel cut the engine and turned around. "Did you check your messages?"

Antoine yawned and rubbed his eyes. "No. What messages?" He stretched in his seat. Had he been sleeping the entire trip? He looked around. Traffic surrounded them. Horns honked.

He lowered his window, and saw large, glass doors across a vast sidewalk and people scurrying about, all in different directions, but most towards the large doors. Some pulled large suitcases behind them. Young children ran to keep up with determined parents. College kids hoisted large, overstuffed bags over their shoulders while hugging crying mothers. He looked up at saw the sign: DEPARTURES.

"Are…we at the airport?" Antoine turned back to face Ramiel.

Ramiel nodded. "Frankfurt airport, yes. While you were sleeping, I called the airline and booked you a ticket to Rome. You'll need to meet up with Delia there. She's with Monsignor Harrison in Vatican City. They're still in session with the High Council, but Delia should be free to go by evening. You'll need to meet up with her there so you both can catch your flight together and head to Miami."

Antoine paused. "Back to Miami. Why so soon?"

Was he ready to return to the city that still held so many memories?

So many fresh wounds that still bled?

"My estate is a burned out shell," Antoine said. "What's the point of going back there?"

Ramiel nodded. "Yes. But you need to find the manuscript that you spoke of. The one Darius wrote. What was it? *The Quest for Immortality?* Yes…that's the one."

Antoine raised the window, leaned back, watching the scurrying people, and sighed. "I wish I could still fly myself. I feel so useless to our kind."

Ramiel turned around and looked at Antoine. "Your powers will return, Antoine. They will return. Spend some time. Recharge. Recuperate. And take stock at the estate. The manuscript may hold answers for you. We'll send for you to come back to Rome when the time comes. But for now, meet up with Delia and get to Miami."

Ramiel opened the driver's door and stepped out. He went around to the trunk and popped it open. He fished out a large, black suitcase and set it on the pavement, extending the handle. Ramiel walked around and opened Antoine's door. Anotine looked up at Ramiel.

"It's time, Antoine. You need to get with Delia. And then head to Miami. Just go. This recharge may be exactly what you need right now."

Antoine nodded and reluctantly got out of the car. "Which airline?" As Ramiel gave him the details of his upcoming flight, Antoine grabbed his rolling suitcase. He joined the throngs of passengers dashing from cars towards the terminal; and as he headed to the large, expansive glass doors, he turned around. Giovanni had lowered his window, his head pointed in the direction of Antoine, his arm draped over the side of the car. Ramiel had closed the rear passenger door and stood, arms folded, leaning against the car, watching him leave.

Delia felt a hand touch her face.

It wasn't hard nor forceful, but a gentle slap. "Delia! Delia, wake up!"

She opened her eyes as the room slowly came into focus. "Wha…I…" Monsignor Harrison was directly in front of her, holding her hands. His face was shifted with worry. "Delia! You're awake!" There was a team of paramedics checking her vitals. A white stretcher was sitting on the floor in front of them.

"Wha…what happened?"

The Monsignor sat in the chair next to her and placed his arm around her shoulders. "You were out. Completely unresponsive. Administration sent the paramedics."

She leaned in close to Monsignor Harrison's ear. "Yes," she whispered. "But I am *immortal*. I do not need all of this." Monsignor Harrison waved his arm and gestured for the EMT's to leave. He turned back to Delia. "Just…please. We don't need any more rumors circulating about. Especially not here."

"I am just fine," she said to the paramedics as they packed up their things and grabbed their gurney. "No need for any of this." She reached into her purse and fished out her phone. "I think there is a message from Antoine." She scrolled through her messages. "Yes. He's already in Rome."

Monsignor Harrison got up. "Just a moment, Delia." He wandered over to the reception desk. He spoke with the agents for several minutes as Delia looked on. As he returned, he smiled. "Well, you'll have to return immediately," he said. "But I bought us some time. They are delaying the inquiry so you can go to Miami with Antoine."

"You can't come?"

He shook his head. "No, I must stay in Rome. Klemmson said he plans to continue questioning me unofficially. But the inquiry will wait until your return. Now go, Delia. Get yourself to *Leonardo da Vinci*. Meet up with Antoine. Get yourself to Miami and back."

Delia nodded and tossed her phone in her purse. She swung it over her shoulder and stood, steadying herself. "Yes, yes. Antoine. He is waiting for me."

"And we will be waiting for you here, Delia. Come back soon. We need you. We need to figure out how to save our kind."

As the first day of the inquiry headed towards a close, Delia found her way outside the basement level of the Sistine Chapel. She walked, as quickly as her elderly legs would allow her, down a wide hallway, lined with old, but highly polished, linoleum. People scurried back and forth, heading in and out of doors that lined the passage. Now that the inquiry was placed on hold, many of the members of the High Council would be preparing for a short trip back to their home sectors. Harsh overhead light panels hung from the ceiling every few feet. The tiny door, which held the small, dark set of stairs up to the chapel, seemed so far away, at the end of the hallway.

She was still well a ways from the door, when she saw it open.

"Antoine!" she exclaimed. He looked tired, but it was the same Antoine. So tall. Ruggedly handsome. She picked up her pace as he stood, smiled and nodded.

"You made it!" she said, giving him a hug. "Let's go! We have to catch our flight. I have so much to tell you on the way to Miami. We had a day of inquiry about *The Hooded Man*. But what's really interesting is what Monsignor Harrison was speaking to me about when we were waiting for the afternoon session to end."

Antoine nodded and assisted Delia up the tiny stairs. They exited into the Sistine Chapel worshipping area. Antoine looked up. His mouth dropped open. "Amazing..."

Delia turned around and saw Antoine had stopped walking next to her, but was standing and admiring the ceiling. He looked at the artistic masterpiece, saying nothing, his eyes wide and his mouth hanging open.

Delia backtracked back to where Antoine was standing. "Michelangelo's work," she said. "The ceiling at least."

Antoine shifted his gaze forward, towards the altar. "Look...at all those people...I see the cross...and others...and the colors..."

Delia leaned on her cane and looked across the chapel towards the altar. She nodded. "Yes," she said. "Michelangelo's *Il Giudizio Universale*. You see it on the back wall? The finality of it is just profound."

Antoine broke his gaze and looked at Delia. "What did you say?"

"It's Italian, Antoine. It means 'The Last Judgement'."

Antoine gasped and studied the mural.

"It took several years to complete. Just that fresco behind the altar. But all of the painting was completed in different time periods. It depicts the Second Coming of Christ."

Together, they stood and looked at the soaring mural, at those in the celestial areas; in the clouds, in the heavenly glory. And those in the center, rising towards the Heavens. And then towards the green grounds below, what could only be a depiction of the physical Earth; the bodies lying; lifeless; grey corpses amidst fissures of flames rising from the ground.

Antoine paused for a moment, looking around the chapel, admiring the ceiling, and the frescos by the myriad artists. But he kept looking back at the work by Michelangelo on the altar wall.

The Last Judgement.

He did not speak, but as they piled into the waiting black sedan, which sat running in La Piazza san Pietro, Delia saw that Antoine looked pained. There was something bothering him. Something eating at his insides. She chose not to bother him with asking about it now, as they were rushing to the airport.

But she knew something was on his mind.

Monsignor Harrison returned to his quarters.

From a distance, he watched Delia hug Antoine and disappear into the tiny doorway to the world above. After a few minutes, he turned, heading the opposite way towards the residences. The hallway, the same polished linoleum. He pressed his access card against a steel plate on the wall in front of a set of heavy, wooden doors, and entered the residential area. Carpet now lined the hallway floors in this area, as well as a more "homey" feel – side tables, couches, and floor plants lined the walls. When he found his door, deep into the residential sector of the catacombs, he fumbled for his keys. Once inside his humble quarters, he opened a small cabinet in his living room. His prized bottled of aged cognac was locked inside, along with several snifters.

Several hours later, the bottle of cognac was nearly polished off. The amber liquid hugged the bottom of the bulbous bottle. Monsignor Harrison leaned back on the couch, his eyes semi-closed. He fumbled in his breast pocket, and fished out a cigarette, when the room went dark.

"What the – "

He attempted to stand but lost his footing, almost crashing face forward into the coffee table. He reached in front of him, and tried to make out his hands. The table and furniture.

Something.

Anything.

The Monsignor opened his eyes, but saw nothing.

Until he heard the voice.

"Chet."

It was masculine. Sounded rugged.

He flopped back on the couch, staring forward, but unable to move. He watched as a spine of light formed in the darkness, reaching from the floor, upwards towards the ceiling.

Alone in the darkness, he knew, moments after the rip closed, the purpose of the visit. He knew, as he had sat in the conference room with the questioners, what had happened.

And then, moments after those thoughts had entered his mind, he saw a light. It seemed that it could be miles, if not more, away from him, but – what it *seemed* to be was his ray of light. Could it be his beacon of hope in the darkness?

And then, in an instant, he was carried back and saw him.

He saw Tramos.

And the Monsignor recognized the bull-stature of the muscular man who stood as a dark silhouette bathed in muted white light, with his head hung down. The Monsignor could see Tramos' hair hanging down towards bare, muscular shoulders, standing in a shadow. Tramos was the one who he had heard about, so many times throughout his long life; the one who had transformed Darius, and the one who had always fought with the Monsignor for control of the immortals.

Tramos opened his eyes, and looked directly at the Monsignor. "I have brought you here," he said.

Tramos was the same as he had always remembered. The same striking, blue eyes, the flowing blonde hair, the chiseled features. But Tramos was not smiling this time. "Do you know why I have brought you here?"

"Into the darkness? Away from the conference room? And the High Council?"

Tramos looked straight at the Monsignor. His eyes were piercing. "I have brought you here to show you…that there is hope for all. For redemption. Even for the immortals."

The Monsignor's mouth dropped open. "I did not think…"

Tramos nodded. "I am more than what you know," he said. "I am from another . I have been living amongst your kind for centuries, but for a specific purpose. And now, that you are facing the end of your kind, I must reveal who I really am."

"And who are you?"

"I am the one sent to protect. To guide."

Monsignor Harrison thought he was drunk. The Tramos that he knew was a conqueror; the Tramos that he remembered always clashed with him.

And then Tramos took the Monsignor's hands, and when they locked fingers, the darkness spilled away. Tramos extended his wings across a new sky, and the Monsignor's mouth dropped open.

"You're an *angel*!"

Monsignor Harrison woke up in his quarters with a throbbing headache. He clutched his head as he swung his legs out over the bed. The finished bottle of cognac sat on the dresser next to a bulbous snifter with a small dash of amber liquid in the bottom. He trudged over to the bathroom and splashed some cool water on his face. He filled one of the glasses with some tap water and took a sip, looking in the mirror.

The bags under his eyes were pronounced today.

But as the fog started to lift, he thought of Tramos. Had he visited? And was he really an angel?

As he walked to the conference room, for an unofficial continued questioning, he remembered the days after they had finally captured Claret. When the days were darker, when the skies had still been active.

When *The Hooded Man* still walked the Earth in search of all of the immortals.

He looked up, it was still dark, angry, burning with crimson red. The painted wisps. Once in the conference room and settled in front of the High Council, Monsignor Harrison continued: "The black clouds raced across the heavens above me. But as I looked down, over towards the barren earth, I saw the result of her crucifixion."

They shuffled in their seats.

"What do you mean? What was the result?"

It was a random, masculine voice. Monsignor Harrison had been looking down at his lap and did not know who asked the question. He looked up and around at those at the conference table. They were each well poised, looking directly at him, with sullen faces, waiting for an answer. Monsignor Harrison shifted in his chair, looked around the room again, and grabbed a handkerchief out of his pocket and mopped his brow. "There was some unity that we hadn't seen before. At least not in our race."

A young man with horn rimmed glasses, who sat near Klemmson towards the center of the conference table, looked down at his notes for a moment, and then back up, adjusted his glasses. And then cleared his throat. "Do you think she was misjudged? That she was innocent of the crimes?"

Monsignor Harrison's arms fell to his sides. "Claret? No! I proceeded over those trials! She was given a fair judgement!"

The young man nodded.

Monsignor Harrison leaned forward. "Do you honestly think it matters? With what she has done?"

The young man removed his glasses. "Fairness matters, Monsignor. In the end and in the pursuit of justice, we must always remain fair and true. Regardless of us being immortal and somewhat separated from the human race. Many of their principles still apply to our kind."

Another male member sitting on the opposite end of the table sighed. "Yes. And we are in these proceedings to also determine if Claret was given a fair judgement."

Monsignor Harrison snapped his head in the direction of the new member of the council. "You all sound as if you are doubting my judgement As if I did not act from the experience that I have. As if I somehow were incompetent!"

"Take us back, Monsignor. Back to when you captured her."

The Monsignor remembered seeing Claret in a holding cell; the walls were made of rock, partially covered in moss. It was dark like a cave, with a layer of putrid water at the base.

And then he saw the hill.

Golgatha.

The famous sandy brown mountain outside of Jerusalem; where Christ was nailed to a cross; where Claret had been crucified thousands of years later.

He heard the sound of boulders rolling down a hill as the sun beat down above with ferocious intent. "Take her," he said to the High Council. "Her hair, I remember, was stone white. But that's all I remember about her. She just hung there, her head down. Blood ran from her eyes, her mouth, her ears. She cried out as she seared in the sun. She had been so weak with dehydration."

Monsignor Harrison recalled his commands to the soldiers: "Take her to the bowels. To the dungeon. The cave. Chain her up. But give her water. She is near death. We must keep her for the trial. No food. Only water. Go now!"

Once in the cave, Claret laid against rough stone, her eyes watching the door. There were heavy footsteps approaching outside.

But the door remained closed.

A fire crackled in the distance.

She reached out for a small, wooden bowl of water. The shackles and chains on her wrist clanked as she moved closer to the bowl. The water looked cool, and fresh. She could see the reflection of the flames in the ripples. She was almost there.

But then a pair of heavy work boots appeared just at the bowl.

She sat back and closed her eyes.

There was a fire in a pit in the center of the holding cell that reflected a warm, orange glow on her cheeks.

Monsignor Harrison sat back, his hands crossed in front of his stomach, and cleared his throat. He waited as the members of the High Council leaned in towards one another and conferred with each other.

The young man in the horn rimmed glasses picked up a piece of paper, adjusting his glasses as he read. "Since some time ago, and over the course of years, there was a man who wore a hood, and he rose from the bowels of the earth. A personification of evil. He wiped out my race. Everyone who I had ever known. And relied upon. Everyone…gone."

The young man removed his glasses and looked directly at Monsignor Harrison.

The young man brought his hand up to his forehead and smoothed his hair back. "Well, Mr. Harrison, it seems from that statement – which you gave to us directly – and from what you just told us about her holding and resulting crucifixion, that we have a question before us."

"Which is what?" The Monsignor shifted in his seat and crossed his legs.

The young man leaned forward and looked directly at the Monsignor. "Was she guilty of the charges? Was she treated properly during holding? It's a moral question, really, isn't it Monsignor?"

He tugged at his collar and took a sip of water from the adjoining table. He looked at the eldest Cardinal, who sat off to the side during this session.

"I stand by my decision," Monsignor Harrison said. "And my holding practices. Claret was treated no differently than any other prisoner who had committed crimes against the immortal kind."

Klemmson stood. "Monsignor Harrison. Do you think those practices are just? Moral?"

He shook his head. "Since when we – as immortals – who have strayed far from goodness…have a great concern about morals? She is gone now. Paid for her crimes. I'm sure she's found her redemption."

Klemmson scoffed. "Redemption? Of our kind?" He laughed, turned and sat.

Monsignor Harrison took another sip of water and watched Cardinal Klemmson settle back into his seat. "We all can find redemption, can we not? And perhaps she has now found hers."

The younger man in the center shook his head and lay his glasses on the table.

He stood and looked across at Monsignor Harrison. "What you are failing to connect with," he said. "Murdering an immortal is a crime against your own kind. You do know the punishment for it, correct?"

Monsignor Harrison slammed his fist on the table. "Yes I am fully aware! And she was tried and found to be guilty!" He looked at the council with wide eyes. "This hooded man attacked our kind. All over the world. And she was tried. And found to be guilty for the same exact crimes that you are speaking of!"

"Then, Monsignor, why did you not escalate this mater to our Council?"

Monsignor Harrison swallowed but did not reply.

Miami.

The brightest city with the darkest shadows.

For the immortals, it was the city that had been central to *The Hooded Man's* wrath. Where it had all began. When Darius had first encountered the villain outside a park in the dark, wee hours of morning in Miami Beach; that was when it had all started.

And afterwards, it spread like an infection.

There were those who talked about seeing *The Hooded Man*. Immortals met in bars, cafes and even churches to discuss their dilemma: who was appearing to immortals offering salvation but bringing death?

And in all of those meetings, it all came back to Miami.

It had been the city of Antoine's leadership; he had an estate in Coral Gables. The city where the infection started and spread. Antoine had called it home for years, and he had once owned and operated a nightclub on Miami Beach called *Sacrafice*.

Coral Gables was also the home of *The Astral*, a research society with offices on Ponce and 5th, which were lost, almost entirely, to an explosion, coinciding with the fires at both Antoine's estate and the nightclub on Miami Beach.

Two of the researchers met in the local library to discuss the situation with the immortals. Hector Tabares led the investigation surrounding the fires and explosion. A short, silver-haired Hispanic man, he had close ties with Antoine.

There was an announcement over the Public Address system that indicated the Library was closing. Hector looked up from his computer screen and saw several rows of bright, florescent lights snap off. He shook his head, returned his attention to his computer, and went to save his work. As he shut down the computer, the screen snapped off and went dark. He started to pack up his notepads and books. His associate Geraldine, a Director of her own Research Society in Rome, had asked a question of him the other night and which now popped into his mind.

"Why do you have this deep fascination with the immortals?"

Hector hadn't had the opportunity to give Geraldine an answer, as she had asked him just as the Library had been closing a few days prior.

Hector saw Ponce De Leon after dark.

The offices to *The Astral,* back before the explosion, the blinds shut tight and drawn, the glass door closed and locked and dark. "I remember meeting with a Sheldon. He was the Director at the time. I remember...yes. That was him."

"Wilkes?" Geraldine pecked at her keyboard. "Sheldon Wilkes?"

Hector nodded.

"He died, correct?"

Hector shrugged. "No one knows for sure. He was *rumored* to have died. I hadn't seen him since he was actively meeting with Antoine. He told me he was writing a book. His car was found sitting outside Antoine's estate in Coral Gables. He was thought to have been visiting Antoine that evening. But never came out. And then after the fire..."

"…after the fire no evidence was found." Geraldine took a breath and looked over some notes on a yellow legal pad. She removed her glasses and looked up at Hector, who sat across her at the tiny wooden table, and looked right back at her. "So…then…what is next Hector? What is the next step?"

Hector fidgeted and bit his lip.

He crossed his arms, leaned back in the chair, and looked up at the ceiling. After a few minutes, he looked across at Geraldine. "How about we visit the estate? Get a look inside? Is it still a crime scene?"

A stern librarian leaned over the table. "We are closed. Please gather your things and exit downstairs. We open tomorrow at ten in the morning."

Geraldine chuckled as she closed her laptop. "You just let me pull a few strings. I know some people in Miami PD. Back before I was sent to Rome. I can get us access. Watch and learn, Hector."

The chatter in the conference room died down as the Elders stood in front of the long table at the end of the room. "Monsignor Harrison, stand please."

He did as instructed.

"For the crimes against an immortal, we find you guilty as charged."

The room erupted in chatter.

Monsignor Harrison's mouth dropped open and the others had to restrain him. Several burly men stood in front of the room, in front of the Cardinals. "Everyone, please! Quiet!" Cardinal Klemmson banged his gavel. "Order, please!" He banged the gavel again as the chatter died down.

"Now for your sentencing."

Monsignor Harrison remained standing as the other immortals were instructed to sit. He kept his eyes focused on Cardinal Klemmson, who looked straight at the Cardinals. They each took their seats behind the lengthy table. As they got settled, Delia sat and Klemmson spoke. "You are herby sentenced to death. We will command your soul and you will navigate the netherworld and find our redemption. The immortals need salvation after this wrath from this 'hooded man', and as punishment for crucifying one of our own kind without an apparent fair trial, or proper prisoner holding procedures, you will be burned to ashes and buried in an unmarked grave here in Italy."

There were some gasps as Monsignor Harrison looked at the floor and closed his eyes.

Klemmson continued. "When you are on the other side, you will meet up with another chosen representative of our kind and go on a mission to earn our redemption."

The chatter swelled again as Klemmson banged his gavel. "Everyone! Please! Quiet!"

After a few minutes of dwindling chatter, Monsignor Harrison looked up at the panel. He looked at each of the men, the eldest immortals save him, and paused on Klemmson. "I did not cause this!" he said. His eyes were wide. "I did not give the order! I didn't recruit George!"

Klemmson banged the gavel again. "Order! Order!"

The chatter died down as Klemmson stared directly at Monsignor Harrison. "Tell me who this George is. Has he been newly transformed?"

Monsignor Harrison looked over at Delia, who leaned forward over the table she was sitting at. She looked back at him and nodded. The Monsignor looked back at the Cardinals and cleared his throat. "George Stanley was a predator, your grace. Of young men. He seduced them and murdered them. Locked them up in cages in his basement."

"And you are bringing this up at the last minute, why?"

Monsignor Harrison shook his head. "Because he was Claret's puppet! He is a man. *Was* a man. A man with a very dark past. And Claret recruited him. Lured him."

"And how did she lure him?"

"She visited him regularly. Some say in his dreams."

Klemmson looked down and shifted through some paperwork. Monsignor Harrison waited patiently and folded his arms. "She had many powers," he said, as Klemmson looked up at back at him.

As Monsignor Harrison told the story of Claret and George to the Council, Delia awoke. She waited for her vision to adjust, but after a few minutes, she heard the hum of the engines. The blue fabric seats expanded in front of her, as most of the interior lights of the cabin were off and the plane was quiet as passengers were sleeping.

She looked across and saw Antoine fast asleep in the seat next to her. His seat leaned far back, and he was wrapped in a blanket.

She could not get the image of Monsignor Harrison out of her mind. She could see him, standing in front of the High Council, getting a death sentence. But had he been guilty? Had it happened?

Delia closed her eyes.

She could remember everything.

She saw the tiny stucco house in the Southern suburbs of Miami. She could still feel the stifling heat and humidity against her skin as if she were standing in George's driveway. She could still see a Styrofoam cooler toppled over with beer cans rolling down the driveway. She could see George passed out in a lawn chair, holding a can of beer in his hand, with his right hand down his shorts.

But in the past, she had stood there.

She had seen George.

She had watched him.

And next to her was the one immortal who would secretly keep tabs on the others. But Antoine had little interest in George. Other than his death and what it meant for the immortals. As for Delia, her mind's eye was like looking at film: she was there, once again, to experience what she had in the past.

And the scene replayed in her mind.

The stifling heat.

The humidity.

Those are the two factors. The sensations that she felt that drowned out her thoughts of Monsignor Harrison back in the conference room in Rome and brought her to the past, in Miami, an ocean away.

She could feel the tall, rugged presence of who had been standing next to her, on the cement driveway, looking up at the tiny yellow stucco house.

Tramos.

IV

TRAMOS THE CONQUEROR

Emaleth cried for three days and three nights.

She would pace across the wood planks of the front porch, usually in the morning, and then finally find her rocking chair on the side of the house. She would rock back and forth in her wooden rocker, holding her coffee by her knees; they were clutched together as she rocked.

The chair would squeak methodically against the silent humid morning, and that was usually the only sound, save the occasional passing bird. She hung her head low, and held her steaming cup of coffee, in the steel cup, just between her legs. She would close her eyes and listen to the silence. She could feel the steam from the coffee across her face, but she opened up her ears on those mornings after Henry had died.

A creek babbled in the distance.

And she was amazed at how much she could hear when she ceased her sight and opened up her ears.

But Daniel never returned.

He had promised. He had said he would come back to their little mountain ranch, but he never did. Emaleth never knew what had happened after the night she saw Daniel last, but that was the last time she had seen him.

She remembered the night.

It felt so long ago.

And maybe it had been.

Emaleth couldn't remember either way. But she could still remember what happened that night, even if she could not place the time.

Despite that, she could still look over and see her bedroom curtains blowing in the wind, as she remembered that she had left her window open that particular night.

And she could still feel the cool wind against her naked body as she lay in the bed; her bosoms heaved as the wind cooled her sweat, and she remembered pulling the sheet up and over herself. There were many details about that night which she could remember, as if they had happened yesterday.

And then, after she had settled back in to try to get some sleep, he had appeared.

She heard him outside the window. He had called in to her. "Emaleth!" He had said. Her eyes fluttered open and she drew the sheets up to her chin.

She snapped her head towards the window.

There was a shadow standing in the frame; it appeared thick, but muscular, most certainly a man.

It was he.

She recognized the long, flowing golden hair from the marketplace. He peeled off his shirt as she reached over and turned on her bedside lamp. The warm glow revealed a cemented chest of roping muscularity. "Let me in," he said.

He grasped the windowsill with his hands, as his arm and chest muscles flexed while he spoke. She heard the wood creak as he grabbed it. "You remember me, I am certain. You have seen me, and I have been watching you. So I know you will let me in. You must let me in!"

She sat up in bed and looked over at him. "You've come calling to me? With no shirt? What are your intentions, dear sir?"

He smiled.

Emaleth shook her head and swung her feet out onto the floor. She winced. It was cold. She pulled the sheet around herself to cover her naked body. Wrapped in the sheet, she walked over towards the window and stopped a few feet short of the windowsill, just out of his reach.

"Haven't you seen enough of me tonight?"

"Never enough!"

He smiled and looked down, but continued to grasp the wooden ledge. She watched his arms, and then his chest, as the muscles roped against his skin as he moved. "Did you honestly think I wouldn't come and visit you? That I wouldn't want to see you after what we experienced? All you need to do is invite me in, and I will be there with you…"

"…I don't know, it's late…"

"…keeping you warm, Emaleth. It's such a cold night! Will you banish me out here to freeze?"

And Emaleth paused for a moment, and looked over at his bare chest. She could see the muscles move under his skin as he leaned in as far as he could. "If it's so cold, then put your shirt on!"

He laughed, drew his arm upwards, and flexed his bicep. "Then I couldn't show you this."

His bicep expanded against his taught skin, like a rock in his arm, it pressed outwards, threatening to tear. Her mouth dropped open as her sheet dropped to the floor.

He stopped moving and looked directly at her. Her nudity, her nakedness, her vulnerability.

And then he climbed through the windowsill.

Once he was inside, he stood next to her, towering over her. She felt his heat, looked up and into his piercing blue eyes. "Take me," she said.

He picked her up and carried her over to the bed, laying her down and straddling on top of her, dwarfing her. She watched as he sunk down on top of her; she gasped at his size, his weight, his muscularity. She grabbed onto his arms and screamed out as he drove himself into her, and when she was near climax, she felt the pierce in her neck, but she was powerless beneath him. And when he plunged his fangs into her neck, she felt the hot wet warmth of her blood spilling onto the sheets, and she felt herself disconnecting as the room turned black...

...and the next thing that she remembered was awakening to darkness. She looked around for the man, but saw nothing.

"Hello?" She called out against the silence.

Do you not remember me?

She stopped in her tracks. There was silence but she heard someone speak to her.

"Hello? Are you there?"

Look into your mind.

She closed her eyes and concentrated on the rough stones she had been standing on. They were cold, wet, staggered and their dull points dug into the souls of her feet. She shook her head, tried to press on, to find her way back, and then the voice came again.

Look deep within yourself.

"What do you mean?" she asked. "Who are you? What are you saying to me?"

And then the mysterious, hidden voice was revealed: as he stepped into the light, and it was him.

The same man, the same one who had taken her.

She remembered now.

"Who are you?" she asked.

"You have known me as Daniel," he said. "But my name is Tramos. I have been known as Tramos for many centuries."

She took a few steps back. "Centuries?"

But then Emaleth woke with a start.

She was still holding her steaming coffee in her lap. Had she been dreaming?

Of Tramos?

She must have dozed off, for it was still the same summer morning, when she had been sitting in her squeaky wooden rocker, crying, hanging her head down low, close to her steaming coffee, and wishing and waiting for his return.

As the sun set on the fourth day, and there was an insurmountable feeling of dread that overcame her; she parted the curtains and looked out the window. The same trees rose from the yard, the same garden reached out towards the mountains on the eastern side of the house.

But he had been gone far too long now.

Emaleth paced across the floor, as the cold stone made the soles of her feet dusty. "Where are you? What are you in my life?" She looked up the ceiling. "Are you my tutor? My lover? Why have you left me? Where have you gone?"

Tramos always thought he had different origins.

But his last memories were of Cairo.

And long days of hard, back-breaking work. Hoisting large blocks of stone, on massive wooden carts, in the searing, hot desert sun.

When he finally slept, he dreamed of his life in Europe. He couldn't place where he was from, but that's what he had felt. He could not remember when he had come from, or when he had last seen his mother and father. But living as a worker south of Cairo transformed him into the hardened physical warrior that he was destined to become.

"Daniel!"

He could remember a voice calling his name.

It was feminine. Could it have been his mother? And had that been his name?

The next morning, he woke as the sun rose from the eastern sky. "Daniel! Wake up! Get up now, it's time!"

He rubbed his eyes and pulled at some of the grit. As he opened his eyes, he saw outside that the storm had come. A giant, billowing dust cloud was approaching.

He swung his legs out of the bed, onto the sandy floor, and dashed over towards the opening of his tent. He looked towards the east. The giant sand cloud filtered the sun, and other workers would scatter and scurry towards their workstations, securing whatever they could, with whatever they could find.

Daniel walked out to the dusty sand yard.

His mother and father were standing there, along with his little brother. They stood and watched him in silence in the morning sunlight.

"Go out now, Daniel," his father said. "Go, make your living. Your life. It is time, my son."

He closed his eyes and shook his head.

And then they were gone.

Darkness befell the land where there was no measure of time.

There was a certain time, and a certain place, that an angel rose from the ashes; tearing through the thorns; rising from the field of skulls. It had been in the days of the altar. The days when Antoine was burned, and Darius had navigated the sea of souls to rescue him.

Angry, dark clouds swirled in the sky.

Lightning flashed as winds howled. Tall, dark mountains rose from a dark and barren landscape like sunken sea-ships rising from an evaporated ocean.

Thunder crashed followed by a flash of lighting, bathing the sky in green. A chorus of wails emitted from below. As he looked downwards, he saw a putrid lake…a sea of souls…pasty white limbs thrashing from the water; the screams wafted upwards as he looked outwards.

The land of the three suns.

The dark light that shined throughout each day and night; the rings of fire that burned incessantly downwards on the beach of the putrid sea; the bodies, some of whom had escaped the clutches of the ocean, littered the beach, surrounding the rings of fire, decrepit, motionless, but moaning.

There was a man crawling on the beach, naked, pasty white, emaciated; his head was looking downwards towards the sand. He crawled a few steps, slowly, and then collapsed.

"Can you save me?!"

He looked down at the man on the beach. There were other bodies in the sea; some appeared lifeless and washed up with the surf and were scattered on the sands. But this one body - this one man with thin, pasty white limbs, crawled from the waterline to the dry sand. He raised his arms up. "Water! I thirst! Please, bring me water!"

And then he prepared to step off the perch he had been standing on. He felt his wings spread and reach across the sky, as he lifted off of the stones, and was carried over the sea.

As he flapped his wings, he heard a hum, if not a chorus, without discernable words, but he remained focused on the body.

His coffin lid opened.

The images that followed were blurred.

Hazy and undiscernible.

"I saw light, indiscriminate light…" Darius opened his eyes as the lid was propped open entirely. Had there been someone there? He waited and looked downwards. The shadows that covered his body were not dissipated by the light.

And then there was a shadow.

Movement across the field of blurred images; the feeling, welcome, joyous, something unexpected. The coffin lid had opened. And Darius spoke. "I had been buried. I had not expected to leave the dark, solitary box."

But then the coffin lid opened.

And the light spilled in…

Darius chose not to sit up.

He felt paralyzed, watching upwards, his eyes open for the first time that he could remember since he had seen the room at the chateau.

But I was lying in there! I was in there for weeks!

And then, in the dark solitude, he examined himself. There were the days before his transformation, which did not figure in to his decision.

Was I selected for the gift? The dark gift? Was I destined for the darkness from birth?

A dark figure appeared in the hazy light, hovering over the casket. Darius looked up, but did not see anything except a dark spot against the light.

Darius tried to speak, but was unable to. He reached up to his throat, opening his mouth. He tasted dry, hot air. Was the coffin lid really opened? Could this be a dream?

And then the darkness extended through the light – as if there were a shadow; an arm reaching out towards him. A finger coming closer, down to where he lay on the pillows and in the satin, deep in his grave in the underground mausoleum.

And then he saw Tramos.

He saw the same morning he always remembered.

The same sunlight shined through the windows, as the wind blew the curtains inwards. Darius huddled under the sheets and pulled them up to his nose. He was still mortal, still yet to be transformed, still a young man, and in some respects, still quite naive in his ways. He had the same brown hair, but it wasn't tied back. He lay in bed, shirtless, his arms behind his head, waiting. The small tufts of hair under his arms caught the breeze that blew through the open window as his sweat dried.

He looked over towards the door, still closed, but he heard rustling through the house.

Bacon was cooking. He could smell that.

But then the sounds came from the window.

He snapped his head around and saw a silhouette of a man in the window. The sun shined behind him, and his hair was long and flowing. Darius could tell from the shadow that he was large and muscular.

"Do you remember me?" he asked.

Darius held the sheet up towards his nose but waited. He could feel his hot breath against the fabric as he heard Tramos pull against the window frame. It creaked under his weight.

Darius snapped his head over and looked towards the window. "Are you coming in *here?*"

Tramos looked up and raised his eyebrows. "I did it for days in demon form. You won't let me enter in my human form?"

Darius sighed and leaned back on the pillows. As Tramos entered, and found his way into the room, Darius raised the sheets and moved over to one side of the bed. "If you're coming in you're coming in here."

Tramos removed his clothing.

He stood in front of the bed, nude, muscular. His chest was that of a sculpture in Rome; his arms, powerful and roping. Darius caught himself staring at the powerful immortal standing before him. He clutched the blanket up closer to his face, looking up at him as their eyes locked.

And then that same face, which had looked down at him as he lay in bed so many mornings before he was transformed, the face that was locked with his as Darius lay on his back, in the bed, underneath Tramos, was the same smiling face that looked down at him as he lay in his coffin.

The vision started to clear.

And Darius recognized the flowing hair, the warm smile, with perfectly white and straight teeth. "You are welcome here," Tramos said, as Darius reached up and shielded his eyes from the light.

"Rise," Tramos said. "Rise and be with me here in the light."

Darius' face shifted. "Who…you're evil…I know you are evil. You have shown me so many times!"

Tramos smiled, reached out and placed his hand on Darius' cheek. "We all can find our redemption. And grow. I have done that. And so can you."

He closed his eyes as the light found its way into the casket. He pulled down the satin sheet, untucked it from the sides of the coffin, and tossed it aside. Darius sat up and saw Tramos right next to him, smiling at him. Darius covered his face with his hands, shaking his head.

I am…

Tramos reached and placed his hand on Darius's shoulder. "Your voice will come to you…in time. Just open your eyes, Darius. Let them adjust. Let them see this new world that you are in now."

He opened his eyes.

Tramos had been a clear vision. The first vision. The only thus far.

Crystal and sharp, his face was the same face which he remembered. But even so, there was something different about his face here.

For where he was, the brightness, the light, and the *feelings* that washed over him since the coffin lid was opened, were very different from what he had remembered.

What type of world was this?

They were levitating in pillow white clouds, and there was a light breeze blowing.

"Come out of your casket," Tramos said. "Rise, Darius. Rise."

He and Tramos were concealed by a veil; pure white, pastel blue, powdery and flowing. And when he stepped outside the coffin, he felt the shimmery rainbows which danced around his feet.

"Take off your shoes," Tramos said.

Darius bent down and unlaced his shoes. He tossed them in the casket and pulled off his socks, and immediately started laughing as he felt the shimmer and the rainbows envelop his feet and glide through his toes.

He threw his head back and laughed.

Tramos smiled. "You will come back to them, to those you loved in life," he said. "You will rise from your coffin, which is already buried in the mausoleum beyond the cemetery. But you will take a different form."

Darius coughed. "I…won't be the same?"

Tramos shook his head. "To them, they will see you as the same Darius…but you are like me now. You are celestial. And now it's time for you to earn your wings!"

Tramos spread his wings, and Darius watched as the wings soared across the sky, piercing the veil. The colors screamed loudly at him; rainbow on white; light before dark, and the music. The unseen choir; the genesis of the chorus as the plumes of white tore through the clouds as they raced across the sky, amidst shining light. There was a hum, a chorus, a crescendo, as Tramos wrapped his muscular arms around Darius, carrying them upwards, farther into the sky.

He looked down at the small coffin, sitting on a cloud, and it seemed so foreign. So dark and dull against the vibrancy of the world he now found himself in. And still, being held against Tramos, and his powerful body, of being wrapped in his arms as he was carried across the sky, it did not matter that he was nude. It did not matter that the wind blew through his hair and against his face.

For the sun, the brightness they flew towards, was warming. Inviting. Reassuring. The treasure had been found. There was no longer time in the coffin. And when he opened his eyes, he saw the brilliant sun, the light fingering its way towards them, as Tramos flapped his wings, carrying him, protecting him, reaching across the sky.

Delia snapped awake as the Captain announced on the PA system that the flight was preparing to land in Miami shortly. Delia looked over, and saw Antoine lying back on his seat, his eyes closed. She reached over and shook his shoulder. "Antoine!" she said. She shook his shoulder again. "Antoine, wake up! We're almost ready to land!"

Antoine's eyes fluttered open and he raised his arms, letting out a yawn. "What...what is it?"

Delia leaned closer to Antoine. "I was dreaming. Of Darius!"

Antoine's eyes widened and he turned to face Delia. "Of Darius? You are kidding me. What was in the dream?"

Delia nodded. "I think he's alright, Antoine. I believe he still exists. And that he is being protected." Antoine leaned back and looked out the window. The morning sun was just starting to lighten the night sky. He saw the white and pastel buildings of Miami rise into the sky. He looked over at Delia and then back out the window as the plane approached. "You know, this place always feels like home to me. For some reason. Forget Badulla. This is where I feel most at home."

"Of course you do," she said. "This is where you found yourself. You came of age here. It's quite profound in one's life. Badulla is full of memories. Of Darius finding you in the Café, of your mother and father…but Miami is where you grew into your leadership role with the immortals. And found yourself."

Antoine and Delia's plane landed at Miami International Airport just as the sun was rising. Delia looked over and noticed Antoine's eyes were red-rimmed. She did not say anything, and they exited the plane in silence. As they meandered through the terminal, Delia gave Antoine a few concerned glances, as he appeared to be moving through the terminal in a trance.

Passengers darted around him as he kept his slow pace. When they reached ground transportation, he finally spoke.

"I have a car here," Antoine said. "It's out in long term."

"How long has it been there?"

Antoine shook his head. "Weeks. Maybe even a few months. I parked it there when we headed to Lyon and I didn't give it another thought."

Delia let out a whistle. "That's going to be quite a bill."

Antoine shook his head as he hailed a shuttle. Within minutes, a white van pulled up to the curb and they climbed inside. "Antoine!" the driver beamed. "I have been watching your show! And look at this! You're in my van! You're back in Miami! Word on the news was you went to Europe and closed your house up."

Antoine smiled wanly and introduced Delia. "With the fires, I thought I needed a break from Miami." The driver said he understood, but remained beaming. As the van pulled away, into the crowded terminal traffic, the driver started asking about Club Sacrafice.

"Well, glad to have you back man!"

The van pulled into morning rush hour traffic as Antoie looked out the window, saying nothing. The driver broke the silence. "It was a shame about the fires, man," he said, navigating a merge. "It was all over the news."

Antoine looked out the window. It still seemed dreary. Cloud cover dominated the sky, which spat rain droplets on the windshield. "They got my house too," Antoine offered. "Not just the club."

The driver's eyes widened and Antoine noticed the driver watching him through a massive rear view mirror that spanned the length of the van. "No kidding! I'm sorry, man. Damn, you need a place to stay?"

Antoine looked up and made eye contact with the driver in the rearview mirror. He smiled. "We'll be fine," Antoine said. "But thank you for the offer."

The driver looked back at the road. "There just seems to be so much chaos that erupted in the city recently. These fires. Not sure what's happening."

"Agreed."

Delia reached into her purse for some dollar bills and handed them to the driver as the van pulled up to the satellite lot. Antoine stepped down onto the pavement and turned around and looked at the driver as he waved and pulled away.

Delia placed her hand on his shoulder. "That's your silver Mercedes, isn't it, Antoine?" He nodded as he fished through his pockets. A few moments later, the trunk raised. He tossed their bags inside and they climbed inside the car. Antoine thought nothing of the parking fees as he pulled out his heavy, metallic Black Card.

Back in Vatican City, Monsignor Harrison dialed the phone and waited for Delia to answer. He looked at the clock, counting back the hours, in an attempt to figure out what time it was in Miami versus Rome. When he was about to give up and send a message, Delia answered.

"They're restarting the inquiry," he said. He grabbed a suitcase out of the closet and started packing neatly folded clothes inside. "There's talk that we must have representatives sent to the astral plane to plead our case for redemption. At least one representative. I was found guilty, but when I told them more about George, they agreed to stay the inquiry. Now they're saying we need a representative."

"But that means…"

"A single immortal. One who can be chosen."

"How can that work?" she asked. "A single immortal to represent all of us? Don't we have different sectors who don't have any desire for redemption?"

Monsignor Harrison paused. "That means whoever goes, must die. I don't know, Delia. That's a steep price to pay."

Delia sighed. "But it's to redeem our entire kind. We go in to Antoine's estate later tonight. Antoine left on his own to check on it, but should be returning to pick me up soon. We're going to find that manuscript. There may be an answer in there. Might help give us some direction."

"You mean *The Quest for Immortality*?"

"We suspect there may be some answers in that manuscript. But fear it may have been lost in the fire. In the meantime, has anyone talked about who is going? Who will represent our kind?"

"Nothing yet. Everything could change once the inquiry reconvenes. Antoine's sector was affected the most, more than any other sector, and I would suspect that he will need to be here for the questioning. They haven't called for him yet, but I can see that coming. Once you both finish your business in Miami, we'll definitely need you both back in Rome."

Delia hung up the phone from her conversation with Monsignor Harrison and moved through her cottage, opening drapes. She and Antoine had been in Miami just a short time, enough time to open up Delia's cottage in Coconut Grove, to remove the dust cloths from the furniture, and for Antoine to head out to check on his estate.

It was unusually cool in Miami and Delia had felt the immediate need to get a fire going. Delia sat back on the couch, hung her head down, and examined her cup of tea. The fireplace crackled as a sudden light rain pelted against the windowsill. She reached for a cube of sugar and spoon. It clanked against the china as she stirred the hot liquid. She picked it up and brought the cup to her lips and paused. There were footsteps in the hallway. She turned around. "Antoine? Are you there? Are you back?"

There was a shuffling of feet from an unseen source. Lightning flashed and illuminated the room in pale blue light. She gasped as the door slid open. A tall, imposing dark figure stood in the doorway. Thunder crashed as the power went out, darkening the room.

Her eyes widened and she dropped her teacup with a crash. "You! You have returned!"

The dark figure did not answer, but moved forward. The darkness from the storm kept the visitor's identity a mystery.

Delia stood and looked at the figure. "I know who you are," she said. "Why have you come for me again?" The fire crackled and bathed the room in a warm glow.

The figure reached his arms up towards his head, reached back, and removed a hood, revealing long, golden hair. "Don't you see, dear Delia?"

"Tramos? I thought…"

"Who did you think I was?"

She looked down. "A dark visitor from my past. He's been haunting me my entire life…"

He nodded as she reached down towards the coffee table and lit a candle. She blew on the match and left it in an ashtray. The candle reflected a warm light on his face.

"Why do you come?" she asked.

Tramos sat in a chair opposite the sofa. Delia sat.

"I have heard you, Delia. Calling. Questioning your sanity. And I know you see me in your dreams."

"Yes," she said. "I have seen you. And I have seen me with you. And I saw Darius. On separate occasions. But just on our flight over here, I saw you with Darius."

"He still exists," Tramos said. "He is out there."

"In the astral world? Does he walk among them? In the heavens?"

"I have brought him out of his coffin. He is in the light, dear Delia."

She nodded and smiled. "You carried him across the sky with your wings?"

Tramos nodded. "I did." And then he looked concerned. He touched her cheek with the back of his fingers. "Have you lost your wings, Delia? Do you remember when we flew together?"

She closed her eyes as a solitary tear streamed down her cheek. She breathed in deeply, reached up, and squeezed his hand. "Yes…" she said. "I remember. Flying above the beach. You carried me. Protected me…."

Her eyes fell. "I've seen her, Tramos. I still see her. Even though she slithered down the cross. She still haunts me."

He sat back. "Claret….the ultimate time traveler…"

Delia closed her eyes and thought back to Jerusalem. "Does she still exist too?"

Back in the days of the dusty, stone room which she shared with her for years. In the days when she would follow her through the market in search of the 'holy ones'; in search of the lost cup, the One who those in those days would be called the Messiah.

"Do you remember the days of Jerusalem?" She felt Tramos put his hands on her knees. "I want you to keep your eyes closed," he said softly. "Go back to the days of Jerusalem.

When she was with you. In the early days – when she had just transformed you. Do you remember?"

Delia's eyes remained closed, but she nodded.

"Go back," Tramos said. "And tell me what you see…"

Delia remembered Jerusalem.

She could still feel the sun beating on her skin; the dust, the dry air. And she could see the sun rays shining through the hanging, colorful tapestry. It was perched over a small, square table, held up by two wooden sticks.

"Come on!"

She heard Claret calling.

Delia could recognize her striking red hair.

Her face was shifted in anger, and her hair was mussed and matted. She reached her hand out. "They are coming with stones! They will stone you to death!"

She followed Claret through the market, dodging the shoppers, until they approached a mob of people, throwing their fists into the air and laughing.

"What is it?" Delia asked. "What is happening?"

Claret turned around and faced her.

Her eyes were wide and she bit her lip. "The square. It's mobbed. They are whipping Atticus!"

Delia's eyes widened. "What?! Can't we do something? How did they find him?"

Claret shook her head as Delia pushed ahead, parting her hands between arms of those wearing colorful robes. As she approached the clearing she watched in horror. "Atticus!" she screamed. A whip cracked on his back, as he cowered to the ground. His clothes were torn and shredded; long, bloody gashes ran up and down the length of his back; an expanding red lake of blood was forming underneath Atticus.

The soldiers stopped their whipping and looked over at Delia. The taller soldier took a step forward, never taking his eyes off Delia. He glared at her. "Is that not Delia Arnette? From the Atarah family? She protects whores!" He pointed at her. "Grab her!"

The crowd chorused. "Whore! Whore! Whore!" Fists were balled and punched into the air to join the shouting.

Two soldiers ran from the side and grabbed each of Delia's arms.

They dragged Delia over to the tall soldier.

She looked down at Atticus.

He slowly raised his head and looked up at Delia. The whites of his eyes seemed almost glowing against his dirty, sandy skin. Blood was caked and dried on his hands and arms as fresh blood oozed from the sores on his back. He reached his arm up towards Delia, his eyes wide and pleading, as he opened his mouth. Blood dripped from the side down his chin.

Delia looked down at him. "How did they find you?!"

She was jerked upwards and was staring the tall soldier in the face.

"Stone her!"

The cheering from the crowd swelled "Stone her! Kill her!"

And then Delia was brought back.

She opened her eyes.

Tramos was sitting before her, his eyes looking directly at her. The fire had died down, as did the storm. It was much quieter, and the power had returned. Tramos reached over and turned on a small lamp on the end table.

"What happened after the soldiers decided to stone you?"

Delia sighed. "It was Claret. She appeared from the crowd. I could feel the pressure on my arms. Her hands grabbing them. Her face. The intensity of her eyes. And her long red hair. The soldiers…they were so strong. Their grip was so tight. I can still feel it. They were dragging me through the crowd, to the clearing. I can still feel the stones piercing my back. And the sand on my arms and face. I could see the people had stones in their hands. They were standing and watching me. Taunting me. They picked them up from the ground while they still had fresh blood dripping from them. Poor Atticus. It's like it had just happened only yesterday."

"Claret came and rescued you?"

Delia nodded. "I looked over and saw her. She was fighting her way through the crowd. The soldiers held me and turned me to face the crowd. They kept shouting 'whore! whore!' all while Atticus lie on the ground bleeding. Like they forgot about him."

"And what became of him?"

Delia took a breath. "Well…"

She thought of Atticus.

Of when she first saw him. Across the market, tending to Camels. She could see him, bent over, holding a wooden bucket in front of the animals, looking away from her.

He was young, sandy, blonde hair, and strapping bare, brown muscular chest. He had removed his robe and wore a wrap around his midsection. He carried a wooden bucket of water and placed it on the sand in front of the camels. He raised his head and looked over at Delia.

He raised his arm and waved.

Delia was jolted back to the present as Tramos placed a platter of teacups and a small pot on the coffee table with a light clank.

"Did you have a romantic affair with him?"

"No, no, Tramos. Nothing like that."

"Why were they whipping him?"

Delia reached for the teapot and a fresh cup. As she went to pour the tea, the spout rested on the brim of the china cup with a slight clank. Steam rose as the hot brown liquid poured out. Tramos sat back patiently, his hands flat on his thighs. He watched Delia intently.

"Atticus was the one who took the cup. *He* was the one."

Tramos stood. He started pacing. "What do you mean? Wasn't that Claret who took the cup? On the night Christ had His Last Supper?"

Delia shook her head. "That is what we have been led to believe," she said. "But I know otherwise. I saw it. I waited in the garden Gethsemane and watched the whole time."

Tramos leaned down close to Delia. He brought his face directly across from hers. She could smell fresh blood on his breath. "So Atticus did it? He took the cup?"

She leaned back and looked up at him. "It was Atticus. Claret never did it at all."

Tramos shook his head. "I don't understand why he would be whipped for that. Why would the people even care? I mean, they had crucified Christ at that point. Why would they care about the cup?"

"Even they couldn't deny the power it holds. And Because Atticus was associated with Judas. Any association in those days was a death sentence."

Tramos shook his head. He reached out and grabbed Delia's chin.

"Come again?"

Delia's face fell. She reached for his arm and pushed it away. He fell back into the chair. "It wasn't Claret," she said. "As I told you. Atticus did it. He was quite close with Judas, and that's how he got access to the cup."

Tramos' eyes widened and he pointed at her. He stamped his foot on the floor for a moment. "You mean Judas Iscariot?!"

Delia was taken aback for a moment. "Yes..." she said slowly. "The one who betrayed Christ."

"Yes!" Tramos exclaimed, standing back up. He dashed over to the other side of the room towards the wet-bar. After a few moments of sifting through clanking bottles, he turned around. "Antoine keeps some Absinthe back here, doesn't he?"

Delia shook her head. "Yes, he keeps some here since the fire at his estate. He has a special spot for it."

"Do you think he would mind if I had a glass of it?"

They both looked up as there was a knock on the front door. Delia got up slowly, found her cane, and walked over to the foyer. She peered through the peephole, and saw Antoine smooth his hair back. He leaned forward as Delia reached down and opened the door. "Antoine! Why didn't you just…"

Antoine stepped inside. "I can't find my key."

She ushered Antoine towards the sitting room and he paused when he saw Tramos standing next to the sofa in the front room. The power had returned, and Antoine reached over and snapped the chandelier on, bathing the room in light.

"I wasn't expecting to see you here," Antoine said. "Talking more about Darius?"

Tramos took a few steps forward. "No, actually. Delia and I were discussing some questions she had about her past. Now I understand you are heading to your estate?"

Delia looked up at Antoine expectantly.

Antoine meandered into the parlor and headed towards the wet bar. He shook his head and let out an exasperated sigh. "I drove past," he said. "That's all for now."

"Are you returning?" Tramos asked.

Antoine looked at Tramos and nodded. "Yes, later tonight." He looked over at Delia and raised his eyebrows.

"I'll be coming along."

Tramos joined Antoine at the wet bar. "You mind if I come along as well?"

Antoine shook his head. "We're leaving soon."

Hector and Geraldine left the library and a staff member locked the doors behind them. Geraldine hoisted her bag over her shoulder as Hector pulled his phone from his pocket. The small screen shined against his face in the darkness, as he typed with his index finger. He adjusted his glasses as they proceeded to the parking lot.

"Do you have the address?" Geraldine asked as they unlocked the car and slid inside.

"I'm looking it up now," he said, turning around to look at the back seat. There was a large box. He turned forward and searched through computer desktop file folders.

She nodded and turned the car engine over.

"Here's the address," Hector said. "One Andelusia Avenue. The high price district."

"That's Coral Gables," she said.

"His house."

She nodded. "Well, rumor is he is going to be there tonight. That's the perfect time. So let's go."

Antoine unlocked his small, silver Mercedes as Delia and Tramos followed out the front door. Delia reached around to lock her cottage, as Antoine waited in the driver's seat. "Let's go!" he said.

Tramos held the passenger seat forward so Delia could slide in the back seat, and Tramos squeezed in the front. He looked around for a minute as Antoine threw the car in gear and backed down the driveway. "Nice car," Tramos said. "Very nice. But small."

Antoine shrugged his shoulders but kept watching the road. "My sedan was destroyed in the fire. That had much more room."

Antoine pressed a few buttons and a chorus of strings filled the car.

He looked over at Tramos. "I love Vivaldi. Such a great use of strings. This is *Winter.*"

Tramos nodded and closed his eyes and leaned back in the seat. Delia watched both immortals, in the front seat listening to the classical music, to the violins; the strings chorused in the passenger cabin as she leaned back in the seat herself, closing her eyes, and wondering what the night had in store.

Before the concerto had ended, the small silver car pulled up in front of Antoine's estate. Delia opened her eyes and looked out the window. Yellow crime scene tape still surrounded the property, reaching from one end of the property at the edge of the sidewalk towards the other. Large green hedges masked the interior of the front gardens, but they were in blood. Delia admired the purple azaleas that carpeted the crest of the hedges.

Towards the center of the property was a large, iron gate, framed by soaring lamp posts nestled in cement columns.

"I can't use the drive," Antoine said. "It's still taped off." He pulled to the side of the street and cut the engine. "Shall we?" He looked back at Delia and raised his eyebrows and smiled, as Tramos opened his door and stood on the street.

Antoine fidgeted with the gate key as the door swung open. The gardens were still well tended; the gardeners still visited weekly. But the house was in a different state. Delia still remembered the soaring, grand mason columns that reached from the front, wraparound porch up towards the roof. The front windows, which once were expansive, floor to ceiling glass, were now broken, and the fingerlings of dark soot reached around on the stucco.

And then there was a growl.

And a rustling in the bushes.

Delia gasped as Tramos stood in front of her and Antoine. Antoine looked up and over at the rustling bushes. "What is going on…"

Tramos stood in front of Antoine. "They are protecting it, Antoine. Just like Darius said. It's the hounds. The Hounds of Hell…"

"The hounds?" Delia's eyes widened as she craned towards the bushes. Desperate phone calls from Darius permeated her mind. And stories of those supernatural beasts; she could smell their rancid breath; their acidic saliva dripping from decomposed snouts.

And their stench.

Excrement.

And the days when Darius would pound on her cottage door, in the middle of the night. "The estate is guarded!" Darius had said. "Those supernatural dogs are there!"

And then Delia remembered the hounds.

She explained what they were to Antoine. "They are called Hell Hounds. They guard the Gates of Hell."

Was Antoine's estate a supernatural gateway? She stood in front of Antoine and leaned close to his ear. "Listen, Antoine. Do you hear?"

Antoine and Tramos stood silently. Antoine looked back at Delia. "I don't…"

"It's the Hell Hounds," she said, as the rustling continued in the bushes. "We cannot defeat them. They will tear us apart!" She placed her arms around Antoine's back and felt his body tense up.

Tramos crouched down and examined the bushes. "We cannot see them…"

"…unless they reveal themselves to us," Delia added.

"Let's just get inside," she said. She held Antoine, her arms around him, close together, as they took several steps back towards the porch.

The bushes thrashed.

Tramos fell backwards as the hounds charged out of the bushes.

"Get them!" he cried. Antoine lunged forward as Delia bowed her head down. She stamped her foot on the ground. "I command you! Be gone!"

The dogs stopped and focused on her.

Their stance was wide, they were muscular and emitted a rotten stench. Their eyes were fiery and red. Drops of acid fell to the ground from their matted, bloodied fur as tiny puffs of smoke rose to the air. "I command you!"

She opened her arms as the dogs froze.

Her breathing was heavy, her chest rising and falling with every breath.

Antoine watched, his mouth open, as her white wings tore through her shirt, stretched across the gardens, crashing against the trees, and soaring outwards from the small of her back. The woman, Delia, the one whom Antoine had known only as a feeble, white-haired senior, bent down, placed her arms around his torso, and picked him up off the ground effortlessly, as Tramos extended his wings and they all soared into the sky.

Antoine looked down as the hounds jumped and howled, their chorus of barking permeating the otherwise silent night. Delia and Tramos reached their wings across the sky, carrying Antoine up towards the roof of his estate. They settled at the peak, gently landing on the Spanish tiles, as the dogs quieted below.

The night became still and silent again as the breeze flew through their wings. Antoine turned around and saw Delia's wings retract into the small of her back. His eyes were wide, his mouth hung open.

"You are!" he said. "You…" And then he looked over at Tramos. "And you!"

"We are here to protect you," Tramos said. "Our assignment is you. And only you."

Delia watched Antoine, who hung his head down, and closed his eyes. "For me…" he said. And then she saw. She saw the inner recesses of his mind; of his time in the cemetery when he was chased by demons. She saw him standing in an open grave.

Wake up, sleepyhead.

Delia reached out and touched Antoine's shoulder. He looked up and looked at her. A solitary tear streamed down his cheek. "What are you thinking, Antoine?"

He shook his head, and looked out at the twinkling lights of the city. Trees surrounded large estate homes on Andelusia, and beyond, towards downtown, a warm glow tinted the night sky.

"I can't even *fathom* having protection. Divine protection, isn't it?" He looked over at Delia. "I can't even understand how I would *warrant* such an order. My coffin sentence came but I don't feel any less evil…"

Antoine focused on Delia. She had grown young. Her hair was long, brown and flowing; her lips were fiery red. She was the Delia that Darius had known so many years ago in Paris, returned to the prime of her youth. Antoine's face shifted as he cocked his head to the side. "And you…look at you. You're young again! How can that even be possible? Didn't *The Hooded Man* seduce you too?"

She nodded as Tramos stood, looked outwards, and scanned the horizon. She turned back to face him. "The body is just a shell, Antoine. When you see what is really inside, that is eternal beauty."

"But what about Darius?" he asked. "He grew old and was mortal again. What kind of death is *that*?"

Delia placed her arms around Antoine's shoulders and leaned her head against his. "It's never too late for any of us, Antoine. You've spent your life searching for answers. I've seen into your mind, Antoine. I know what you think. What you believe. And I want to tell you, I will walk with you. And it's never too late."

He looked up at Delia. "Do you think the answers will be in his manuscript?"

"You mean *The Quest for Immortality*?"

Antoine nodded.

"It depends on what answers you are looking for. Darius wrote that book when he was mortal and dying. His gift of immortality had been stripped from him. When fighting for you. *For you*, Antoine. But the answers...Darius was very bitter during those days. He was distressed. Running from these things he called 'the dark ones'. I don't know what type of answers will be in that manuscript. But you need to consider his state of mind when he wrote it."

Antoine placed his hand over his eyes. "I just…don't understand. Maybe reading his words will give some insight?" He let out a sigh. "Then what am I looking for? Does it even matter?"

"Of course it matters," Delia said, rubbing his back. "You have to go back in there – back down to the basement – and face your past. You need to redeem yourself. Free yourself of the chains you have been wrapped in for as long as I have known you. And if it means finding that book and getting some answers about what happened when you were gone, then that is what needs to be done."

Tramos turned around. "And the time to do it is now," he said. "I haven't heard the hounds. This may be as good a time as any to go inside. I can carry you both. We can fly down and head right into the front door."

Antoine craned his neck and looked down into the yard, and Delia joined him.

The bushes rustled again.

Antoine looked up and shook his head. "There's an attic. We can go in that way."

Delia placed her arm around him, and looked directly at him. "Are you ready?"

Antoine nodded. "Yes…"

"Then it's time to face your past, Antoine. When we go inside, I will be with you."

Delia turned to face Tramos, who looked up at the sky, in an apparent study of the moon, as Antoine sat on the edge of the roof, leaned back, and closed his eyes. "Let's go inside," he said. A group of blue-tinted clouds floated by, as Tramos sighed. Delia placed her hand on Antoine's shoulder. "Just a few moments," she said. "I need to take care of this. Before we go to where we are going." She turned away from Antoine to face Tramos.

"You are so passionate about finding justice," Delia said.

Tramos broke his trance and looked down at her. "Justice?"

"For the assault on our kind by *The Hooded Man*."

He returned his gaze towards the moon and nodded.

"But you seem so distant," she said. "And even though I have not spent a great deal of time with you, I can tell that you have something on your mind."

He looked back at Delia. She smiled.

"Are you looking to enter my mind?" he asked. He turned and sat on the edge of the roof, never breaking eye contact. "How can you help me by exploring my past? And why are you doing this now?"

"Because I am being willed to do so."

Tramos sat down next to her. "What do you know, Delia? What is about to happen?"

She shook her head. "Everything isn't always revealed to me," she said. "But there are certain times where I am willed to do something. That I feel a sense of urgency to fulfill. And for you, I must learn more about you. Right now. Before we enter the house."

Tramos looked out at the city and nodded.

"And it gives me a better idea of who you are," she said. "And by facing your past, you can receive redemption too." She looked down at his hands. They were muscular, rugged, a workman's hands. "In life," she said, "I can tell that you were a hard worker. Tell me about your life, Tramos. We have all been placed in one another's lives for a reason. And I believe the reason why we have been placed with one another is about to be revealed to me."

Tramos grasped Delia's hands, as they sat across from one another, on the edge of the roof, under the moonlight and floating clouds, above the rustling bushes and the Hell Hounds, and Tramos started speaking to her. As he spoke, he started to tell her, for the first time ever, about his past. And when she listened, she looked deep into his eyes, past the retinas, deeper into his mind…

…Tramos had always thought himself to be one of the eldest immortals. There were times that he had seen Claret – who was believed, at least by most, to be the absolute eldest, and when he saw her, their interactions were, for the most part, amiable in nature.

But the nature of Tramos and his story stretched back further than ancient Jerusalem and the days of Christ.

There was an approaching thunderstorm on the night that Tramos entered the world. It was long ago, in ancient times, before the days of Claret, before the days of Christ, and when the world was governed by the ancient Egyptians and rulers of the land. It was those rulers who commanded the pyramids be built, on the backs of muscular men, in the searing sunlight; as giant, squares of concrete were hauled in the powerful, desert sun, on rickety wooden wagons, Tramos discovered himself, along with the men of Egypt, hauling concrete.

Tramos doesn't remember how he found Cairo.

Or how he wound up building pyramids with an ancient Egyptian army. But the early years of his life, before he became a young man, had been a blur. He knew, at some point, he was transported from his life in Europe, to the hot desert and the sweaty, brown culture and the pyramid building, but, no matter how hard he tried, he could not remember who, or what, brought him there.

Later in the evening, when he had been laying in his bunk, he pulled the tattered sheet up towards his neck, as a cool, night wind blew in his hut from the darkness outside. The winds tore across the desert, blowing sand and hot air against the flaps.

He closed his eyes and tried to sleep, but sleep did not come well for him that night.

Tramos, I am speaking to you. Do you listen?

He opened his eyes and threw the tattered cloth off his body. Sweat dripped down from his neck and his chest, as the winds and heat roared outside. He looked over and saw his tent mate was sleeping soundly.

Tramos…do you hear me?

He sat up as the wind blew the tent flaps open. He rushed out of bed and tore the flaps closed, as he felt the sting of sand against his bare chest. His tent mate turned and faced the other side of the tent, but did not rouse.

Do you remember me, Tramos?

He looked towards the corner, shrouded in darkness.

Was someone there?

Lie down.

Lie back in your bed, Tramos. Pull up the covers. And remember me…

He climbed back into his small cot, the sweat now dried on his strapping chest, his small, white flax linen which wrapped around his middle. He lie, flat on his back, watching the wind whip across the tent ceiling, as he felt a pair of hands wrap around his ankles.

He raised his head and saw the outline under the sheet; it was, perhaps, a woman, from the light feel of the hands along his calves and thighs.

But the mysterious woman moved further up his body, her hands exploring his developed thighs, his abdomen, and massive chest. He was pinned to the bed and threw his head back, his eyes closed tight.

She lay on top of him, her weight pressed on his; he could feel the heat of her breath against his face, but when he opened his eyes, the appeared to be no one there.

As he felt the searing heat around his cheek, breath after breath came closer to his ear: "You are right where I left you!" her voice was deep. Raspy.

And then his eyes widened.

He shot up to a sitting position, looked down at his lap. Only the linen on which he slept; and he was pulsating and massive. His chest heaved with each breath.

But no mysterious woman.

The wind still tore against the tent flaps.

His tent mate slept soundly next to him.

And he lay back down, pulled the small piece of linen back over him, and closed his eyes once again.

Antoine clapped his hands in front of Delia's face. "Wake up, Delia! Let's get going!" he said. "They're climbing the drainpipes!"

Delia's trance lifted. Her eyes widened as she leaned over the side. She look down at the bushes below. They were thrashing around violently as twigs snapped and leaves rained on the ground.

And then there was a scratching.

Like nails on wood.

She turned to Tramos. "They're climbing the side of the house. We have to get inside. Fast."

Tramos stood next to Antoine as they faced the side of the house. Antoine grasped a small, square ventilation shutter and pulled. "Dammit!" he cried. "I didn't think it would be jammed like this!"

Tramos stepped forward as Delia turned to keep an eye on the approaching hounds. The monstrous dogs tore up the side of the house. They would approach, full force, tearing into the side of the house, growling and howling, and then fall to the ground.

And then start climbing the house all over again, tirelessly.

Delia looked back at Antoine, who had stood aside as Tramos eased his fingers around the sides of the shutter and pulled. "They're making headway!" she said.

"I've almost got it!" Tramos said.

He turned his head around and looked directly at Delia. "You just let me know what they're doing."

Antoine reached up and eased his fingers under the edge of the shutter, and pulled with all of his might, they both grunted, as it popped off, sending both of them spilling down towards the side of the roof.

Delia gasped and lunged forward. She leaped on both of them and grasped the gutter on the edge of the roof. Antoine spilled over the side as Tramos grabbed his arm. He hung over the side. "Pull me up!" he said, eyes wide. "I can feel their teeth! They're getting my feet!"

Delia pulled herself downwards as Tramos hooked his feet on a vent. He reached his other arm down. "Reach for my hand! Reach for my hand, Antoine!"

They pulled him up back to the roof, as Delia spilled backwards and lay on her back, trying to catch her breath. Tramos pulled Antoine up and laid him down, and then he lay down next to him. Delia sat up. "Let's get inside, Antoine. I'm getting too old for this."

Tramos looked at Delia and cracked a grin, as Antoine got up, still panting, and headed back to the shutter. The dogs resumed their attempt to climb the house, as their nails scratched on the walls and the twigs and branches snapped as they fell back down on the shrubbery.

Delia leaned over the side and looked at the Hell Hounds. As she craned her neck, their assault hit a crescendo. The growling was deep, throaty and demonic. Their harried and repetitive attempt to climb the house suddenly became more urgent, like dogs barking louder and more insistently when an intruder nears the master's house. She leaned back. "Let's get inside. Now."

Antoine climbed through the small opening, and Tramos, far larger and more muscular, had a bit of difficulty, but managed to squeeze through. As Delia eased herself though, she reached out and picked up the shutter which Antoine had left leaning against the side of the house. She pulled it back into place and snapped it in position.

Antoine looked at her, his face shifted a bit. "Um…locking us in here?"

Delia shook her head. "No, but where we are going, we won't need to come back here." Antoine sighed as Tramos moved boxes out of the way with his feet. He bent down and scattered some books off to the side. "There's a lot of old things in here," he said.

"Just keep clearing the path towards that way," Antoine said. He pointed to the far end of the attic.

The power no longer worked, but several other ventilation shutters which surrounded the area cast pale rectangles of moonlight and highlighted the boxes, books and old furniture.

"It looks like the place was ransacked," Delia said, standing in the center, under the sloping ceiling. She reached up and held on to one of the wooden beams to steady herself on the unfinished wooden floor.

Antoine shook his head. He stood, his hands on his hips, and looked around at the old, dusty boxes and piles of books. "I don't know *what* happened here." He bent down and picked up a book, held it up close to his face, and examined it. He reached out and ran his fingers across it. His fingers scraped away a dark film, dust. "Soot," he said, tossing the book back with the others.

"I'm surprised the attic wasn't burned," Delia said.

Antoine shook his head. "I can understand the soot. But I have no idea why everything is such as mess." He tossed a few boxes aside. "If I'm right," he said, "it should still be here." He carved a path through some of the boxes. "Ah ha!"

Delia looked over at Antoine, tossing boxes aside. She watched as he revealed a dark, rectangular box — or something that looked like a box — against the far wall of the attic. She saw Antoine reach down and let out a chuckle.

"It's an old kerosene lamp. Anyone got a match?"

Antoine dug through his pockets and produced a lighter. He flicked it and held it to the small wick in the base. After a few moments, a small flame rose from the enclosed clear chamber, and he held it over the mysterious dark, long box.

Delia gasped.

She saw the reflection of silver on the sides. Which looked like handles. "That's a casket!"

Antoine chuckled. "Of course it's a casket! I had this placed up here years ago!"

Tramos returned. "I found the door to the house!"

Antoine scoffed. "I lived here. You could have just asked me where it was."

Tramos shrugged his shoulders. "Yes, but you and Delia were busy. So what is it you guys found?"

Delia looked at Tramos. "We found a casket. Back against the wall. Behind those boxes over there." Delia nodded over towards Antoine, who was rummaging through some of the boxes.

"Hey Antoine!" Delia said. "Are you going to open that?"

He shook his head. "It's locked. No key."

Tramos went to the casket and looked up at Antoine. He nodded. Tramos raised his right arms and slammed the casket lid with the side of his hand, splintering the lid. He tore the wood away, as it splintered and cracked against the otherwise quiet attic. He tossed the pieces aside.

Delia joined them. "Look inside there Antoine. Look in there. It's full of stuff."

Antoine dropped the boxes he was rummaging through and diverted his attention to the coffin. He grabbed a piece of the splintered wood from the lid and pried it away with a snap. As he did, the interior was revealed.

There were piles of papers and composition notebooks. Antoine rummaged through the papers. He picked up a black and white composition notebook and examined it. Tramos knelt next to Antoine, also looking at the book, as Delia moved closer.

"What is it?" Delia asked.

Antoine smiled. "It says *The Quest for Immortality* on the front."

Delia's mouth dropped open as Tramos snapped his head around and looked at her. She nodded.

Antoine's face fell as he opened the notebook and paged through it. "But it's just notes. Most of it doesn't make any sense to me."

"But it means that we are getting close," Delia said. She rose to her feet and placed each of her palms on Tramos and Antoine's backs. They both looked up at her. "I think it's time we moved on. It's time to go inside and get what we came here for. This was a great find, but we have to stay on our mission."

Antoine and Darius nodded and slowly got up.

As they got up, Delia continued, looking at Antoine. "I think this was an amazing find. Make sure to take that notebook with you."

"What about the rest? There's a lot of other papers here. Charts and diagrams. Bunch of stuff."

"Whatever you think you can carry," Delia said. "Do you have a bag or backpack somewhere that you can put all this in?"

Antoine shrugged. "I haven't been here for years. I don't know how Darius changed things around."

Delia nodded as Tramos passed by them, moving through the attic and clearing more boxes to the side. He held up a small bag. "Look here!" He handed it to Antoine, who stuffed in the small composition notebook and the piles of papers. "I'm going to take as much as I can fit in here," Antoine said. "Who knows what it could mean, I just need to find the manuscript. I have to read it. Have to."

"And it's time to go, we shall look for it, Antoine," Delia said as she followed Tramos to the darker side of the attic. "Tramos! Are you still up there?"

She heard rustling and the sound of cardboard boxes sliding against a wooden floor. After a few minutes, they heard his voice. "Yes!" Tramos appeared, slightly out of breath. "Sorry!" he said. "There was a large angel statue blocking the way. Almost as tall as you, Delia. It must weigh a ton!"

They made their way to the entrance to the house below.

It was small, square opening in the floor, with a set of retractable wooden stairs that would be stored in the attic when the homeowner did not need attic access. Tramos led the way, as Antoine assisted Delia down the steps.

They looked around the second floor as Antoine's mouth dropped open.

The upstairs hallway looking nothing like it had in the past. What was once opulent and well-appointed, with a gold railing that spun around a rounded cathedral foyer, lined with a marble staircase, and Greek statues at each pedestal, was now a shell of its former self. The once impeccably clean white carpeting was now stained with black soot; water stained walls, with dark patches, burned away, filled with holes. There was a large, burned out area in the ceiling. Electrical wires hung down towards the floor like tentacles.

Antoine paused at the top of the stairs, hung his head, and closed his eyes. Delia approached him and placed her hand on his shoulder, leaning in close to his ear. "We must keep moving," she said. "Take us there."

Antoine sighed and nodded, wiped his eyes with his fingers, and started down the stairs. The debris crunched under their feet and as they entered the foyer below, Antoine paused and looked back at Delia and Tramos. They stood in the rounded foyer; the marble floor was filled with debris; the walls were burned black, and more wires hung down from holes in the ceiling.

Above them, the chandelier still hung.

What was once elegant, with many spires, with candle light fixtures in circles in several layers, was now partially melted. It still hung above them; but haphazardly. Wires fingered their way out of the hole in the ceiling.

The foyer was rounded, and the round table still sat in the center, although it was burned and had fallen into two pieces, crashing in on itself. Broken glass littered the floor around the table.

"The basement is just beyond the kitchen over there." Antoine pointed towards the back of the house.

They all turned as there was a crash against the front door followed by a deep, demonic growl. Tramos rushed to the door and placed his weight against it. "It's the hounds!"

Delia quickly ushered Antoine towards the kitchen. "Let's go. We have to go inside. Tramos! We will back up towards the kitchen! Antoine! Are we almost there?"

They entered the kitchen and where the basement door once stood now was a large, gaping hole. The wooden stairs were still there, but quickly vanished into darkness. "There!" Antoine said.

Delia craned her neck to see in the foyer. Tramos held the door closed as the dogs scratched, jumped and howled. The hounds flung themselves against the doors, shaking the frame.

Delia called out to Tramos. "Can you come now?"

Tramos looked up towards the top of the door as the hounds catapulted their bodies against the wood. The door shook again. His massive body kept the door closed. His face was red, veins popped out of his arms and beads of sweat formed on his forehead. "Go! Just go! If I move they will break through!"

Delia turned to Antoine. "Go down. I will meet you at the base of the stairs. I need to help Tramos." But when she said those words, there was a thunderous crash and splintering of wood from the foyer. Nails on marble as she heard growling and a demonic throated chorus of barks. "Tramos!" she cried.

Tramos stood in the center of the foyer, his wings extended upwards, reaching towards the ceiling. He raised his arms upwards as the hounds tore at his clothing; the shreds came down as they tore at his skin. Bright red blood splattered up on his wings, which remained open and outstretched, crashing against the ceiling, against the walls, and continued to reach upwards, reaching towards the sky. His arms remained outstretched, as the dogs tore at his body, tearing it apart.

Delia's eyes were wide and she gasped. "Tramos!"

He looked over at her as the dogs ripped him apart. One ripped his arm off as his screamed. He shut his eyes tight and craned his neck upwards, as a solitary tear cut through the bright red blood on his cheek. "Go! Go *now!*" he said.

Antoine appeared in the doorway, a look of horror on his face. "But he's an *angel!*" Tears streamed down his face as the dogs ripped him down to the floor. A lake of blood formed around Tramos, the wings, now torn, tattered, bloodstained and ripped now lay on the floor, as Tramos took his final breath as the front doors slammed themselves shut with a deafening boom.

She turned and rushed back to the kitchen. "Antoine!" she cried. Tears flowed down her face. "We must go! Head downstairs. Go quickly! We must leave! Just go, Antoine! Go!" She pushed him forward, looking back several times, as the hounds tore apart Tramos' body. Her face fell as she saw the wings in a desperate, final attempt to reach up towards the sky.

But in the end, the bloodstains remained.

V

BLOODY MARY

It is better to conquer yourself than to win a thousand battles. Then the victory is yours. It cannot be taken from you, not by angels or by demons, heaven or hell.

– Buddha

THE STORY OF THE ANGEL, the *War Angel*, continued.

And as the story was told throughout the generations, told over years, and decades and centuries, the rumors circulated, still, throughout communities. The talking and the whispers remained. The wonder endured. There were still those who experienced the spiritual event of the appearance of an angel – and there were others who experienced but did not see. Both mortal…and immortal.

And those who saw, and not only experienced, were thought to be the gifted ones. And those were the ones who had a mission – whether they were mortal or immortal. Some for a greater purpose. A means to live, for certain. But also a means to live…for others.

And those chosen people, whether mortal or immortal, were the special ones.

For the angels were sent to protect.

To interfere when necessary, but never to intrude, or encroach on one's free will. The people would have a different mission.

One of proactivity.

One of protection.

And of purpose for existence…and prevention. The idea that: Could the actions of evil be prevented? Would the actions of evil be prevented with a small, otherworldly interference, causing events to progress differently?

The analysis continued.

The questions remained.

And still, there were others who had the approach of skepticism.

There were those in the human population that not only chose not to believe in the presence of angels, but also chose not to recognize the existence of evil.

Antoine's estate, which sat on Andelusia in the heart of Coral Gables, had once been the home of a wealthy investment banker from the International Bank of Venezuela. And the owner's son, Roberto, became quite enamored, at one point, with a certain Antoine Nagevesh, who had come to Miami, in those days, as a spiritual healer and, later, a nightclub promoter.

Antoine had met Roberto late one evening on Washington Avenue in the heart of boisterous Miami Beach, and the two started a torrid affair.

Antoine's origin was little known, and how close Roberto had gotten to Antoine was unknown entirely. But there were people – and immortals as well – who would talk about Antoine and Roberto's infatuation with one another. For it was a thought-provoking topic to discuss.

Because Roberto disappeared one day.

When it first happened, it was all over the Miami news stations. As Antoine had become a local celebrity of sorts (his local fame catapulted after he was discovered by Sheldon Wilkes and The Astral; Mr. Wilkes made it very publicly known that he had been writing a book on 'The Integration of Immortals into Everyday Society'). But when Roberto disappeared, Antoine was cast into a negative spotlight.

Some say Roberto was observed entering a secret side door to the nightclub Antoine owned and operated called *Sacrafice*, built in an old, repurposed cathedral. And the same people who claimed to have seen Roberto disappear through the door also said they never saw him again. So the news stories became somewhat less infatuating and more fear-inducing: Who was this Antoine? And why did evil always seem to surround him and his life?

After Roberto's disappearance, the Andelusia residence remained quiet, but also after some time, the owner at the time, Hernan Perez, was brutally murdered in the upstairs Master Bedroom. The local news stations were not permitted in the residence, but some locals who claimed to have accessed the mansion insisted that the bed was stained red as if Hernan had lost all of his blood.

And then a mysterious new resident started to appear, but not often.

One Antoine Nagevesh.

And with the disappearances of Roberto and the mysterious death of Hernan Perez, the locals started to think the house was cursed. And, perhaps, that Antoine was as well.

The activity, though, remained.

Cars lined the streets at all hours of the day and night. Some were reporters investigating Antoine, others were paranormal researchers, mostly from *The Astral* which held offices just a few blocks away from the Andelusia estate. Residents who lived directly on Andelusia noted one particular small, silver sedan was regularly parked outside the gates. People started talking…wondering who the sedan belonged to, what the purpose of their repeated visits was, and where the previous owners had gone.

The mansion managed to stay out of the news for some time, until the fire.

The fire, which caused significant damage, was determined to be arson from the resulting investigation. Then, the estate sat, empty, surrounded by yellow crime scene tape, windows broken, black soot staining the white stucco. The grass started to grow high and the trees and shrubs concealed the massive wraparound porch. At one point, only the four columns, which reached up towards the roof, could be seen beyond the cement wall that bordered the sidewalk.

After the fire, the house still remained a center of activity, despite the apparent absence of residents. The neighbors were waiting for an appearance of the mysterious Antoine, who had been rumored to own the property, but all the while observing the occasional news van and various parked cars that appeared from time to time.

Until the neighbors saw one particular parked car, that sat on the side of the road, just outside the gates. A small Mercedes.

And the residents of Andelusia suspected that it might be Antoine's car. For they doubted that the researchers and news folk who would drop by on occasion might not be driving so luxurious a vehicle.

And so the rumors would start again.

And when the stories intermingled with that of the celestial, there were those who chose to follow, to act on intuition alone; they learned to guide themselves through the land of spiritual warfare…

…Hector leaned back in his seat and closed his eyes as Geraldine pulled the car away from the library parking lot. Several palm trees that lined the edge of the entrance started to sway as thunder clapped overhead.

Hector opened his eyes and looked over at Geraldine. She was focused on the road, but he knew where they were headed. Hector looked down and examined his notes.

There still seemed to be the celestial mystery regarding the presence of angels.

And of the supernatural.

For those who experienced the phenomenon, the idea of celestial beings (and evil beings) became second nature: there was a large group of the population, both immortals and mortals alike, that chose to believe.

"I don't think Antoine is an angel," Hector finally said, in the otherwise silent car. Geraldine shot a glance over at him. "Rereading your notes?"

Hector nodded and sighed. "I just don't think that these immortals are as evil as some believe."

Geraldine nodded, still looking ahead, but said nothing.

"And this whole thing about angels," Hector said. "What is it about? Do you think the angels are real?"

Geraldine scoffed as they continued on the darkened streets. The golden streetlamps reflected against the pavement, now wet from a light falling rain. She looked over at Hector for a moment, shaking her head. "Do *you* believe in angels, Hector? Do you believe?"

He sighed.

"None of this can be verified," he said. "Nothing. Not one bit of it."

Geraldine laughed and shook her head as she pulled the car towards the quieter residential side streets. "It's not about that, Hector! It's about believing. About faith, right?" She alternated between looking over at him and looking at the road. "So whether it can be verified or not is really insignificant. It's whether you believe or not. So…do you believe?"

Hector paused for a moment.

He leaned back on the headrest and closed his eyes.

He sighed.

After a few minutes, as Geraldine was on Andelusia, preparing to park in front of Antoine's estate, Hector finally spoke. "No, I don't believe in angels."

After they parked and exited the car, Hector slammed his door with a thud against the night, which had grown quiet. "Where did the storm go?" he asked, looking up towards the sky. The clouds raced past as the moonlight tried to fight through. And then lightning illuminated the clouds. He gathered Geraldine and their bags and approached the front door. As they climbed the steps Hector looked over at the line of shrubs across from the front porch.

"They say there are Hell Hounds in those bushes guarding the entrance," he said.

"But there is nothing," Geraldine said. "That would explain the mystery. For we are simply mortal."

"And we do not believe," Hector added. "Good…and evil…rely on the belief. If there is no faith in goodness then evil can't exist, can it?"

Geraldine sighed as Hector looked towards the bushes. "Oh, it still exists, Hector. Even if one doesn't believe."

The bushes rustled.

Antoine walked further into the darkness, and then turned around. He saw light filter in from above, from atop the set of rickety wooden stairs, the same stairs that led down to his basement from his kitchen. Delia was walking down the stairs, and then she stopped.

"They won't come after us down here," she said. "This is what they are protecting. They won't go beyond that area up there."

Antoine sighed. "What about Tramos?"

Delia looked downwards. "He's gone." And then she looked up at him. A tear streamed down her cheek. "He died protecting us, Antoine."

Antoine gasped and looked up the stairs. He saw pale light filter from the kitchen, and thought of Tramos. Of the blonde warrior. He could still see him throwing his head back in laughter, during one of the many occasions he had visited Antoine in the kitchen above.

Antoine looked forwards, deeper into the darkness. After a few minutes, he turned back to Delia. "I've taken others through here," he said. "A long time ago, there was a man – a Sheldon Wilkes – who came with me down this very same dark passage, and was never seen again."

Delia moved past Antoine, further into the darkness. She turned back. "Do I need to show you what I am? Or who I am? Or how I protect you?"

Antoine shook his head.

"Then let's proceed."

Delia nodded.

As they walked into the darkness, Delia watched Antoine. He walked ahead, like a child, but also someone who had been there before. As he walked through the darkness, fingers of light appeared around them, and she got a better idea of her surroundings.

They were walking on stones. A path made of large stones, surrounded by shallow water. But the walls surrounding them – walls which might have been earthen – which might have lent to the feel of a cave – were not there.

It was Delia who first noticed the darkness.

As she looked forward, she watched Antoine, who walked several feet ahead of her. The air was musty; their feet splashed in a layer of water. And they navigated stones.

And then Antoine disappeared.

"Antoine!" she called ahead.

There was no answer.

She stopped, one foot on each stone, and stood, facing the darkness. The silence permeated, until she felt a presence. She knew that she was surrounded by walls, but she could not see them. She reached out and felt dirt.

Earth.

Like an endless cave.

Murky water below, a damp smell.

But darkness.

Complete blackness. Devoid of light.

"Antoine! Where did you go?"

She closed her eyes and shook her head. *I have failed again. Another assignment that I have failed to do.*

She raised her head and opened her eyes, squinting. There was no opening to this tunnel. Her skin erupted in goosebumps as she felt a chill pass through her. A voice called for her.

Delia.

It was a voice she could not place. A voice…that perhaps…had no distinct origin? But she knew where she was. And how she had gotten here. And then she tensed herself.

"It is I."

She saw a light in the distance. Like a sphere, or a star. And it crept closer to her, but did nothing to alleviate the darkness.

And then the voice.

"Did you not know that I would come calling? It was your despair that called me."

She looked ahead and strained to see. But a sense of dread washed through her. Her voice croaked when she spoke. "You...you are not the light I seek."

There was laughter. "Do you think He would come? Your God? Do you think that you – a fallen angel – is even on His mind?"

She remembered the voice. It was deep and demonic. "We can all be redeemed," she said. "But you...I have no homage to you. I am here to protect. Nothing more. It does not involve you."

"Would you not think that I would be here? As my hounds have alerted me of your arrival?"

She tensed. "Where is Antoine?" She took a deep breath and exhaled. And waited.

"Where...is...Antoine?"

"Antoine is where Antoine is," he said. "You two chose to come here. To enter through the portal which I have protected. This was your choice!"

Light flowed around her until she was in a veil of white. He laughed as she felt the ground fall from beneath her, as she fell, further and further. She looked down as the ground, of some new, unseen world, appeared below her, traveling faster towards her –

– until she was yanked upwards as her wings shot out of her back and soared across the sky. She instantly flew across the sky, looking at an unknown sea, with calm waters, and a desolate beach surrounded by a forest of tropical trees.

The laughing stopped.

"You do not leave me! You chose to follow me!"

She hovered in the air and looked at the darkness ahead of her. The sky was bright, but the light felt cold. Dank.

And the darkness hovered ahead of her as she flapped her wings, across the sky, and then she was ready. She drew her sword, held it upwards, in front of her face. She saw the darkness ahead swirling.

The same deep, demonic laughter. "You think you can tease *me* with a trinket like that? How are you going to pierce me? I am darkness. Swirling. Penetrating!"

She took a breath as the sword ignited in flames. She swung it across the sky. "I will make you light! The light *always* destroys the darkness!" She flapped her wings and soared towards the darkness, swinging her flaming sword across the sky. "Good will triumph over you!" She swung again. "You will retreat!"

"I am light too! Look into my light, little Delia!"

She swung her sword back around her head and thrust it forward, piercing directly into the center of the darkness.

Wails of torment chorused as the darkness retreated.

And she paused, examining the sword, as the flames extinguished themselves.

And the light became blinding. She dropped her sword with a clank as she felt her wings retreat into her back. She started falling. Faster and faster, until she opened her eyes with a start.

She gasped.

Her head still fuzzy, and her vision still hazy, she raised her head. Had she landed on the beach? By the calm, mysterious sea?

Her head pounded and she brought her open palm to her forehead and winced.

But as her eyes slowly focused, she saw light. Squares of light, and then she recognized her surroundings. Two windows. On the opposite side of the room. She recognized the drapes. The cranberry shears concealing the light.

And then she saw Antoine.

Sitting on the chair in her front living room. It was her cottage in Miami.

His leg was draped over the arm, his hands twirling his locks as he paged through the manuscript. She scoffed. "How...how did we get back here?"

Antoine looked up from his reading. He raised his eyebrows and shook his head.

She stood and walked over to Antoine. She sat in the overstuffed chair next to him, her hands on her knees, as she stared straight ahead. Her face was shifted as she bit her lower lip. Antoine had returned to his reading as she sat in silence. She turned to face him. "So how did we get here?"

Antoine set the manuscript down. "We got the manuscript, as you can see. And then we left. Pretty plain and simple. We got in the car, we came back to your cottage. And that was it."

Delia sighed and projected a calm demeanor. "It couldn't have been that simple..."

Her mind was racing.

She sat, replayed the events in her mind, and tried to remember. What was the last thing that happened to them? She remembered Antoine disappearing into the darkness. And falling to the beach.

She opened her eyes.

The side of her face was in the cool, wet sand. She heard the dull roar of the surf in the background. Her head pounded. And her back. She reached around and winced. It felt warm and wet. She brought her hand in front of her face and gasped.

Bright red blood.

She shot up and sat, her hands propped in the sand, and looked up towards the sky. The greenish tint reflected against the clouds, which meandered by. "Why have you abandoned me!" She cried, then jumped to her feet, shaking her fists to the sky. "*Why have you abandoned me?!*"

And then she fell back in the sand.

She lay on her side, her eyes open, concentrating on each breath. The air was salty. The sun was warming. And then she saw a dark figure, well down the beach, standing in the sun, walking towards her. The image seemed like a mirage…

Hector returned his attention to the door. He turned the handle.

Locked, naturally.

Geraldine looked outwards, towards the bushes. She reached around and tapped him on the shoulder. "Hector," she whispered.

He was focused on getting the front door open, which appeared to be jammed.

She was more insistent the second time. "Hector!"

He snapped around. "What is it *mami*?"

"Look over there."

She pointed out towards the bushes. Hector looked, adjusted his glasses, and craned his neck forward. "It's nothing. Just some wind blowing the branches."

She shook her head. "Are you sure?"

Branches snapped and there was a deep growl.

Geraldine's eyes widened. "Go! Get us inside! It's the hounds!"

"They...don't...exist!" Hector fumbled with the door handle as Geraldine dropped their bag to the floor. She reached on her side pocket and drew a long machete from her sheath, waiting, watching.

The bushes thrashed, but no supernatural hounds appeared.

"Get the door open!"

Hector took a step back.

He charged the door and crashed into it with his foot.

It didn't budge.

"Do it again!" she cried. "They're coming!"

Hector felt his breath quickening as he lunged for the door again. It splintered open as Geraldine bent down, grabbed their bag and followed him into the darkness inside.

Hector slammed the door behind him as they heard the dogs running towards them, racing and howling, barking and growling. They catapulted themselves across the door.

It shook in the frame.

But the assault from the hounds was short lived.

For once they were inside the foyer, the dogs retreated and quieted.

Geraldine gasped as they both froze in their footsteps.

The saw bloodied wings.

White, feathered wings, extended, and which were large; they reached upwards towards the ceiling of the second floor. Huge, feathered, broken wings. What the wings were attached to was down towards the shadows, still a mystery, but the wings were what they were fascinated with. Slender feathers. White, greyish hue.

But then, when they looked closer, they gasped at the bloodstains. Tiny, red droplets dotted the upper portions of the wings, and the bottoms were completely drenched in blood.

They looked down at the floor and saw they were standing in a lake of fresh blood.

Geraldine gasped and raised her foot. Viscous, bright red blood dripped from the sole. She looked at Hector with wide eyes.

Hector crouched down. He reached his arm out, and saw a torso. There was a large gash on the one arm, which seemed to be where a great deal of the blood loss had occurred. But this body was completely torn up.

Macerated.

The body was still almost completely shrouded in darkness, as Geraldine reached out and touched one of the wings. She looked down at Hector. "Now do you believe?"

After Delia retired, Antoine sat on the sofa in Delia's cottage and fished the manuscript from his bag. It was a large, white binder. He placed it on the coffee table and opened the cover. Darius had prepped it for publication. What was he intending to do with this story?

Antoine poured himself a glass of wine and settled in to the sofa, the manuscript in his lap, and started reading. When he approached "the letter", he paused for a moment, and set the manuscript back on the coffee table. He didn't bother to refill his wine glass. He leaned forward, close, and read the letter.

If you are reading this, I am dead.

I don't exactly know in what way I will have died, but I can be certain that it won't have been under the most pleasant of circumstances. Over the past few years, I have become consumed with a coven of immortals, immortals who are much more than your typical vampire. And I have been researching their ways and lifestyle as part of my work at The Astral, which I joined in 1985.

Several years ago, I came across the subject of my inquiry, a young Antoine Nagevesh, of Sri Lanka. He grew up working the coffee fields outside of Badulla, but that was well over two hundred years ago. He was transformed into an immortal shortly before his nineteenth birthday, and has remained in that physical state since. Some might think of him as a vampire, but in actuality, he is much more than that. I have experienced this first hand.

Antoine and I met at his estate over the course of many months, and I gathered notes, tapes and everything that I could about his story. My intentions were to write a book integrating immortals into everyday society;

but those intentions were never realized. Too often and too soon, I became consumed with his story and his way of life, and I wound up becoming swallowed up in the madness.

When I listened to my tapes, I went mad. I drank feverishly, I ate everything in sight, I slept at the office night after night, and I smoked a steady stream of cigarettes. Because his story was addictive.

Antoine is pure evil.

Please heed warning in that. He has a gift, a power, and is one of the most charismatic gentlemen I know. He is very well learned and he is very well traveled. But I write you this letter to give you a warning.

You must do three things for me.

I ask you to do these things, as my friend who I lost so long ago, my friend who I have always loved and cared for, and who never understood my work.

Now you will understand.

Now that you have come to Miami, you need to erase my existence from that city. You need to start at my office, at the corner of Ponce De Leon and 5th in Coral Gables. Have your hotel arrange for a car to take you; they will know the way. What's important though – have the car leave right after he drops you off.

When you get there, go into my office, close all the blinds, close all the doors, turn off all the lights, and dump the contents of my files on the floor in a giant pile of papers and folders. And then I want you to open the bottom right hand drawer in my desk. In that drawer, I have a jug of lighter fluid. I want you to douse that mound of papers and soak it – get *it wet! And then take my ashes — take the urn and dump it on the pile of papers and light the fire. Let it burn and let me go down with it. Then get the hell out of dodge and let the building burn.*

Then quickly walk down Ponce De Leon until you get to the corner of Andelusia.

This is so important, so pay attention.

You will see all the stately mansions, the magnificent royal palms, and the stunning canopy shading the street. This street is so beautiful but so evil. You need to go to One Andelusia Avenue. You will recognize the house with the giant mason columns out front from the photos that I have sent to you.

That is where Antoine lives.

It is so necessary that you destroy this house. It must be burned to the ground. But you will see houses in Florida are made of cinder block because of the violent storms, so you will have to go inside. You won't be able to just douse this house in gasoline or lighter fluid; nothing will happen.

And this is where it will get difficult for you, and I apologize for it.

The last time that I saw Antoine, he was guiding me down into his cellar; and his cellar led down a set of stairs framed by white plaster walls like any other cellar, and it had a hanging lamp at the foot of the stairs like any other cellar, but that light did not penetrate the darkness. It hung from the ceiling, and it cast a warm, yellowish glow — but that is where the light stopped. And beyond there was blackness. And I have been there. And you don't want to go there.

But you have to burn the house down, Douglas. You have to burn it to the ground, and you have to make it seem like the fire wasn't started intentionally. The Miami FD is very adept at determining arson and what is not, so you will have a challenge ahead of you. But, please…see that it is done. You do not want what will be coming out of that house to be coming out into your dimension.

And, as Antoine's house is burning and in smoky ruins, you have to travel to Miami Beach. You will need to find a way to get there completely undetected. You will have to find a nightclub that opened recently. It's called 'Sacrafice'.

The club was built in Saint Peter's old Cathedral on Washington. After the fire, it sat for several years abandoned as the diocese opted to close the church due to low attendance.

But our fine friend Antoine snatched it up.

But it's the pure personification of evil now.

He uses it as a magnet to draw the lost and forbidden – and it must be destroyed. I don't know how you will get rid of a Cathedral. Burn it down, plant a bomb, find a way, Douglas. You are a smart man. I know you will find a way. Just do it, please.

I never understood the need for my organization. I would sit in my office, lay back in my chair, and always look to people like Antoine. He – his kind – was one of the purposes of my organization. But, to be totally honest, The Astral did not exist to interview. We did not exist to write books. We had a deeper purpose.

At least I thought so.

I remember the night that I first met Jean Carlo.

I saw him across the room. And I think he saw me. He was sitting at a long banquet table, and I don't think he knew what exactly The Astral was about.

But he is key. And he can be of great help to you, Douglas. He was initially brought to us when he first arrived on the astral plane. He can help you, Douglas. Take heed in that.

And now, the third task.

I have booked you an open ended First Class plane ticket. All you need to do is call the airline listed on the accompanying paperwork and choose your travel dates.

I need you to fly to Frankfurt, Germany.

Darius flew to this city to bury Antoine's ashes not long ago. But Antoine was a demon. He was an immortal.

So he could come back.

He could come back and undo everything I have been trying to do to stop him. The interviews, everything. I wanted Antoine to feel like he was a celebrity. And he did. And he was stopped.

But his heart remains.

He died an immortal, and could always return one day. His heart is the source of that.

Antoine was buried in a small, unmarked grave in a cemetery near his and Darius' chateau near Lyon in France.

You need to travel there, south, into France and to their Chateau. Darius most likely will not be there as he is mortal at the time of this writing and only travels to Europe via commercial airliners. Most likely, the chateau is closed.

But you will need to get inside, Douglas.

You will need to look through the basement, and find the map to Antoine's grave.

And when you do, you need to dig up his casket, find the heart, and destroy it.

Our lives depend upon it.

Darius is aging quickly and will die a quick and final death if he cannot get Antoine's son, Roberto, to resurrect him.

The heart is the key. And you must destroy it.

For if Antoine returns, so will Darius to immortality. And Darius must be stopped.

Our future depends upon it. Darius may be humbled as a human, but as an immortal…he will transform.

Please do these things for me, Douglas. I need you to ensure that Darius never walks in this world again.

With Warm Regards,

Sheldon T. Wilkes

VI

ANIMA CHRISTI

MY WINGS were clipped.

My God has forsaken me.

I tried to drink but there was no water; I tried to eat but only took blood. My eyes saw nothing; the demons were tearing at my flesh.

I reached my arms to the sky as the blood ran down my skin.

I felt my wings extend outwards.

And then the crash; my confinement was real. I felt the crash; the rumbling of the house; the splintering of wood, the thunder above and the shaking. My abhorrent reality.

But my wings were clipped.

Torn and dripping with bright, red blood.

I remembered the hounds.

And could still feel the sharp pierce of their fangs as their claws tore into my flesh. I still saw the blood splatter on my wings as it shot from my wounds.

And on the walls. The walls were covered in blood. The bright red blood that dripped down towards the floor in a network of bloody lines.

It was hazy, but starting to come into focus.

I had been in the foyer of a mansion.

In Miami.

That's where I had been. But where was I now?

I could no longer fly.

I raised my head towards the sky, but all I saw was darkness.

But I knew who I was.

For the sky spoke to me.

The clouds raged and tore across the sky, as purple light filtered through the darkness. The light felt warm, it felt reassuring…but it ignited memories.

Memories of me.

And through the darkness I watched, a scene pierced through, and I saw a woman, sitting on a rocking chair, in front of an old, rickety wooden house…

…The chair creaked as she craned her head back towards the screen door behind her. She turned around in her chair, staying seated. "Need me in there, Henry?" she called in her deep southern drawl.

But there was no answer. She returned to her washing, took a few more strokes, and stopped again.

She turned again in the creaky old wooden chair. "Henry?!" she called, louder and more insistent this time.

No answer again.

Laying the wet clothes down on a towel, she dropped the washboard in the basin and wiped her hands on her apron. It was time to go inside and see what Henry was up to.

The screen door creaked as she opened it slowly, giving way to a silent house.

Even as she bent her head inside the door and strained to listen, she did not hear anything but the ticking clock nearby in the kitchen.

She peered inside and waited for the blackness to clear and her eyes to adjust to the darkness of the foyer.

"Henry, I'm gonna come up and see what she is doin'."

She called up through the winding stairs, which rounded the foyer and the spokes in the railing, like fingers of dark wood posed as bars in front of expansive oil paintings of the owners of the mansion that reached upwards towards the darker cranberry colored walls of the second floor.

A door handle from the second floor clicked open, a door creaked open for a moment, and then silence.

"Henry?" she called again. "Do you hear me?"

The squeaky door slammed. Heavy footsteps followed, moving towards the edge of the dark wooden railing, as Mary looked up at the clear crystal chandelier as it shook from the rumbling of the footsteps.

Henry dashed down the stairs, his bight white eyes contrasting his very dark skin, his eyes open as wide as saucers, his light brown button shirt covered in bright red blood.

"I'm leavin'!" he yelled, taking steps two at a time and jumping down to the foyer, shaking the chandelier as he did so. Mary grabbed his arm and stopped him just as he placed his hand on the knob of the front door. He turned his head to face her. He paused for a moment, breathing heavy, his mouth partly open and salivating, eyes still wide and the look of fear on his face.

"What is goin' on up there?" she asked, determined for an answer.

Henry grabbed her hand, ripping it off his arm. "I am not staying in this house!" And he stormed through the door, and ran out to the backyard into the coming sunlight. Mary stood and watched him run past the dead garden, farther off to the edge of the garden towards a path that led towards the mountains.

Mary shook her head, let out a deep breath, closed the door, and turned her attention to the upstairs. She wondered why Henry might act like this, but she was concerned about Emile.

"Emile?" she called once she got to the foot of the stairs. "You alright up there?"

There was no answer.

She ascended the stairs, each one creaking under the weight of her foot as she did so; her determined methodical course of taking each step, one by one, ate at her sanity. What was Henry so upset about? The calm, quiet, normally reserved man had just stormed past her down the stairs, running for the door in a desperate attempt to leave the house and the woman upstairs who he loved and served so loyally, the woman with whom he was so close with that he agreed to deliver her child.

Mary reached the top of the stairs and looked down the hallway, past the numerous photographs and paintings to the last white door at the end of the cranberry colored walls, shut tight with no sound coming from it.

"Emile?" she called one more time, craning her head to see past the edge of the wall.

Still no answer.

The floorboards creaked as she moved towards the door in the silence of the early morning; the new and infant light permeated the hall from a nearby window, but that light did not deter Mary's rising fear any more than the silence added to it. So many days before, she had walked the distance from the top of the stairs to the door of the master bedroom so many times in so little time. The distance on other days seemed so insignificant. Today, it seemed almost insurmountable.

But she made it.

After a series of methodical creaking steps and racing heartbeats, she stood in front of the door, and she held her breath for a moment, moving the side of her head close to the door, listing in an effort to hear anything that might give a clue.

Silence.

"Emile, I'm comin' in," she said quietly and carefully, as she turned the squeaky doorknob, the concern showing on her face. "I hope you're ok cause I'm comin' in right now."

Tramos cried out.

Emile was lying flat on the bed, her head back, her eyes wide open, seeing nothing. The baby wailed as the wet nurse held the little boy, comforting the baby while it cried. But the bedsheets were no longer white.

For in between Emile's legs was a lake of blood.

Bright, red, viscous.

And her eyes were open, yet they saw nothing…

…Darius' face fell, but he understood. Tramos looked and saw him through the darkness, a smiling, familiar face, painted with concern.

"Do you understand, Tramos? Do you see?"

Tramos sat up. "She died. When I was born. I had repressed that memory."

"How did you know?"

There was a cascade of colorful pastel light that soared beyond them. "I didn't. Until you showed me. Until I could see. I had so much…hatred…for my mother," Tramos said.

"Why?" Darius asked.

"I thought she abandoned me," he said.

"She clearly didn't."

Darkness surrounded Tramos, yet the light highlighted Darius, who smiled down upon him.

And then when Tramos looked up, and saw the illumination behind Darius, he saw the wings, the white wings soaring out from his back, flapping behind him.

"You're…an *angel*" Tramos said, as his mouth dropped open. "Were you one all along?"

Darius smiled as he stepped back. "You were one once too."

Tramos got up, slowly, as the scene shifted before their eyes to a small café. Tramos sensed the familiarity in the small wooden tables and chairs. There were no patrons, only Darius and Tramos. As Darius sat in the small café, he looked up and smiled across the small, round, wooden tables and chairs. He looked up and gestured for Tramos to come. "Sit."

Tramos could see now. The darkness abated, and he saw that he had been sitting in a small, plain, wooden coffin. The coffin of a pauper.

"That's the coffin I was confined in for years," Darius said. "I was in chains. Wrapped around my chest. The blood had dried on my skin after Antoine plunged the dagger into my heart, but I only existed in my mind. When Antoine tore the coffin lid away, I was merely ashes….and dust."

"And you came back in physical form?

Tramos exited the casket and walked over towards where Darius sat. The floor did not feel like it would have felt back on the day that he had been in that small café. There was something different. Like he was walking through a painting, or on clouds.

"This is all just a recreation of our minds," Darius said. "We all have our own individual experience here. This is yours."

Tramos sat at a small table opposite Darius. "So why this café? How does it figure in to my experience?"

"The café connects us, Tramos. You, me, Antoine. Even Delia. It's a location where we had all been in life, and where each of our lives took a turn...a transformation."

A transformation.

Could it be?

Could they have evolved through death?

Taken a journey to another realm of existence beyond the end of their lives?

"When did you discover you were an angel?"

Darius looked down, leaning forward, closer to Tramos.

"It was after I passed," he said. "I learned that I was on a mission the entire time. I had no idea. When I accepted the gift as they call it – the immortals – I had merely been misguided. I had strayed from my true mission."

"And what mission was that?"

Darius chuckled and lean back. He looked up into his eyes. "Well, it was to save you, Tramos. My mission was for that."

Tramos looked up, opened his eyes, and looked up at Darius. He was not the same Darius that he had remembered. This was not the Darius who had killed for sport. This was not the same

Darius whose clothes were painted with the blood of his victims.

Yet it was the same smiling face that he remembered. The same brown hair, about shoulder length, sometimes tied back; this time it wasn't. It flowed down towards his shoulders.

His teeth were perfect.

They always had been.

His smile was seductive.

There was just something about Darius. Something about his face, his smile. And as Darius gazed downwards, as he opened his mind, his inner being, he smiled again.

"Darius," he said. He shook his head back and forth, looking for an end to the darkness; but he found a wall of sorts, the edge of the box; some indicator that he was in a coffin, some confines; restrictions that said he was lying in a casket.

But he wasn't.

He was in some, strange afterworld. A life after a life, and this time, he realized it was for real. Darius had been sent to guide him, to ease him into a spiritual existence.

"You are…an angel." Darius reached out and embraced Tramos. "Now listen to me," Darius said. "Delia is in trouble. Lucifer, the fallen angel, has been haunting her and pursuing her for the majority of her life."

Tramos' eyes widened. "The devil has been after her? For what purpose?"

In an instant, they sat in the café in Badulla. They were the only patrons there.

Darius ushered Tramos towards the bar. The café was devoid of patrons or a bartender. He walked behind the bar and set two bulbous wine glasses on the bar. And then he placed a slender decanter, filled with red wine on the bar top. "She drank from the decanter. They called it *The Blood Decanter*. You remember the talks about the man in the hood?"

Tramos nodded.

"There were rumors of him being directly connected with the devil. And Delia had drank from it, just like I did."

"How did you survive?"

Darius smiled. "I didn't. I lost my gift. And my passion for life. When I was a mortal – for the second time – I saw that I was quickly dying. I aged rapidly."

"And then what?"

"I died. But after I died, I was given a choice. A decision to follow light or darkness."

"And what did you decide?"

Darius smiled. "If I had chosen the darkness, I can assure you, I would not be sitting here with you, nor would I have revealed my wings to you. I would not have been able to recreate this tiny little café which you remember so well. There would be no wine. No light. No color."

"What would there be?"

"There would be nothing."

Tramos thought of the beach, the bodies, the sea of thrashing limbs. "What about the sea of souls? I saw the thrashing bodies for myself! Did they choose the darkness?"

Darius looked downwards and ran his finger along the rim of his wine glass.

"You were given those visions," he said. "To prepare you. For your destiny, Tramos. And your destiny is to be with me. To protect."

Tramos thought of Delia.

He could still see her sitting in her cottage living room.

Darius placed his hand on Tramos' shoulder. "She has been pursued by Lucifer, the king of the fallen angels. For her entire life."

"How did it happen for her like that? I know you had a life changing event from drinking from the decanter. You became mortal again. But Delia? Getting visits from the devil when she was a child? Before she drank from the decanter?"

Darius nodded. "For her, it was different. Her gift is somewhat different. She is called to different time periods based on a mission that she is assigned to. So her life is always out of order. And when she was a child in France, she had already experienced periods of being an adult in ancient Jerusalem."

Tramos shook his head. "I can't seem to comprehend..."

"You will...in time...but it confuses your mind. It will. It did with me. There is no sense of time or space here. Most humans can't comprehend that. Even immortals have difficulty. But now, that we exist in the same level, I can explain it to you."

Tramos waited in the darkness.

He waited for the end to Darius' tutorial.

For this was not what he had expected about death; he had not imagined that he would be sitting in a bar with someone, who in his life, had been a protégé.

But just so happened to pass before him.

Was Darius an instructor?

A guide?

Had the tables been turned?

Antoine tossed the manuscript towards the fireplace.

The pages flew around the room as several flew into the flames. Delia shot up and started yanking them from the fire. She stamped on the pages. She looked up and over at Antoine, her eyes wide. "What are you doing?! This is our only account of his life when you were gone!"

Antoine sat back on the sofa and scoffed. He looked around the room, examining the drapes. "It's interesting how you still have curtains on your windows," he said.

Delia dropped the papers in a pile on the floor and shook her head. "What…are you talking about?"

Antoine got up and went to the window. He leaned his head against the cool glass and listened to the falling rain. He let out an exasperated sigh, and then looked back at Delia. "Did you read the letter?" he asked. "The letter that Sheldon wrote before he died. In the manuscript. Did you read it?"

Delia thought of the manuscript.

And the letter. She'd remembered Darius visiting her on several occasions discussing it. It was a letter to a certain Professor Douglas Khan of Boston College. Written by Sheldon Wilkes, then the Director of *The Astral*.

If you are reading this, I am dead.

And she remembered when Darius had sat with her, in the very same parlor, next to a fire in the fireplace when he had visited her so many times.

"It's the letter," Darius had told her on a similar night so many moons ago. "The first assault on the immortals is detailed in the letter."

Delia remembered sitting on the sofa, right next to Darius. "And you say that you must report this? Chronicle it? Will it change anything?"

Just after Delia had asked him, Darius had shook his head.

"Perhaps not," Darius had said. "But I am compelled to report it. And if it helps — in any way — that we have been brutally attacked. Our heart...our well-being...our way of life...just utterly destroyed. At least in this city."

"And Antoine's estate?"

"Burned. Along with the club. The offices for *The Astral*. Our stronghold in Miami."

"Where are you keeping this manuscript? Will you be publishing it?"

She couldn't remember how Darius had answered the question. But she knew he had sat, the printed manuscript resting on his legs, watching the fire burn away until it died down.

Delia was jolted back to the present when the phone rang. Antoine was at the wet-bar making himself a cocktail. He looked up and made eye contact with Delia as she answered.

"Monsignor Harrison! Yes?"

Delia sat forward as she listened to the Monsignor.

"We need you back in Rome," he said. "The council is deliberating and we all need to be present for the ruling."

Delia looked over at Antoine as the Monsignor hung up from their conversation. She lay the phone down in her lap and sighed. "I know we just got here, Antoine. But we have to get back to Rome." Antoine walked to the sofa with two, large bulbous glasses of red wine.

"Book us some tickets," she said. "On the first available flight. We have the manuscript. We've done what we came for. We need to get back and finish this."

"I will, but I am booking us a flight to Frankfurt. I promised Giovanni that I'd take him to Paris for his sight procedure. And I'm going to keep that promise. You can go straight to Rome if you like."

Delia nodded as Antoine phoned the airlines.

As the first fingerlings of light painted across the Miami sky the next morning, the pink pastels and powder blues reached towards the darkness in the West.

Delia stood on her back deck, overlooking the Bay, towards the lighter skies ahead. Their stay in Miami had been brief, but she knew that she was needed back in Rome.

Antoine managed to book their flights, but they were flying separately. He to Frankfurt, she to Rome. Antoine planned to drive back to Lyon and take Giovanni to Paris for his eye procedure, and then catch the train to Rome. She would fly directly to *Leonardo da Vinci* and meet with Monsignor Harrison, who had called her again in the wee hours of the morning, to ask for an update on her return, as the High Council had stayed the proceedings for her and Antoine's return.

Together, they put the stark white dust cloths over the furniture, without speaking. The thunder rumbled overhead as they finished the final preparations for closing up Delia's cottage, and Antoine carried his small, black suitcase into the small front foyer.

"Your flight takes off an hour after mine," he said.

Delia nodded as she closed the bedroom doors, joining Antoine at the front door. She raised her eyes and looked up at him. He clutched a bag on his shoulder and looked down at her, sunglasses pushed up on his forehead.

"You know what we are going there to do, right?"

With his hand still on the doorknob, he paused. He turned to face her, his face shifted. "We are heading back to Europe. After only a day in Miami. And then we will face the High Council in Rome. Am I correct?"

Delia nodded slowly. "Yes..." she said. "But we also must address the redemption of our kind, Antoine. And now...that we are taking separate flights on the return....has me concerned."

Antoine opened the door and stepped out onto Delia's small front porch. A light wind blew through the oak canopy. "What are you talking about?" he asked. "I'm not going anywhere."

Delia kept a close eye on Antoine as she watched him load his suitcase into the trunk of his small, silver Mercedes coupe. She turned and locked her cottage, checked the mailbox one last time, and joined him in the car.

The trip to the airport was uneventful, and when they got their tickets, and set to part ways as their flights were in two separate terminals, Delia reached out and grabbed Antoine's arm. "Meet me in Rome," she said. "We need you. Don't forget about me."

It seemed dreamlike as Delia let go of Antoine's arm, passed through security, and found her flight to Rome. She could scarcely remember finding her seat, the cabin announcements, take-off or the in-flight service. The next thing she remembered was waking up with a start, her head leaning against the window in her cramped economy class seat, as the captain announced their arrival at *Leonardo da Vinci.*

There was a pain in her neck.

She reached up and massaged her neck as she stood in line after the plane had stopped at the gate, and again as she dodged scurrying passengers through the expansive terminal, and met the black sedan waiting for her outside of baggage claim. A driver in a back suit popped the trunk and assisted her with her bags as she eased herself into the backseat, leaning back into the dark interior.

The driver closed the door and the outside took on a smoky appearance from the dark window tint. As the car pulled away, she received a message:

THE INSPIRITI. WE'RE WAITING FOR YOU.

She placed her phone down, leaned her head back, and closed her eyes. She listened to the rumble of the tires move across the road, and the occasional honking horn.

And as soon as she closed her eyes she saw Tramos.

He was before her, looking down on her, smiling, with his brilliantly white teeth, his long, blonde hair framing his head as it always did.

The wings were not there.

There had been no blood.

But she knew – Delia knew – even in her dream, that she was not experiencing Tramos in the same state of mind that she always had.

Do you feel me Tramos?

Are you looking at me with eyes that do not see? Do you listen to me with ears that do not hear? Are you able to reach out and touch me? Do you feel me?

Do you listen to me?

Delia opened her eyes as the car pulled into *La Piazza San Pietro*. Despite her other locales around the world, this square felt most like home. She saw the familiar columns reaching around the large, open plaza; the large fountain in the center which looked like a giant mushroom with water cascading from its crown; Maderno's fountain; built in the center of the plaza. Tourists gathered around it taking photos. And then when she turned her attention towards the doors to the Cathedral, she saw all of them, the High Council, standing motionless in black suits, stern-faced and expressionless, waiting.

For her.

She recognized Monsignor Harrison who walked up just outside her window as the door to the car swung open. The cloud cover had increased the closer the car approached Vatican City, and tiny droplets of rain started to fall. Monsignor Harrison reached around and assisted Delia with her bags as the members of the High Council turned, filing back down a small set of stairs at the side of the Cathedral.

"Why do they go in that way?"

Monsignor Harrison looked over at the High Council members and then over at Delia. "They have special quarters," he said. "For their stature. Not down in the catacombs with the rest of us."

"Why were they out here? Waiting for me to return?"

"For the both of you," he said. "Where's Antoine?"

Delia sighed. "He flew out an hour earlier than I did. To Frankfurt. He has a car waiting there and is handling Giovanni's sight procedure."

Monsignor Harrison shook his head but said nothing.

Delia and the Monsignor walked through the chapel. Delia raised her head, once again, to look up at Michelangelo's masterpiece, which she had appreciated just days before. "It doesn't even feel like I left," she said. "Such a quick turnaround."

The hallways were the same, dimly lit, with stark, brown walls and black and white linoleum tile on the floors. The activity that had been there previously had ceased. Monsignor Harrison led Delia through the administration hallways, marked with small signs, and she paused, for a moment, on the sign that said "Conference Area".

And then the Monsignor took her deeper, towards the residential hallways, where the carpet lined the floors. He paused at a door at the end of the hallway and fumbled in his right pocket. "Ah ha!" He produced a set of jingling keys and jiggled the lock open.

His quarters were small and unimpressive.

It appeared like an undersized hotel room, but sparsely furnished, save artwork hanging on the walls. A crucifix hung above the bed, and there was no kitchenette, for all of the members ate in a common dining hall.

"So Antoine's in Paris."

She fumbled with her purse, sat on the bed and reached for her phone. "That's where he was going. Eventually. I haven't heard from him yet. Let me check my messages."

The Monsignor sat on the bed next to Delia and looked on as she scrolled through her messages.

She shook her head. "Nothing yet."

"But he is en route, right? You said he went to Paris to have a procedure?"

Delia tossed her phone in her purse. "It was for their servant Giovanni. Their loyal houseman. To get a new pair of eyes."

Monsignor Harrison nodded. "Ah, yes. I do remember that. Well then he will be along directly then? I don't know how much longer I can stall the High Council."

There was a knock on the door and they both raised their heads to look. Monsignor Harrison sighed and hoisted himself off the bed, pausing at the door. "Yes? Who is it?" he asked.

A muffled voice replied. "We cannot wait any longer. Please locate Antoine and return to the conference chamber."

They were led back to the conference room, which was filled with immortals. The long, wooden table which lined the opposite side of the room remained empty. Monsignor Harrison was shown to his seat and they sat, waiting for the High Council to appear. He loosened his collar while the Cardinals deliberated in their chambers. Delia sat at the table across from him and looked up at him and smiled. He crossed his legs, and then a few minutes later uncrossed them. He leaned against the table and drummed his fingers against the wood, just as he raised his head and saw the small, wooden door at the opposite end of the room.

The Cardinals filed in, taking their seats at the long, expansive table that stretched the length of the room.

"Your highness," Monsignor Harrison said. Cardinal Klemmson looked up from his paperwork and raised his eyes at Monsignor Harrison, but did not say a word. He raised his hand.

"I have discussed this with several of the other high ranking immortals," Monsignor Harrison continued. "We are in agreement that a chosen one needs to represent us. To save our kind from annihilation."

Cardinal Klemmson leaned forward. "Monsignor Harrison. The immortals have nearly been wiped off the face of the Earth – on your watch, I might add. And now you are suggesting sending a representative – to where?"

"To Heaven."

The room erupted in chatter.

"To Heaven? Are you *mad*? Do you even realize what that would require? To send an immortal to Heaven?"

Monsignor Harrison nodded as he looked over and made eye contact with Delia. "It means one of us would have to voluntarily die."

Antoine exited the terminal in Frankfurt to brilliant sunshine and throngs of passengers exiting cars and buses, carrying suitcases and wheeling small bags. Moments later, his silver Mercedes pulled up to the curb as the trunk popped open.

Ramiel popped out of the driver's seat and waved to Antoine and smiled. "Right on time!" Antoine dropped his bag and hugged him. Antoine was about to let go when Ramiel hugged him tighter. His muscular arms wrapped around Antoine, and Antoine returned the embrace. Ramiel's eyes were closed, he shook his head as a tear streamed down his cheek. After a few moments, their embrace loosened, and Ramiel tossed Antoine's bags inside and shut the trunk. They slid inside the car and Ramiel navigated the heavy traffic.

After they had made it to the Autobahn, cruising West, Antoine felt Ramiel's hand on his chin. He looked over at Ramiel, who was alternating between looking at him and watching the road.

"I'd heard about what happened to you in Miami," he said. "With the Hounds. We thought we had lost you, Antoine! And Delia too."

Antoine sighed and looked at the other cars pass by. "We did lose Tramos." They drove through the rolling green hills of western Germany as Antoine leaned back in his seat and closed his eyes. "It's all gone," he said. "Everything. And the estate…guarded."

"Tramos. I never saw that one coming…"

Antoine opened his eyes and looked over at Ramiel. He noticed his salt and pepper hair was getting longer.

"He died protecting us." Antoine turned his head and gazed out the window.

"To the chateau, right?"

"Yes. Giovanni is waiting for us there. It took all of my energy to block the thoughts from her about this."

"Delia is a powerful immortal."

Antoine nodded. "Yes, I know. And I never told her that Gio already had his procedure before I met her in Rome in the first place. Took a lot of effort to block that out of my mind. If she had known I was planning this, she would do everything in her power to stop me."

"And you feel you must do this? Journey to the other side?"

Antoine nodded. "I must make amends. This is my day of atonement. It was my sector where it started. Hell, it started with Darius. How did I not *know*? How did I not know about *The Hooded Man*? Or his coming assault? I was supposed to be a leader of the sector!"

They drove through the French countryside, through green rolling hills and tiny, white houses that dotted the landscape. Every so often, Antoine would look through the window, study the cattle, or admire the colorful palette.

Once back in Lyon, Ramiel sighed as they approached the chateau.

He pulled the car in the expansive, tree -lined driveway and pulled the car in front of the steps. When he cut the engine, he looked over at Antoine, who stared down into his lap.

"You've always been so quick to forgive others, Antoine. I see it in you. I've seen it since before you were transformed. And that's a good trait to have. But have you forgiven yourself?"

Darius looked up at Ramiel. He looked back with a warm smile. After a minute, he raised his eyebrows.

Antoine opened the door and looked back at Ramiel as he exited the car. "I'll be heading there tonight. Giovanni is already gathering the equipment. I'd like you to come. I need you to."

"I will come."

Antoine did not have to say anything. He looked at Ramiel, and he smiled and nodded. And then he turned and headed up the front steps. Ramiel followed, slamming the driver's door behind him. He pressed the lock for the car and the alarm automatically engaged.

When Antoine opened the soaring front doors inwards, there was the smell of cooking. Giovanni appeared almost instantly. "Master! Welcome back! I am making some chicken soup!"

Antoine set his bags down against the wall and started to head down the hallway towards the Master bedroom. Giovanni lunged forward and gently grabbed his arm. "No, master. If we are doing this, and you are going where you are going, we need sustenance. And then we need rest."

Antoine looked up and over at Ramiel. He nodded slowly.

Antoine shrugged. "Okay."

Antoine changed his clothes and they convened in the kitchen. Giovanni had three large bowls of soup along with fresh bread in the center of the table. He walked around the chairs pouring hot brewed tea in each of the cups as Antoine sat. Ramiel pulled the chair out opposite him and looked across at Antoine.

Antoine gestured for him to sit.

The three ate in silence and shortly after, Antoine went to the master bedroom to rest, as Giovanni cleared the dishes. Ramiel watched Giovanni run each bowl under the water, washing and drying each piece of china with care, and returning them to the cabinets. He then wiped the countertops, ensuring everything was back in its assigned place.

"You have been quite loyal to Antoine and Darius," Ramiel said. "Don't you ever want to go out and find your own way in the world?"

Giovanni turned off the running water and looked back at Ramiel. "This is what I know. This is my home. Why would I want to leave it?"

Ramiel nodded and nursed his cup of steaming tea. "They've been good to you."

Giovanni nodded and joined Ramiel at the table. "I did not know love in my human life. When I was transformed, everything changed. And Antoine and Darius have shown me that love."

"Antoine cares about you a great deal."

"He does. And for that, I am eternally grateful."

AFTER THEY RESTED AND WAITED for the sun to set,

they readied themselves without further conversation. Ramiel and Giovanni joined Antoine in the foyer. They proceeded outside without a spoken word.

Antoine locked the front door of the chateau as Giovanni and Ramiel waited at the bottom of the front steps.

The sun was waning in the sky; the dark blues and purples had nearly taken over as the exterior lights snapped on.

The forest at the edge of the property looked uninviting and dark. Antoine joined the others as Ramiel placed his hand on Antoine's shoulder. "Are you sure about this?"

Antoine nodded. "Certain."

Giovanni chewed on his lip and watched Antoine with wide eyes. Antoine took a deep breath and looked out towards the thick forest. "It's time to go."

Antoine led as the others followed.

There was a certain method to their footsteps; they were quick and determined; their feet crunched through the gravel, and when the gravel gave way to grass, and then gave way to leaves and twigs, their pace remained methodic and steady.

Their silence was interrupted by the call of a loon from deep within the woods.

Antoine looked up and saw the tops of the trees blowing in a light breeze.

Look deep within yourself.

Their feet crunched on the dry, dirty leaves and fallen twigs. The darkness had now permeated the land as the sun had retreated from the sky. Antoine didn't wish the darkness on others. And he wished he could escape it as well.

The light seemed so far out of reach for so many.

The transgressions were too many; addictions to the physicality of the material world. A feeling – if not a need – to do work that in the end, did not matter. Bank accounts were filled with cash, bills were paid; fantastic homes were built; luxurious vacations were taken.

But what could the answer really be?

Was this – this physical world – all that there was? Was death the 'end all' when one were to die in the physical form? Antoine thought of Darius, now buried down below the Earth in his coffin. Would they be able to communicate with him as they had in Miami? Might redemption be found? Could Darius ever come back to the world of the living?

Ramiel stopped ahead and held out his hand. "Do you hear that?"

Antoine looked around the forest. "Hear what?" The same trees stood, reaching upwards, that had been there during the years that he had visited these woods in the past.

"I thought I heard a snap."

And it was in those years, many years ago now it seemed, that he had run through these same trees, on this very forest floor, escaping Asmodai's wrath.

"What was that?" Antoine caught up with Ramiel who stood in a clearing and scanned the woods. Antoine stood next to him and looked over at him. "He could be here," Antoine said. "Legend states that he appears when the winds start blowing, when the moon is high, and the…"

Look deep within yourself.

Antoine stopped walking and looked up and deeper into the forest. He cupped his hand around his ear. Their footsteps stopped crunching in the leaves as Giovanni and Ramiel stopped behind him.

"What is it?" Ramiel asked, looking in the same direction as Antoine.

"It's around here. We are close."

Ramiel pointed out a faint blue light in the distance. "And that? Do you know what that is?"

"That's the entrance," Antoine said. "There are pale blue lights surrounding the door. Gives off a glow at night."

Don't look into my lights...the square lights...for you will certainly go mad.

Antoine winced and closed his eyes. He smacked the side of his head.

Ramiel and Giovanni rushed to his side. "Antoine! What's wrong?"

He opened his eyes and shook his head. "He's close. I can feel it."

"Who's close?" Ramiel asked as Giovanni stood watching the forest ahead of them, where the lights glowed a pale blue in the distance.

They continued forward through the crunch of the leaves and twigs, heading towards the pale blue light that reflected against the moonlit sky, as Antoine explained. "Back when I resurrected Darius...when he was buried under the tree at *Les Enfantes*...I conjured up some sort of a ritual that summoned Asmodai."

"A ritual? You performed a ritual when you resurrected Darius?"

Antoine shook his head. "You know about immortal lore, I'm sure. Sometimes we're coffin-sentenced. But in the end, yes, we return. But in this case, I freed Darius before his time. And Asmodai was summoned."

Ramiel nodded. "I had heard about him."

"He's one of the core demons," Antoine said.

"And he has been haunting Antoine ever since," Giovanni added.

"Ever since then he's been tormenting me," Antoine said. "As if I could settle the score."

They approached a clearing in the woods.

At the opposite end, towards a network of large trees, was a stone, windowless building with a set of stairs leading downwards into the ground to a small door with an ornate wrought-iron cover. The door itself was also made of stone.

Antoine brought the others over to the entrance.

Ramiel reached out and touched the iron cover. "Is this some sort of a stone mausoleum?"

Antoine banged the pickaxe against the mausoleum lock, sending a shower of sparks down towards the ground. "That's exactly what it is. Been a kept secret for centuries. Many of our bloodline are buried here." Giovanni gasped. "Master Antoine! Careful Master Antoine!"

Ramiel stood back and looked on as Antoine continued the assault with the pickaxe. "And the biggest secret is inside."

Ramiel held Antoine steady as the pickaxe sent another shower of sparks to the ground. The lock gave and fell to the ground, in pieces.

Antoine turned around and looked at the group. "So Monsignor Harrison is saying that a representative needs to go to the other side – to Tartarus – to represent our kind. This is my choice."

"To Tartarus? How did you know this?" Ramiel asked.

Antoine started pushing against the heavy stone door. "I can feel my power is slowly returning. I can sense it. Delia might be thinking it, not sure. But I can sense that is what we are going to find out in Rome."

Ramiel stood, arms crossed in front of his chest, eyebrows raised. "And you think you can accomplish this?"

Antoine nodded. "It is my duty. I brought this on to our kind. I must earn our redemption."

Ramiel helped Antoine push, and the door rumbled open.

Antoine turned around again and smiled. "Are you ready?"

A set of stone steps was revealed that led downward into darkness. Antoine tossed the pickaxe off to the side and gestured for the others to follow him. Once a few steps down, he whistled. "It's musty down here. Gio, you have the masks?" His voice echoed against the stone.

Giovanni handed out several white masks for each of them. Ramiel fixed his around his head, adjusting his head through the plastic tubing around behind his ears. "Is this really necessary?"

"Better safe than sorry," Antoine said. "It's musty and wet. Lots of mildew. Plus rotting corpses. The stench..."

Ramiel scoffed. "We're immortals, Antoine. This should not affect us."

There was a deep thud coming from above, sending dirt cascading through cracks in the stone, showering on their heads.

Ramiel's voice sounded rushed as he brushed the dirt from his hair. "What was that?!"

Antoine, Giovanni and Ramiel all studied the ceiling. The sound most definitely came from above ground.

Then a snap pierced the silence from outside the door.

Antoine closed his eyes and shook his head. "You've got to be kidding."

"What?" Ramiel asked. "What is it?"

Giovanni looked upwards, his eyes wide and mouth hanging open. "Master? Is this..."

Antoine leaned against the side wall. The torch that Giovanni was holding reflected a warm glow on his face. "The same thing happened when I resurrected Darius before. Years ago. Asmodai came."

Ramiel fidgeted with a brown bag. "You think that is him? Coming for us?"

Antoine shook his head. "I don't know. We're not exhuming a body like I did with Darius so long ago. We're not bringing anyone back to life. I'm not doing any incantation or ceremony like I did before."

Giovanni started pacing. "Do you think that matters to him?"

Antoine looked up at the ceiling of the mausoleum as the ground rumbled again. "No," he said. "Asmodai thinks he has a score to settle with me. When I last saw him, I had just resurrected Darius, but I escaped. He still thinks there is a payment due."

Ramiel grabbed Antoine's arm. "So is there?! Is there still a payment due?"

Antoine shoved Ramiel's arm down. "He's a collector of souls!"

The ground shook again as Antoine eased himself back into the corner.

The ground shook as dirt showered down on their heads again. Antoine looked at Ramiel who glared back at him.

"Will we be safe down there? If we go all the way in?"

Antoine shook his head. "I don't know, Ramiel."

The group continued down into the darkness. At the foot of the stairs was a small, square room with walls of stone. They stood in dirt. Antoine looked up the steps. They were deep enough that the pale blue light from outside was no longer visible.

They now only had Giovanni's torch, which burned weakly, from the low levels of oxygen.

Antoine gestured for the others and led them into a larger room. "This is where Darius now lies," he said. "He is with the other members of the blood ancestry who have passed as mortals."

Ramiel joined Antoine who held the torch over the wooden coffins that lined the walls. "So wait a minute…you mean this assault on our kind has happened before?"

"Many times," he said. "*The Hooded Man* is not a new phenomenon."

"So why wouldn't Klemmson know this?"

Antoine ran his hands over one of the coffin lids. There was a large cross carved into the wood. "Oh, I imagine he does."

Old, wooden caskets lined the opposite side of the mausoleum, each tucked into a cubby. Some were sealed with stone, others were not. Antoine stood and honed in on the center and then gave the torch back to Giovanni. He drew it close to the small, wooden coffin. But that coffin was not the crumbling wooden box that Darius had been buried in years ago. It was not the same watery grave under the giant oak tree. And the cemetery did not fill up with demons.

Had it?

Antoine spoke with wide eyes fixated on Darius' casket. "No, Ramiel, no. Asmodai has been chasing after me for years. I thought that after I was burned at the altar that payment was rendered!"

"No, you fool! He wants your soul! He will take nothing less!"

There was another rumble, closer this time. The caskets rumbled in their crypts as some dirt fell through cracks in the ceiling.

"He is waiting for you! And he will stop at nothing to get it!" Ramiel said.

There was a deep thud as Giovanni gasped. He looked over at Antoine with wide eyes. "Is the ceiling going to cave in?! Are we going to be buried alive?!"

Ramiel stood and placed his arm around Giovanni. "Come and sit. Next to Antoine and I." Giovanni looked over at Antoine. "Antoine? Who is this Asmodai? Is it who you think it is?"

Antoine leaned his head back. "He's the protector of everything evil. The demon of lust."

"The devil's right hand," Ramiel said.

Antoine raised his eyes towards the ceiling and shook his head. "There was always a certain way he came," Antoine said. "Through the trees. With heavy footsteps that shook the Earth. Branches would snap. Whole trees would topple over. And the winds would roar."

Antoine didn't look at the caskets on the opposite wall. He hung his head down between his knees, down towards his feet, and closed his eyes. He attempted to ignore the rumbles in the ground; he tried to ignore the falling of the dirt in between the ceiling cracks.

But in his mind he wasn't there.

He wasn't in the mausoleum.

He was in *Les Enfantes.*

He was lying in his maker's grave.

He could still smell the stench and feel the wet, cold water at the base underneath the coffin.

Back then, it had been so simple.

When Darius had died then, he simply placed him in a plain wooden, quite simple coffin and buried him underground. Now, that Darius had passed as a mortal, a human, it was more difficult. His heart was no longer beating. His body would rot, and could not regenerate.

But that did not matter.

The shaking stopped.

After a few minutes of silence, Ramiel looked at Antoine. "Shall we continue?"

Antoine took a deep breath and exhaled. He hoisted himself up to his feet and looked over at the coffins. Each casket was neatly placed in a square cubby; lengthwise as the head of the deceased was deepest inside the opening, and the end of the casket handles were in view. "Should I just pull the casket out?" Antoine asked. He looked back at Ramiel, who gestured his hand. Giovanni sprang to his feet and dashed over to Antoine's side, still holding the torch. He shined the light towards the coffin. "I must help you," he said. "You shouldn't do this alone."

Antoine looked at the casket and shook his head. "I don't think I can do this." He looked back at Ramiel. "Can you help me? Darius is inside. But what we are coming for is behind the coffin."

Back in Rome, Delia gasped.

"We have a problem, your highness." She whispered across the room. The High Council was conferring to their notes. Delia waved at him where he sat near the conference table. Monsignor Harrison was reading through a yellow legal pad filled with handwritten notes, which Delia had given him after the first day of his trial. He slowly flipped the pages up as Delia got up and walked over to him. She poked him in his arm. "Monsignor!"

Startled, he dropped the pad and looked at Delia. "What is it?"

She leaned in close to his ear. "We've gotten word that Antoine and Ramiel have joined forces."

The Monsignor shook his head. "I don't understand. Joined forces? Against whom?"

"Not against," she said. "For."

Delia stooped down and looked up at the cardinals. They were still conferring amongst each other. She knew that Antoine was trying to access the portal. She knew he wanted to take on the task of redemption alone.

She also knew that Daius was buried in that same mausoleum. And she knew that Antoine had always been connected to Darius in some form or another, even in death. Would he try to exhume him? Attempt to resurrect him?

But at this point in the juncture, she felt she agreed with the Monsignor, when they had spoken earlier. That Darius should be left to rest. There should be no more incantations, or spells, or anything else that would get Hell's Angels back on their backs. Wasn't it enough to have demons chasing them after Antoine resurrected Darius the first time, years ago?

Now, things were different. Darius didn't die this time in possession of the gift. The gift was gone. He died of old age. And Delia discussed it with the Monsignor.

Darius was meant to die. It was his time.

"It's time to let him rest," Monsignor Harrison said, as they closed up their books. "Exhuming Darius and attempting a resurrection – when he died as a mortal – will accomplish nothing. Don't you think Antoine knows that? He died without the gift. His body is rotting in the ground as we speak. There's no magic anymore."

"Unless he invokes the demons," Delia said.

"Do you think he will? Do you think Antoine would attempt something like that?"

Delia shook her head. "I don't think so. But I do know he is down in the mausoleum. And I'm getting concerned for his safety. Something doesn't feel right."

Monsignor Harrison nodded. "True. But why would we want to go down that path again? I just got finished protecting him from Asmodai recently. That's a bastard of a demon. And when these incantations take place…when the demons are summoned to resurrect someone…payment is demanded. And I know, for a fact, that they want Antoine's soul."

"That's why I'm concerned, your highness. I don't *think* his intentions is to attempt to raise Darius. But I don't *know*. But I also know what's there. And so do you. Do you think he's trying to access it?"

"You mean the portal? I thought that was a secret. How would he know about it?"

Delia shrugged. "He's been coffin sentenced in the past. You know that when an immortal returns from a sentence that they come back quite enlightened. No telling what powers he will have now. At least of knowledge."

"So he is not conspiring against us? You are certain?"

Delia shook her head. "I don't believe so."

"Then what do you believe?"

"I believe that he might be in danger."

Back in the mausoleum in France, the ground shook again. Dirt rained upon them and covered the casket.

"I think the ceiling is going to cave in!" Giovanni cried. He jumped to his feet. Antoine reached up and pulled him back down.

"Stop!" he said. "Asmodai will not come down here! There is no way he can!"

"How?!" Ramiel asked.

Antoine raised his hands up and shook his head. "No! Wait! I have to look at him one last time!"

Ramiel grabbed his shoulder. "Let him rest, Antoine!"

Antoine pushed him away. "No! Once I enter through there I won't be back! This is my last chance to see him!" He pointed into the center cubby where Darius' coffin had been.

Giovanni looked up at the ceiling as the rumbles became more methodic and centered. Each shake felt more spaced and determined, like giant footsteps. "Is he coming here? Is he coming down here?!"

"He cannot come down here!" Antoine screamed.

But the rumble got closer.

Deep, heavy, grating footsteps.

Heading down the stairs.

Getting closer.

Giovanni dropped the torch, ran towards Antoine and held onto him tightly. "Please! He is coming!"

Ramiel grabbed the torch and held it out towards the opening from the stairs across the chamber.

The steps continued.

Ramiel shook his head and retreated back to the wall. "Antoine!"

But Antoine did not answer.

He was focused on the approaching shadow. The dark shadow which shrouded the room in darkness; the darkness which led to the green, muscular legs, the canine snout and horns. Antoine remembered the last time he had seen the lumbering demon; the time he had listened to the slow, methodic approach; as he lay in a grave of putrid water, so many years ago, in the same cemetery they were close to under the tree that Darius had once loved so much. As Giovanni cowered closer to Antoine, Ramiel retreated back to the wall, and the three of them sat against the hard stone, as Asmodai lumbered towards them.

Look deep within yourself!

The thunder rumbled as each who had been gifted, and all those across the world who were angels raised their heads to the sky; each at the same precise moment, throughout the astral plane and the other parallel worlds, across space and time, at the very same moment.

"Antoine!"

Tramos was waiting in the other world and also raised his head, seeing light shine down from the heavens. There was a crash, he could tell, he could sense it.

Darius extended his wings, his face painted with fear, his eyes wide and flew to Tramos.

And at the same precise moment, Delia sat in Rome, as the conclusion of the proceedings were drowned out, she raised her head towards the ceiling but saw a vision of angels cascade and soar towards one another, their wings spread, joining each other in chorus, painted and organizing across a brightly lit sky:

Antoine was in danger.

VII

CHORUS ANGELORUM

DELIA RUSHED BACK to the Monsignor's side as the Cardinals looked up. "What is this? Go back to your seat!" Cardinal Klemmson took off his glasses and tossed them on the table. His eyes were wide and his cheeks were flushed. "We are not finished with these proceedings!"

Delia ignored them. "We must get to Lyon at once! Antoine is in trouble! It is confirmed! We must go now!"

Monsignor Harrison rose from his chair and started leaving with Delia. Klemmson banged his gavel against the table as the obeservers started chatting amongst each other. As they reached the doors, they turned and Delia transformed; her aged appearance shifted and her skin became more tight, taught, soft and youthful. Her snow white hair lengthened and turned dark brown.

The Cardinals all looked up in their direction. "And where do you think you're going? We are waiting for Antoine's testimony and you cannot leave!"

Delia stood forward as Monsignor Harrison stood behind her. Her wings rose from her back; they reached towards the ceiling and stopped, folding inwards.

"You're an angel!" Klemmson exclaimed. "You *are* one of the chosen ones!"

Delia nodded. "And Antoine is in danger. I must get to Lyon. He is our salvation, and I must save him!"

Klemmson nodded. "Go. Go now. Save him! We will wait."

As Monsignor Harrison reached around her chest, she soared upward, crashing through the ceiling; her wings broke through the concrete and stone, they splintered the wood and broke through the roof, showering tiles on the piazza below. The Monsignor held tight to her back as they flew above Rome, reaching upwards, towards the sky and towards the sun.

Her wings spread through the clouds, tearing them apart, letting the sun shine through.

They carried them over the land, up towards France, and down into Lyon. She flapped her wings up as they eased themselves to the ground. The sun shined on *Les Enfantes*, the headstones were pronounced, like grey patches in green grass. But her focus was on the forest nearby.

"Antoine!" she called out as she retracted her wings. "Antoine! We have come for you!"

But there was no answer, only silence.

Monsignor Harrison stood and scanned the area as Delia watched him. "Listen to your senses, Delia. They are far heightened now. Don't let yourself be run by adrenaline."

She nodded and looked in the same direction. After a few moments of silence, she nodded. "That way."

They walked to the edge of the graveyard together, deeper, away from the clearing and monuments and towards the forest. There was something about the forest, Delia had said. And so Monsignor Harrison had followed her, deeper, through the woods, in the midst of the silence, until they approached the mausoleum.

Delia pointed. "The door's open! And Antoine would not have the key! Come on!"

They approached the small, stone structure, and looked down the stone stairs towards the darkness. Delia saw the small pickaxe off to the side.

"Well I see how they got inside," she said. She turned around and looked at Monsignor Harrison. "Let's go. You ready?"

He nodded.

They descended the stairs down into the darkness, and when they approached the large room, they saw Ramiel and Giovanni, laying on the floor. The light that emanated from Delia cast a cool, pale glow in the room. They saw the caskets, and the one particular coffin that sat in the center of the room. Ramiel and Giovanni lay next to it.

Delia rushed to Ramiel and slapped him on the face. "Wake up! Wake up, Ramiel! Are you okay?"

His eyes fluttered after a few minutes.

"Where is Antoine?!" she asked. Her voice reverberated against the silence. "Where is Antoine?!"

Ramiel raised his arm slowly, pointing towards the wall. Delia and Monsignor Harrison turned around to where he was pointing. "It's the portal," she said. "We must go." She looked down at Ramiel. "Are you two okay to come? Or would you rather stay?"

Ramiel coughed and got up to his feet. Giovanni shifted as Ramiel approached him and placed his hand on his shoulder. "Come on, Gio. We're being rescued!"

They all approached the cubby where Darius had lain. Delia looked back down at the casket, sitting in the middle of the room, untouched. She turned and focused her attention on the darkness at the end of the cubby, as she assisted Monsignor Harrison, Ramiel and Giovanni crawl into the darkness.

And then she crawled in herself.

The darkness held fast.

"Monsignor!" she called. Her voice reverberated against the silence. "Ramiel!"

No answer.

"Giovanni!"

Still no answer.

She was in a silent blackness; she could see nothing, nor could she hear anything.

Only silence.

Until she saw a wing, a white wing cut across the darkness. It reached from her left view to the right, and then closer. It transformed from white, to feathers, to the fine lines and details that she had come to expect from her own wings.

And then he was in front of her.

His long dark hair looked familiar.

His smile.

But now his skin was different; it was more translucent. Like glass.

"Darius!" she cried. She hugged him. A tear streamed down her face. "I am so glad to see you here!"

Darius looked down at her. He looked her in the eyes. "I know what have come here for," he said. "And Antoine is not here. He is farther in. I saw him. Asmodai dragged him through the muck. Antoine's body was tattered and bloodied! How can a physical being survive in this?!"

Delia gasped and drew her hands over her mouth. "But where is he? How *did* Asmodai get him?"

Darius looked down. "Asmodai came to settle the score from my resurrection."

Delia turned to face Darius. "You mean from years ago? From your coffin sentence?"

Darius closed his eyes and nodded.

Darius leaned in closer and turned Delia around to face a new darkness, when a scene painted itself in front of her. Of writhing bodies. Limbs thrashing in a vast, dark ocean. Near a beach littered with more bodies.

"Now watch," Darius said.

Delia fell to her knees as she saw Antoine spill to the ground from a dark, muscular force in a red sky painted with dark clouds.

"You!" she said. She lunged forward towards the vision. "You have been tormenting me my entire life!" She turned to face Darius. "Can I enter the vision?"

Darius nodded. "If you do you will become it."

"I don't care. Antoine is in there! We must save him! I must stop that dark force!"

She jumped into the vision, above the sea, as her wings soared from her back. Her sword shot into her hands and ignited in bright, orange flames. She flew across the sky, swinging her sword, showering the land with light. she saw Giovanni and Ramiel, standing on the desolate beach below, their faces looking upwards and shifted in a swirl in torment. Their eyes were floating around their faces as their skin dripped from their skulls. Delia snapped her head to their direction. "How did you get here?! Why did you come?!"

Ramiel raised his arm silently and pointed his finger out towards the sea, towards the thrashing limbs and crashing waves.

She saw a rectangular, dark silhouette.

The altar.

There was a stone island, in the center of the sea. She squinted to see, but she could still see the darkness of his body. She snapped around to Giovanni and Ramiel. "He's out there. I can sense it. Where's Monsignor Harrison?"

They looked up at her but could not reply.

She hung her head as Giovanni ran to her side. She screamed towards the sky. "I have failed!" She fell backwards and lay on the dirt as the clouds swirled above her. "I have failed you again!"

She took deep breaths, concentrating on each one, knowing that Antoine lay dead on the altar in the center of the sea. Delia lay on the beach, flat on her back, her arms draped over her head, and cried out as the tears flowed down her cheeks. Her wings were spread out on the sand, reaching out; Giovanni placed his arms around her shoulders, down around her back, and started to lift her up into a sitting position. "Don't punish yourself!" he said. "You *are* the war angel! You went to battle for him the entire time you knew him!"

Once sitting up, she hung her head low. "I am cursed! First it was my father. He was lying in a lake of blood. Then Antoine. And now he's dead."

Giovanni knelt next to her. He grabbed her chin and turned her head to face him. His eyes were wide and pleading. "No. You are the war angel. The chosen one. Your protection is infinite!"

She shook her head. "No, Gio. It was never me. I never was the war angel. I know everyone has wondered. But it was never me." She raised her head and looked out towards the sea. Towards the dark, stone altar where Antoine lay. The limbs still thrashed as the bodies emitted wails around him.

"It was always Antoine. It was always him!"

Her wings soared outwards, reached across the sky, and carried her over the thrashing limbs in the sea. She soared down towards the altar, and saw Antoine lying, motionless, eyes closed, as a fire burned beneath him.

But before she could reach Antoine, the darkness filtered through. And here, in this realm, in Tartarus, in center of Hades, she could see him. The one standing guard over Antoine; the one who was no longer the swirling dark cloud he had been. He was no longer the muscular red-skinned demon sitting in the rocking chair in her room in Paris.

For here, it was a much darker presence.

It was much more sinister. It was not only the darkness swallowing the light; it was what was fighting for the capture of her soul. She saw the darkness. Swirling before her in an angry, dark cloud.

But what she felt was far more profound.

She felt the disappointment. It held her like a vice. She hung her head low. "I have failed my God," she said. "I do not deserve to go on." And then the discouragement. "I do not have the courage to move forth."

"I cannot save anyone. I could not save Antoine. Could I?"

And the cold reached her.

The feeling of loneliness.

She looked at the darkness, her hand at her side, holding the sword in its sheath. She closed her eyes, hung her head, waited and cried out, her hand gripping the handle. "Give me strength! Even I need strength!" She tore her sword out from the sheath, raised it up towards the sky as it burst into flames A torrent of brilliant light filtered across the sky.

And she thought she saw movement in the showering light. Was it the appearance of rainbows? A show of colorful pastels?

But then she saw the upwards and downwards motion – the carrying of feathers; of white upon white, swirling the light throughout the sky.

In that instant, Tramos appeared, his wings extended, soaring and reaching across the sky. "Raise your sword!" he said. "Do it again! You have the power! It is within *you*! Draw…your…*sword*!"

She gritted her teeth and tensed her muscles.

She dared not open her eyes and look at the swirling, dark presence. For when she saw in her mind's eye, there was no darkness. Only light. In her mind, the darkness was gone.

And she tore her sword from its sheath, raising it to the sky as it burst into bright flames.

"Believe!" Tramos cried. "Believe, Delia, *believe*!"

She lunged forward, piercing the darkness. The flames swelled and spread, burning brighter and hotter than she had ever seen them. The light grew larger, brighter and hotter, as the aura changed.

She released her sword and turned to face Tramos.

The sky had lightened.

"Now go down and get him," he said. "Complete your mission."

Delia flew down and knelt next to the altar.

She reached the altar. "I will lift you from the flames! I will carry you upwards, soar you across the sky!" She spread her wings outwards.

The writhing bodies had burned to ash and charred, as if they were in the center of a field of stones. The water splashed against the altar as Delia leaned forward and eased her arms underneath Antoine's burned and charred body. She looked down at him and sighed. She looked up for a moment at Tramos.

He looked downwards and nodded in approval at her carrying Antoine upwards towards the sky. Light filtered down from the heavens, reaching down to Delia and Antoine, as she flapped her wings against a lightening sky; the oranges, yellows and reds fingered their way through the darkness; painting the light against the pastel pallet.

And as she soared higher, the angels filled the sky.

Their wings spread, interlocking with one another, carrying their hymns across the sky. Love wrapped around them like a warm blanket as she raised Antoine further upwards, as the light shined down on his charred body, it reached around him, like a mist, but one of compassion and love. It wrapped around his body and Delia looked down at him.

His skin started to regenerate.

Slowly, bit by bit, as the light moved over his body, the musculature returned as the cells regrew and multiplied; as the light wrapped around his hands, and quickly moved to another area, Delia saw movement. His hand balled into a fist, flexed, and released.

She looked at his eyes. They were still closed, but she could see his eyes moving beneath the healing eyelids.

A plume of light filtered down as Delia raised Antoine higher and offered him to the heavens.

"He was the true *War Angel*," Tramos said.

The clouds parted as Delia looked downwards.

The planet below looked bright; green and blue; so fresh, so very new. It as if she were floating in the celestial heaven, but not in the dark vastness of space. For there was only light. And color. And song.

As she listened, she felt she could hear the babbling of a stream.

And it did not matter how far she was from the surface – for as soon as she looked towards a location, it zoomed up to her, instantly painting a crystal clear image: bright, colorful tropical foliage. Oranges, pinks, yellows, smattered amongst brilliant green plants and towering trees. After standing amidst a tropical forest, she heard a familiar voice.

"Is this the new planet? The new age?"

She turned around and her mouth dropped open. Her eyes welled with tears.

"Antoine!" she said.

He was smiling a brilliant smile, he was vivid, clean, youthful and vibrant.

He stood in a clearing in the forest and looked up towards the sky. She looked down and saw his face, his eyes as open and wide as they had ever been. The days back in Lyon, Badulla and Miami seemed a distant memory.

"It's a new Earth," she said. "Do you see? A physical world. The sense of familiarity is still there."

Antoine nodded. "Yes...yes I see. So fresh. Uncontaminated."

"But here...everyone is immortal. And you will live in complete harmony and happiness throughout eternity."

"There will be no war?"

She shook her head.

"And no famine?"

"No. Everything will be perfect."

"I won't need sleep?"

"No. Unless you want to sleep, then, of course, you can."

Antoine sat at the edge of the brook and looked at the water.

It was crystal clear, bubbling.

And after a few minutes, he saw a colorful school of fish swim by. He raised his arm up.

It was the same familiar arm that he always remembered from before. But it was somehow different.

Glowing

Yet still physical.

"This is your new physical body," she said. "You are a human. You are *not* a monster. You are not a demon. And you don't have to run from them anymore. But you are still immortal. You will always be immortal, Antoine, in the light, and in great love. A physical immortal who will never, ever die."

The End

9/14/16 10:16pm ---- 10/14/16 1:17pm final correction run.

VIII

PURGATORY

ASHES: BOOK ONE

Present Day.

Antoine gathered his equipment - a shovel, brown tarp, pickaxe (in order to pry open the casket) and a flame oil lantern; carefully and quietly he entered the graveyard through a layer of swirling, early morning mist - the type of white cloudy mist that would leave a layer of dewdrops on the earth like a cool, wet blanket. The plot Antoine headed toward, located in the center of the graveyard, housed Darius' casket, encased for two centuries now in layers of earth - sealed by six nails, and placed in a thick cement liner with a crest of a lion on the marble-topped cover.

It was Antoine who put Darius here two centuries ago, and Darius has been in this graveyard ever since. In this cemetery and dead, yes – Darius was dead. But Darius had been dead before Antoine had ever put him there. And when the coffin was nailed shut, when the darkness enveloped satin interior, there was more of changing a state of existence.

It was Darius who had heard the nails being pounded into the edges of the casket; he had felt the shaking as the coffin was picked up – most likely with ropes tied below the bottom, but he couldn't know for sure – and lowered into the deep, dark grave. He had felt the sides of the coffin scraping the cold, hard earthen walls. The dirt fell onto the lid of the casket – each shovel of earth inundating the coffin further with a deep clump.

Blackness.

The sounds from above now seemed more distant. The coffin had been buried. Darius knew that. He even felt the weight of the dirt above him, as if the entire casket would fall on top of him in a cascade of splintering wood and falling sand. But it held. The coffin was holding fast against the pressures of the earth, and would prove to be his holding place for…how long?

The stagnancy of the air inside the small confines grew more insistent, as the heat overtook the darkness and caused him to cough and choke on the thickness of the air that was so quickly fading. But Darius knew. He knew that no matter how fast the air would dissipate, no matter how faint the sounds of the earth above would be – no matter how *dead* he would be – he would be just that.

Dead.

But death is just a state of existence. And Darius knew - all too well - that his death had been many, many years ago – and not so recently in his foyer. His death had been much earlier when he was a very young man passing into his newfound immortality. Not at the hands of Antoine.

As time passed, he became more aware of his surroundings, although all he saw was total darkness. He could feel the softness and smoothness of the satin liner, the pillow at the head of the casket - which grew hard and cold over time and dusty with mold.

Above where he lay, Darius on occasion could hear the faint, muffled voices above the cold ground expressing words of condolence, the grating of a casket being lowered into a freshly dug grave, or the pitter patter of children's feet; ceremonial instruments would play from time to time, signifying the passing of a loved one. All this, he experienced, lying in the cold darkness of the casket, as time passed by above.

Time passed with an eternal slowness until Antoine returned.

At one point, Darius knew the time had come. He continued to lie in the casket as he felt and heard snippets of the outside world over time, but there was one quiet day when he heard those familiar footsteps; the methodic, determined stomps coming closer and closer to his unmarked resting place. The footsteps stopped, just above. Darius could sense it. He knew who it was. No one knew of his grave except one soul. Only one.

Antoine.

~~*

Topside, Antoine reached the grave.

It was the only unmarked grave in the entire cemetery. Located under a tree, the plot was not originally used as the caretaker had been afraid that the roots of the massive tree would grow to a size so immense as to unearth a coffin. But that did not deter Antoine. It had been the perfect resting place for Darius.

It had been Antoine who dug the grave, in the middle of the night, so many days ago. But even then, as he had been digging, Antoine knew that a day of resurrection would come. Even as Darius burned into ash, even as Antoine drove a dagger directly through his steadfast heart, he knew that the day would come that he would need to channel Darius once again and ask for his assistance...no, *expect* his assistance...and receive the help and guidance from the one who created him so long ago.

And now, deep in the night, Antoine set down his tools. The tools were just as dull and rusted as they had been the night he buried Darius. He paused to the left of the grave, and looked to the sky. Night held steady.

I have come for you, Darius. Yes, the day has finally come. The day has finally come when I need you, I need you by my side. But please, please don't come to me with malice or ill-will for putting you here. I love you, Darius.

The moon burned brightly and cast a blue glow on the headstones, illuminating them like tiny, square lights a dark, dank sea. Opening the brown cloth bag, Antoine grabbed the shovel, trying so desperately to pull the tools from the bag in silence. His head snapped towards the direction of the woods as the shovel clanked against the other tools in the bag.

But he rose to his feet and pointed the shovel towards the earth, shifting his weight and breaking the ground. He stopped for a moment as he tossed the first bit of dirt to the side.

Darius…will you ever forgive me?

And then he dug - he dug and dug, hoisting shovelfuls of earth, one after the next, to the right of the grave, next to the bag of tools. The digging continued for quite some time, as Antoine broke through roots and clay. Darius had been deeply buried.

Bury them deep, Darius had once told him. *If you are extinguishing an immortal, bury them deep.*

Antoine finally felt the scraping of the grave liner, the impenetrable cement beneath the thin layer of caked dirt and sand. A black snake slithered from the side of the earth, slinking across the grave liner and re-entered on the other side. Antoine stood above the grave for a moment and looked down at the liner, and then scanned the area around him. The sky began to show the faintest hints of light blue, signifying that he needed to hurry, hoist the casket out of the grave, and head to safety.

The swirling mist was subsiding as the night was ever so gradually waning and giving to the very first peeks of the eastern sun, which slowly yet surely revealing itself way on the far horizon. Antoine had been digging for the better part of the night. He estimated that he had another hour or so of semi-darkness, and then the sunrise would occur. The sky was surely awakening.

Antoine jumped down into the grave and stood on the liner. He just was able to see over the threshold of the earth, and reached out and grabbed the pickaxe. He swung it down into the hole and smacked it against the lock on the grave liner, with a loud *clank!* which reverberated against the quiet early morning silence. But the one assault had not been enough to break the seal of death. He had to break the silence and take another risk of possibly being discovered by a mortal, and again *clank!*

With the second rap, the lock gave. It amazed Antoine that it had still held so prominently after so many years, and despite it being covered in rust, dirt and grime.

Antoine tossed the pickaxe out of the grave, and winced as it clanked against the other tools in the bag. It was time to open the casket.

The grave liner was caked with dirt and mud, the insignia was rusted out, but overall it was still intact (as was the lock) and it held together like an expensive grave liner would be expected to. As Antoine shifted the lid with a deep grating and rumbling, the small, wooden casket slowly came into view — rotted from years of decay. And there, beneath the six nails, beneath the wood and satin, would be Darius.

THE QUEST FOR IMMORTALITY: BOOK TWO

_S_tephen died on a Tuesday.

It was his destiny with death.

But still, he got his wish.

He didn't die in a hospital connected to machines.

He was in his backyard in the bright warmth of the sunlight, surrounded by his family and friends, and, just as he had requested, at the moment he passed and his death was declared, a flock of white doves was released, flying upwards towards the sky. Stephen's body lay on a large lounge chair, spread out and overlooking the expansive gardens that he had tended before his health had failed him.

Now that he was dead, the eyes that overlooked the yard saw nothing, but in essence, the presence of his body still took command of the gardens. And as the doves flew ever farther away, and spread out towards the blue heavens, there was a silence that fell over the small group on the terrace that sunny morning. As Stephen's closest family members fell into each other's arms in tears, not far from the lounge chair, Darius stopped and stared at his friend. He looked down at the frail arms, the sunken cheeks, and the sullen eyes.

He knew that Stephen had been ready for a long time.

For Stephen had been angry with the world since he contracted his disease, and ever since they had formed their friendship and fought together, he got another reason to live, to forage on, and to get just one more day in the world, even if the ending was inevitable.

~~*

The morning sun kissed the sky two days after Stephen died.

The warm rays touched the sidewalks and evaporated the morning dew, the orange fiery beams of light awakened the world, as the sky to the west gradually transformed from black, to blue, to pale to brilliant – and then to the growing shadows that ensued elongated; the warmth and the heat, the sweat and the caffeine.

The sun warmed the city during the midst of a wintertime cold front. It was a rare presence these days, and the citizens of Miami were out and about reveling in its warmth and hospitality, even treasuring the cooling shadows that each building formed as the sun rose farther into the sky. Some shoppers would find respite in the cool shadows, others sought the ocean and the beach. But there was one shadow that formed throughout the morning, somewhat separated from the others.

But it was there, and many didn't take notice of what created the shadow until they didn't want to face it.

It was the shadow of the Heavenly Slumber Funeral Home. It wasn't terribly large, considering it was a one-story building. But it was imposing nonetheless. And the shadow covered cars as they passed by. The shadow successfully blocked the sun, and, when one were to look at the front doors, one might wonder if there were a permanent shadow.

Stephen's body had arrived at Heavenly Slumber Funeral Home just before dawn from the Morgue. Ned McCracken was clutching the autopsy report in a manila folder in one hand, as he hovered over the body of Stephen Henry Drake. The report contained some hastily written notes, but what stood out to him was the cause of death, *Pneumonia as a Complication of AIDS*.

Ned McCracken grabbed a white coat, grabbed some rubber surgical gloves from the kit and placed them on each hand, paused and looked at Stephen's face.

The man looked at peace.

Very smooth skin on his face, thin lips, and manicured eyebrows. The eyes were already closed, but Ned secured them anyway with white medical tape, by placing a strip across each eyelid. He picked some cotton from a jar on the counter next to the preparation table, and pulled it apart into wispy strips. He stopped a moment at the lips.

The man seemed to be smiling.

Was he?

Ned looked throughout the preparation room.

The pale green tiles were the same that they always were. The room felt very clinical. Like it could have been in a hospital. There was the cold and dusty tile on the floor, the heavy, steel door with the small window in the center, and the stark, steel countertops.

The chill was always there.

The striking smell of alcohol, mixed with the stench of rotting flesh, and the overpowering scent of formaldehyde.

It was always there.

Everyday.

And when he left each night, he carried the smell with him on his clothes.

The smell of death.

He couldn't get away from it. It followed him everywhere. But he knew this was the life that was he was meant to live.

And then Ned looked down at the body again. At Stephen.

What did you do, my friend? To get something as devastating as AIDS?

But the man seemed to be at peace.

He longed not to disturb that peace, but he needed to fill the cheeks. They were sunken dramatically on both sides, to the point where the cheekbone was highly visible through the thin layer of flesh. This man was clearly dying for a long time.

Ned shook his head and paused for a moment. He took a deep breath and exhaled. Some of these cases were some of the most complex. AIDS, Cancer. They were all wasted away. And it was his job to make them look like they did before they got sick. So he fished for some gloves from the box on the counter, and started to pry open the lips.

Dead skin.

The cold, hard, uninviting flesh of the corpse. Tough, firm, cold.

It was so difficult to manipulate, to form into something that wasn't horrific.

He knew that he had to handle the face with care. For if he didn't finish this task soon, the face would freeze in a state of surprise and that just wouldn't do. The time to manipulate the skin and flesh and prep the body for viewing was very finite. And Ned knew that he couldn't waste any time with this one. The corpse came in wasted away, and he had to fill the fill and get it ready for display.

That was the everyday task at Ned McCracken's job.

As he stood over the body, bending down towards the face, he took great care in parting the lips, and the jaw, using both hands to pry each layer of lips and teeth away from each other, he placed a wad of cotton in the left, and then the right cheeks. He removed his hands and let the jaw close.

He stood back for a moment and looked down at Stephen.

Ned nodded for a moment, and reached down to adjust the chin. He stood back again and studied the corpse. His forehead wrinkled and he reached up and stroked his chin. "More to the right," he said, and reached down again, pried open the jaw, and stuffed some more cotton on the right side of the mouth.

"There."

He stood back to admire his work.

The cheeks looked noticeably fuller. The man now looked like he could have been sleeping. But there was a large, purple lesion at the base of his hairline above his right eye. Ned reached for his makeup kit, and searched for a foundation that would match Stephen's skin tone.

It was pale, but he had a camouflage crème that would work. He searched through the plastic box and found a shade that might match Stephen's skin tone. He knew that the family would be wanting to view their deceased loved one as if he were sleeping; sometimes, Ned achieved that goal. His mind started to wander as he started to apply the makeup to Stephen's forehead.

He remembered, a while back, a boy was wheeled in after getting hit by a car riding on his bike. He was thrown fifty feet. His skull was crushed.

Ned had felt the boy's head, and it felt like a bowl of jelly. The bones were shattered underneath his scalp. The family had begged for an open casket. But Ned knew that the possibility existed that he would not be able to prevent the corpse from being grotesque. There were large gashes on the side of the boy's head. But the mother insisted.

And Ned was one of the top Morticians in Florida.

He was able to work his magic, he applied the just-so shades of makeup to cover the gashes, filling the wounds with cotton and covering it with a layer of clay, smoothed over very delicately with the detail and precision. And then, the makeup would come into play. The foundation, his artistic palette. While the gashes on the sides of the cheek were there, it did not matter. They were not visible once he was finished; Ned worked his magic.

And when the family was ushered in to the Biscayne Room for the initial viewing, there was no indication that the boy was anything other than asleep. The body lay in a small, white casket with rose tinted lighting and flowers surrounding the coffin, and when family members passed by the casket, stopped for a few moments to shed tears and view the young boy, no one noticed the line on the side of the face – where the makeup met skin, where the clay was covering the cotton, there was just the slightest imperfection if one were to look extremely close at the finest of details.

But Ned was not worried.

Because the family was not concerned with that tiny detail.

They knew that their boy was mortally wounded. They knew that Ned was behind closed doors, working his magic, preparing their boy's body for viewing one last time. They didn't care about those little details. They longed for the big picture. They wanted to see their son as if he were sleeping, and that's what they got. The details, Ned was able to conceal. Because concealing is what it's all about, that's what Ned had always been taught.

And that is exactly what he was doing with Stephen and his purple lesion on the forehead just at the hairline. Because Ned knew that Stephen would be having an open casket.

There was no reason not to.

"The cheeks are sunken," Ned had said to his assistant, Pat, when Stephen's body rolled into the morgue on a shiny, silver gurney which gleamed in the harsh florescent light. "They have to be filled." Ned pushed some hair away from the forehead. "I have something that can cover that."

"Says he had AIDS," Pat had said, his southern drawl still eminent despite living in Miami for several years.

Ned looked up. "Oh did he now?" He returned back to the body, examining all parts that would be on display in a coffin. He paid close attention to the hands. "He had nicely manicured fingernails. That's surprising for an invalid."

But after Stephen's body was prepped, ready on the table, Stephen had seen exactly how macerated the man had become.

The purple lesion on Stephen's forehead at the hairline proved to be one of many.

Pat had cut the pants and shirt away from the body with a pair of scissors. As the clothes fell to the floor, each rib was taught against the skin, and several more lesions on the torso were revealed.

Ned stepped back, and Pat looked up from his clipboard. Pat looked over at Ned and raised his eyebrows.

"A little more than you were expecting?" Pat asked.

Ned shook his head. "No, no." He looked up at Pat, directly in his eye. "You know how many of these AIDS queens come through here? Please. Just another day at the office."

But these days at the office were what Ned had signed up for. He remembered when he was sitting in the front office at Heavenly Slumber, just upstairs, several years ago, interviewing for the role that he was now in.

"I demystify death," he had said to a grey-haired stoic man sitting behind an expansive mahogany desk. The man's face twisted a bit. "What do you mean?" he asked.

Ned shifted in his seat, tapped on his shiny loafers for a minute. He bit his lip as the man sat back in his chair with a creak.

"So many people are afraid of death," Ned said, leaning forward. "I am here to make things a little easier for them."

The man nodded, breathed in through his nose, and picked up Ned's resume again, and read it for several minutes until Ned finally broke the silence. "There are a lot of people who fear death. And fear taking care of their dead. That's where I come in.

THE BLOOD DECANTER: BOOK THREE

Miami.

The Devil's city.

The land where the sun sets later, and the days are hotter, brighter, sweatier, and filled with more caffeine. Where the tall royal palms line the sidewalks; where the manicured lawns are a deep, forested green all twelve months of the year; where the water remains blue and bright and brilliant.

But the darkness of the Devil –

Miami.

It's the crystalline jewel on the tip of the Atlantic coast – hugging the Caribbean, surrounded by tropical waters and majestic million dollar mansions that line the docks and the inter-coastal waters which were usually scarcely used, except by Hollywood elite and celebrities. Most of the time, the waterfront palaces remained empty. And not far from the mansions and high-rises one finds the tiny, shoebox single level cement homes, dirty, bars covering the windows, litter on the lawns and too many cars parked along the streets.

Ah, Miami.

The brightest city with the darkest shadows. Yes, the city has a dark side. But it's the place that I call home. The place where I work; where I follow my calling. The city I love, and have come to love. And it's the city where I truly feel that I came face to face with the Devil himself…

Do you remember me?

Have you possibly seen me before? I always wear my black suit and tie. My hair is gelled, slicked back, cut tight and cropped to the sides. I most likely tower over you. I am quite tall. I am also somewhat quiet and reserved. Most of my chatter takes place inside my head. But I still can exude charisma. Can't I?

But if you have seen me before, you probably won't ever remember meeting me. Especially if you are wheeled in to my preparation room, just waiting for my trocar. Some of you may recall when I first met you when I was embalming in the preparation room.

Preparing a body. It's what I do.

The whole process relaxes me.

The cleaning and sterilizing, and then the actual procedure where I plunge the trocar – that long, reflective needle – with its wide mouth, into the neck, pumping the pink fluid into the corpse.

But my descriptions aren't always so clinical. For when that body arrived, there were always relatives waiting – those who were devastated, awash in loss and despair.

But that is when and where the art really begins.

For then, when a body arrives in my preparation room, that is when I can allow my creativity to run wild. I have a kit – a small, plastic box filled with makeup. Creams and foundations, even lipstick and nail-polish. I apply the foundation to both men and women, bringing life back to the skin, making it appear as if blood still flows through the empty veins, as if the person lying in the casket is not really dead; but just merely asleep.

For that is my calling.

But there was a time, not long ago, when I had a visitor. I only remember it because it was the same day that the man I described above moved through my chambers –

There was a day when I was not in Miami, but across the ocean, thousands of miles away, in a small preparation room in a similar chamber, for the body that I was called to prepare was a close friend. And I was asked to fly to Frankfurt – and so I called upon my fellow Mortician; the one family member who understood me so well. And I was able to use his quarters.

The sun shined through the small, square window in the little preparation room. It was small and boxy, the walls a stark and pale green, the overhead florescent light was harsh that morning as it had been every other morning. I would pick at the grit in my eyes that was usually there every morning. But that particular morning, there was a knocking on the door, it broke the silence.

It wasn't the door to the long, barren hallway covered in the noxious green tiles.

It was on the door to the outside.

And the only one who would come knocking on that door was either the coroner – or better have a pretty damn good reason. I set my coffee on the table.

I lay my clipboard down on the black body bag before me, and looked towards the door. I didn't see anyone in the small, square window. But then, I usually don't. There aren't too many people who will peek inside the lower levels of a funeral home.

I placed my hands on the cold, steel handle, looked out the window, and saw a small man standing in the frigid air; his clothing devoid of color and dressed in black and grey, with a black hat, and dark sunglasses. He looked up towards the window, and smiled. "Can you open for me?" His voice sounded muffled through the glass, like he was speaking into a pillow.

"We do not accept outside solicitations, sir."

The man took a few steps back.

He didn't seem very tall or imposing in the slightest, standing there in his black coat and grey pants. He shoved his hands in his pockets, then looked down at the pavement, and then back up. "You will want to let me in, Mr. McCracken. I have spoken intimately with Monsignor Harrison. I just returned from Rome."

I stepped back and swung the door open. The cold air was striking. The man took a step towards the threshold and looked up at me. He had wisps of grey hair under his hat. But I could not see his eyes through his dark lenses. "Are you going to let me in?"

I stepped aside and he entered the preparation room. He stopped just short of the stainless steel table in the center of the room, and looked around. His mouth dropped open slightly, but he did not make a sound. I closed the door and moved towards him, and he spoke. "I have never been inside a room like this before."

"Understandable. Most haven't, until the one time at the end of their lives when they come into this room."

The small man stopped and looked directly towards me. He removed his dark glasses, and his eyes pierced me. Dark brown, against an olive complexion. Much more noticeable under the florescent lighting, without the sun shining in my eyes. "Oh, Mr. McCracken, I have heard many things about you."

"What kind of things? And from whom?"

The man folded his sunglasses and placed them in his coat pocket. "Rome sent me. Antoine sent me. Because I have a warning. A warning of the greatest importance for the immortal kind."

I grabbed the clipboard from on top of the body bag and flung it on the counter. "Do you have identification?"

The visitor looked at the clipboard as he fished through his pockets. "Who is in that body bag?"

"That isn't any of your business until you have shown me identification that proves that it is."

I waited. And watched for him to fish his ID out. And then I remembered. It was such a distant memory, but it stuck out in my mind nonetheless. It was of Stephen. My, brother, who died on the side of Telegraph in Michigan. "I have had a lot of experience with Funeral Homes," I said, accepting his ID. "And it says here you are a Mortician as well?"

The man nodded and removed his coat and placed it on the counter. "Yes, Ned. Yes I am."

I nodded and handed him back his ID.

"I'm Hector Tabares." He started walking around the preparation table as he talked to me. "Rome sent me, as I said, with a warning." He looked down at the body bag on the table. "You see, this man here, I know who is in there. That is why Rome sent me."

I took a step back. "Okay. So Rome sent you. The Monsignor? Can you tell me a little more about the purpose of your visit here today?"

"I come with a warning."

Look for other exciting Books Published by Parchman's Press

www.ingramcontent.com/pod-product-compliance
Lightning Source LLC
Chambersburg PA
CBHW022238020726
47496CB00004B/965